My Little Brother, My Little Life

Dee H. Gordon

Dee Gordon, enjoy !

First Published in 2015
by GWL Publishing
an imprint of Great War Literature Publishing LLP

Produced in United Kingdom

ISBN 978-1-910603-05-5 Paperback Edition

GWL Publishing
Forum House
Sterling Road
Chichester PO19 7DN
www.gwlpublishing.co.uk

Born and brought up in the East End of London, Dee wrote teenage picture scripts during boring spells in secretarial jobs after leaving school, her stories published widely in *Romeo, Mirabelle, Marilyn*, etc. However, writing went on the back burner after a visit to an employment agency, where she was offered a job and she ended up in recruitment for thirty years, including seventeen years with her own agency in London. She sold her business in 2000 to concentrate on finishing her Open University Literature degree and start writing again, which also meant she could spend more time with her handicapped son, whose care needs have increased as he's grown older. She has focused primarily on local history books about Southend (where she lives with her husband and son), Essex and the East End, but has a list of unwritten novels in her head.

Acknowledgements

Thanks to my writing friends who have such faith in this book, and to Wendy at GWL Publishing for all her hard work and spot-on editing getting *My Little Brother, My Little Life* into print.

Dedication

To my autistic son, Ben, who has been an inspiration in more ways than
he knows – and to anyone caring for someone with autism.

Chapter One
1957

My mum left home today. Before she went, she left me a book with blank pages and the word *JOURNAL* on the front in fancy capitals, and she told me I should write down whatever comes into my head: "Not a boring diary, Linda, but your hopes, dreams, sad things and happy things." It hasn't got dates or anything in it, so I don't have to write every day, which is good, and I don't have to write about what happened that day. And that's good, too. Because some days, I suppose nothing much happens. And some days, like today, a lot happens.

She didn't tell me she was going, or where, or why. She just smiled and gave me the journal before walking me to school, just like any other day. Except that when I came home, wondering why she had left me to walk home alone, she was gone.

At first, I thought she had just gone out. When she hadn't been there to meet me in the past, I'd walked home, like today, along Roman Road to the tall house we shared with two other families, one on each floor. We lived on the ground floor and, if the door wasn't on the latch, somebody upstairs was sure to be there to let me in. I wouldn't be alone for long. Mum would soon rush in, out of breath, tugging little Douglas along behind her, holding a bag of doughnuts or Belgian buns, and the three of us would tuck in straight away, laughing, covering each other in sugar or sticky icing. "Sorry, Linda, there was one hell of a queue. And don't you go saying hell."

But today… Today was different. Mainly because Douglas was at home. He'd never been left alone without Mum before. He was sitting on his bed with his legs crossed, the pieces of a jigsaw puzzle in front of him. He smiled at me when I went into his room. "Fifty pieces."

Something was wrong. "Where's Mum?"

"Fifty pieces."

"Yes, Douggie, but where's Mum?"

"Fifty pieces."

It was no good. As Mum put it, he wasn't 'right in the head'. So I just said, "Good boy," and went on a hunt for food.

The biscuit tin was full – and so was the larder. She must have gone shopping that day, because it had looked a bit bare that morning when I had taken out the jam for my toast. There was an envelope in the middle of the kitchen table with the word 'Frank' on it – in her writing.

I took the biscuit tin into Douglas, thinking about the envelope. Why would my mum write a letter to my dad? And why would she leave Douggie alone? Something was going on.

Douggie tried to take a handful of custard creams, but I stopped him from eating more than two. "Mum will be cross. You don't want to spoil your tea."

He said something through a mouthful of biscuit. But I think it was just, "Fifty pieces."

I tried another tack. "What time did Mummy go out?"

"Not forty pieces." Douggie waved the lid of the jigsaw box at me, looking very pleased with himself.

I hugged him. "Good boy. But I don't think the bed is a good place to do a jigsaw. Let's go next door."

I settled him at the kitchen table. We never used the table and chairs in our third room, which was kept for Sundays and special occasions.

I checked the room, anyway, just in case Mum was there for some reason. Not that it was very likely. We lived in just the two rooms, the kitchen and bedroom. I suppose it was a bit of a waste, but it had always been like that, as long as I could remember. When I poked my nose around the door, I noticed straight away that a couple of photographs had disappeared from the mantelpiece. And Mum's purple velvet cushion was gone. That's when I began to get really worried. Otherwise, the room looked just the same as usual, and it was just as cold as usual.

I went back into the bedroom we all shared and opened the wardrobe door. The few remaining things belonged to me, Dad and Douggie. I looked under the bed and our holiday suitcase was gone. The blankets kept in it had been tipped out on the floor.

What was happening? What should I do? Should I read the letter? I went back into the kitchen and picked it up. But I couldn't do it. My dad had never hit me, but he could sure shout. I turned it over. Perhaps I could open it and seal it up again. But what if I couldn't do it properly?

I had an answer. "Douggie, I'm just going upstairs. I'll only be five minutes."

He turned around in the chair and now he was looking a bit worried, too. I tried to smile. "I'm just going to see Mrs Cohen. Five minutes."

"Douggie come." He got up.

"No, it's okay. Five minutes. I promise."

He sat down again, holding up five fingers.

"Yes, five minutes."

When I asked Mrs Cohen if she'd seen my mother that day, she didn't seem very interested and she didn't answer straight away. She folded her arms. "Why do you ask?"

"Because she didn't meet me at school, she's not at home, and all her things have gone." Saying it out loud suddenly made it real, and I could feel tears starting in my eyes. Immediately, Mrs Cohen pulled off her apron, threw it behind her and called out: "Be downstairs, Dad." Mr Cohen wasn't her dad, he was her husband, but she always called him that.

She followed me down the dozen shiny (thanks to her) stairs and I showed her the near-empty wardrobe. She didn't say anything but her mouth seemed to get smaller somehow. Then I showed her the letter. "Do you think I should open it, Mrs Cohen?"

"Is it poo-poo time?" We both looked at Douggie, who had appeared in the doorway.

"It's not five o'clock yet, Douggie."

He went out again. I was a bit embarrassed. But Mrs Cohen just smiled. "I know 'e likes a timetable," she said. "But I didn't know it went that far."

He came back again. "Where's Mummy?"

"She'll be back later, son," said Mrs Cohen in a very kind voice.

"What time?"

She looked at me. "Er, about eight o'clock, son."

"Who puts Douggie to bed?"

I reassured him. "Don't worry, I'll do it."

He went off again and Mrs Cohen was looking at me. "Have you put him to bed before?"

"Lots of times. Usually on Saturdays. When Mum and Dad are in *The Globe*."

"I see. What time does Frank get home?"

"Earliest is seven o'clock. Sometimes nine, sometimes later."

"And what time do yous have your tea?"

"At half past five. On the dot. Because Douggie…" I didn't need to explain.

"Tell you what, Linda. I'll help you sort out your tea, and then I'll send Dad down to Mr Blake to use his telephone. He can get in touch with the brewery and make sure Frank's coming home early, so he can read this letter and so's you'll know what's going on. Okay?"

What a wonderful idea. I knew Mrs Cohen would know what to do. But then… "I don't know the telephone number."

"No, but I do. Audrey gave it to me for emergencies. I'm not sure Frank's boss will let Dad talk to him, but it's worth a try."

We started buttering bread on a wooden board beside the kitchen sink, she doing the slicing and me the buttering. There was something I just had to ask. I spoke really quietly, with my back to Douggie: "Mrs Cohen, what do you think has happened to Mum?"

She patted me on the head and pushed my pigtails back so that they wouldn't get in the way of the butter knife. "Don't worry. I'm sure she's fine. Looks as if she's taken herself off on a bit of a holiday."

"To Ramsgate?"

"Ramsgate?"

"Yes. We always go to Ramsgate. Well, apart from hop-pickin', that is. But it's not hop-pickin' time, so it must be Ramsgate. We usually go together. In August."

"Well, perhaps this time she needed a bit of a holiday on her own, like." She looked up at the clock. "Five o'clock. Will Douggie...?"

"Oh. I'll see to it."

"Douggie. It's five o'clock."

"Poo now." He climbed down from the chair happily and I could see he'd finished the jigsaw.

I smiled at him. "You've finished. It's Punch and Judy. Well done. I'll ask Dad if he can find you a sixty-piece one next." We looked at the picture of Punch thumping Judy with a stick.

"Mummy and Daddy."

But surely he'd never seen Dad hitting Mum? Only heard it, like I had, after Dad had a few too many drinks.

I looked over at Mrs Cohen, but she just asked if I'd like to use her toilet upstairs.

"No, thanks, we've got our own just outside." Mum didn't like us using anyone else's toilet. "Nothing wrong with an outside lav," she always said. I don't think Mr Cohen liked sharing, either, because he hadn't looked very happy when he once caught me upstairs, even though it was in the middle of a thunderstorm.

Back in the kitchen, Mrs Cohen made sure Douggie washed his hands properly. Then she opened a tin of sardines and put a couple of eggs on to boil on our little kitchen range. "Now, keep an eye on those eggs while I go and have a talk to Dad."

I thought I could hear Mr Cohen's raised voice, saying what sounded like "that no good" and then his heavy tread on the stairs and then a slammed door. I was pleased because that must mean he was going to try and make sure Dad didn't get home too late from the brewery. I didn't know what he did there. He came home smelling of beer, whether he'd been drinking or not, and with his clothes stained and grubby. What I did know was that I wanted to hear what was in that letter.

I heard Mr Cohen come back just as I was taking the eggs carefully out of the saucepan. We like them hard-boiled. "Half past five. Tea," said Douggie.

There was a tap at the kitchen door. Mr Cohen didn't walk straight in like his wife. When I opened it, he just nodded, fiddled with his tie which he always wore, even indoors, and said, "Frank's on his way."

"Thank you, Mr…" But he had turned away. He didn't talk as much as his wife either. Couldn't get a word in edgeways, according to Mum.

Douggie and I ate our tea in silence. I saved some sardines and some of the bread for Dad to have with his soup. He always had soup or stew when he came back from the brewery.

After we'd had yesterday's left-over rice pudding, I was nicely full and feeling happy enough to sing as I started to wash up. Douggie was putting the jigsaw pieces back in the box, counting them carefully.

I thought Dad would be angry when he came in. Perhaps shouting. But he opened the door slowly, and he looked small and sad. "Linda. Are you okay?" he asked.

"Yes." I swallowed and handed him the letter.

He held it in his hand for a moment and then kissed Douggie on the top of his head. Douggie didn't move. He was on his third recount.

"I'm just going to read this in the bedroom, girl. Has she taken… everything?"

I nodded, feeling the tears coming back. I don't know why. Just a holiday, like Mrs Cohen said.

Dad closed the door quietly and I heard the bedsprings creak. Ten minutes went by and I was getting worried. It would soon be time for me to put Douggie to bed.

Douggie looked at the kitchen clock. "Bed time?"

"Five minutes. I'll just sort out your bedtime nappy." Luckily, Mum had left a huge pile of clean nappies in the wardrobe. I'd spotted them earlier.

I tapped on the bedroom door and crept in. Dad had his back to me, his head in his hands, his donkey jacket on the bed beside him, and the letter on the floor in front of him. "Dad? It's Douggie's bedtime. Is everything all right? Did Mum decide to take a holiday?"

He turned around slowly, and his face was wet. I'd seen him look like that a year before when Grandma died. "Oh, Dad, is it bad news?"

"For us, yes. For Audrey, no. And not a holiday. No. What made you think…?"

"Mrs Cohen said perhaps that's where she's gone. The clothes… the suitcase…"

He picked up the letter and put it in his pocket. Then he gave me a smelly hug; something he didn't do very often. "Your mum's fine. But she's had enough. Of me, of us, and, especially, of Douggie." I heard him sob, and I felt it, but I couldn't see his face, he was hugging me too tightly.

"You mean, she's not… not coming back? She's gone? She's…"

He let go of me and bent down so that his face was close to mine. He needed a shave. "Your mother thinks she's too good for the likes of us. She thinks she can do better. And when she comes crawling back, when she realises what she's lost in you, in Douggie… I'm not letting her back in this house, do you hear me? I don't want to hear her name. You don't know what a tart is right now, but you will. Luckily, and I thank God, Douggie will never know."

I couldn't believe what I was hearing. That was it? Just like that? My beautiful mother gone, without a word, no letter for me, no message for Douggie. But where? Where had she gone? I wanted to grow up to be just like her, but how could I if she wasn't going to be around? What did he mean, *she can do better?* How? How would we manage? Cooking, washing, cleaning, shopping, sewing – who would do it all? I could find out what a tart was. And what would happen to Douggie? Would Dad really stop her coming back?

So many questions. I didn't know where to start. I felt as if my happy world had disappeared. Just like that.

"Doesn't she love us any more?" That was the most important question.

But that was when Douggie came into the room. "Fifty pieces."

Dad didn't answer my question. He picked up Douggie and swung him round.

"Are you ready for sixty pieces?"

"Sixty pieces. Yes." Douggie, back on his feet though none too steady, looked delighted.

"Don't worry, Linda. I'm going to *The Globe* for an hour. But there's nothing to worry about. We're all going to be just fine. Just fine."

"But Dad…"

He looked at me. A funny look. "Audrey loves Audrey. Audrey has always loved Audrey. Can you imagine how she felt producing a son like… can you imagine what that did to her? I knew this would happen. I just didn't know when. I'm sorry, Linda. I'm so sorry. But we'll be fine." He hugged me again. I was doing well for hugs.

I kept smiling while I put Douggie to bed. Pillow exactly in the middle, sheet turned back the same distance left and right, clothes piled up at the foot of the bed in the usual order – trousers at the bottom, pants the last thing on top. Little things made Douggie happy. It didn't take much. He gave me his usual tiny kiss on the cheek. For him, nothing had changed.

For me, when I closed the bedroom door and went back into the kitchen, everything had changed. My beautiful mother. I thought about how she looked. Dimples in her cheeks that Dad liked to kiss. Lots of black curls. "Gipsy," he sometimes called her. She never had curlers in her hair out in the street, not even with a scarf on top. She was very special.

I sobbed for what seemed like hours, until I heard Mrs Cohen's voice in the hallway.

"Linda? Can I come in?" she asked.

I poured it all out. I don't know why. Mrs Cohen had never been a friend of Mum's. But she'd heard Dad leave and she wanted to hear all about it and I think she wanted to help, but she didn't know how. It was up to me and my dad to sort it out.

"And if Audrey... I mean your mother... really does stay away, what's going to happen to young Douggie?"

"What do you mean?"

She was looking at the floor. "Well, nothing, but it's going to be difficult for your dad to look after both of you, ain't it?"

Difficult, yes. But what choice did he have? Surely there was no choice? My tears had dried up and I swallowed to keep them away.

"We'll be just fine. Auntie Ivy likes to take Douggie out on Sundays, and he starts school in September, so..."

"How old are you, dear?"

"Ten. Why?"

Mrs Cohen sighed and rolled up her sleeves. "I'll help you finish clearing up. Is this soup for your dad?"

I'd forgotten about the soup. I peered at it in the saucepan where it had been for a few days and took the saucepan off the heat. It looked a bit black around the edges, and not very nice. Mrs Cohen answered my unasked question: "If we give it a good stir, there's enough there for one more bowlful, but don't try and keep it warm any longer tonight. I expect your dad will be happy enough with beer and pork scratchings at *The Globe*, though how anyone can eat them things beats me, I'm sure."

While Mrs Cohen washed and I wiped, I wondered if Dad would tell everyone at *The Globe* about Mum, or keep it to himself. I didn't want everyone to know, especially if he said horrid things about her. "Mrs Cohen, what's a tart?" I asked.

She pulled a face. "Is that what Frank called Audrey?"

"Yes."

She pulled the plug out and watched the water disappear before she answered. "Your dad is unhappy, angry. He will say things he don't mean. Audrey wasn't perfect, but I don't think she deserves that. Not that I ever got to know her very well..."

"But what does it mean?" I could see she was trying to avoid answering.

"It means... a woman with no morals, a woman who doesn't stay faithful to her husband."

I wasn't much the wiser, but that seemed to be all I was going to get. Mrs Cohen was on her way out. "Good night, Linda. And if there's anything you need while… well, anything… you know where I am."

I didn't wait up for Dad, because I didn't want to hear him saying bad things about Mum, perhaps using that word, 'tart', again. I slept in the middle bed, between Douggie and my parents. I pretended to be asleep when Dad came in. He wasn't singing as he usually was when he came back from *The Globe* and he didn't come straight into the bedroom. I fell asleep before he came to bed, but was startled awake as usual by the noise of the rag-and-bone-man's horse across the street, whinny-ing for his breakfast.

Dad's bed had been slept in, and I could hear him in the kitchen, noisily making tea just like any other day. Mum liked her cup of tea in bed.

Douggie was still asleep. There was no clock in the bedroom, so I got up and went into the kitchen in my pyjamas. Half past six.

Dad was holding a cup of tea with both hands, looking at another cup on the table. "I forgot," he said. "Just for a few minutes, I forgot."

I picked up the cup and drank Mum's tea. "There. It's not been wasted. Delicious."

He still hadn't shaved, and rubbed his chin. "I can't be bothered to shave. It's Saturday, so you can look out for Douggie until I get home. Half day today. Do you want some money for Saturday morning pictures? The O's ain't playing at home today, so I've got a bit of spare."

"Wow, thanks, Dad."

"And I'll bring fish and chips – or would you rather pie and mash?"

"Pie and mash, please, with lots of liquor." My favourite.

"Does Douggie like pie and mash?"

"Loves it."

"That's settled then. I'll go and see Auntie Ivy tomorrow and see if you can drop Douggie off on your way to school for a few weeks till the end of term. She's hardly likely to say no."

"Because she's Mum's sister?"

"No. Because she's Douggie's aunt." He stood up and pulled on his donkey jacket, which suddenly looked a bit too big for him. "See you later, girl."

With his hand on the door handle, he turned around. "I heated up that soup last night. Thank you."

When the door opened, I could hear the faint strains of a Pat Boone song, probably coming from Mrs Cohen's radio, as if everything was normal. But it wasn't.

Douggie liked to be woken at half past seven – on the dot. I would have time to write in my new journal before waking him, because yesterday had been an important day. Not like all the others.

Chapter Two

1964

"Come on, girl. Time for a cup of tea. That is, if I can find the kettle."

"I know where it is. I packed it separately with the mugs and milk and sugar."

Luckily, the gas cooker – a gas cooker! – was working, although I didn't feel too confident about lighting it just yet. We'd only moved in, what, three hours ago, so even Dad was a bit wary, standing well back when he struck a match. The last thing he wanted to do was to set light to his old-fashioned Brylcreemed quiff.

"There." He looked pleased with himself. "Instant. Bloody marvellous. What do you think, girl?"

"Magic." At this rate, the kettle would boil before I'd found the sugar and teaspoons.

We smiled at each other, hugging our mugs. "Come on, let's drink this outside."

The council flat had a small balcony with metal framed French doors – French doors! – opening out from the living room. A living room, which hopefully we'd actually use. Although the 'view' from the balcony was just of Whitechapel rooftops, it didn't matter.

"I feel like the King of the castle," Dad said.

"As long as I'm not a princess."

"What's wrong with being a princess?"

I shuddered at the thought. "Have you *seen* what Margaret wears? I can't think of a way to describe it."

"Classic?"

"That's as maybe. But it's hardly the kind of thing a mod would be seen dead in…"

Dad wiped his mouth with the back of his hand. "You and your mods. But seriously, girl, what do you think?" He waved an arm, spilling some of the dregs of his tea, and cursing under his breath at his own carelessness.

"'Ere, watch what you're doing." I moved out of range before I answered his question: "Put it this way. Only if Paul McCartney knocked on the door to help us finish the unpacking would I be happier."

"Blimey. Praise indeed."

Dad laughed loudly enough for people passing in the street below to look up in surprise and then remembered the time. "Linda, what does that church clock over there say?"

"It says it's time you got some glasses. No, it says half three. Shall I go?"

"No. I'll go for a change. I like to show my boat-race now and then at the school, so that they know what Douggie's old man looks like. And I don't often get the chance. This is my first day off since…" I couldn't help him out. Neither of us could remember the last time he'd taken a day's holiday. And he'd worked just as hard today as he did any other day – helping to load and unload the van had kept the removal cost down.

Out here, I felt like Juliet in that play of Shakespeare's we'd done in my last year at school, a year ago now. Although this balcony was solid grey concrete with flower boxes full of weeds, and Juliet didn't spend her days cleaning and cooking. There weren't any part-time jobs that left me free to take Douggie to and from school every day, and Auntie Ivy had been so pleased when I'd finally taken over after leaving school myself, that Dad and I didn't have the heart to ask her if she'd carry on.

I rubbed the gooseflesh on my arms. It was a bit parky out in the shade, even though it was May. No good feeling sorry for myself: it was Douggie who'd drawn the short straw. Poor little sod. Twelve going on seven.

The thought prompted me into action. I downed the tea and went on a hunt through the boxes in his bedroom to find bedlinen. If I made his bed before he got back with Dad, it would help him recognise his room. Douggie's room. His very own room. And one for me, and one for Dad. A bedroom each. And a bathroom. Unbelievable.

The next thing I ought to unpack should be Douggie's lists. The teachers, especially Miss Drake, knew what he liked and were really good at sending home carbon copies of any lists that were typed up at school – dinner menus, names and dates of birth of the children in different classes, timetables, test results. Douggie spent hours looking at them over and over again, working out his own links – five boys called Robert in Class 2A, six children out of thirty in Class 3B were born in March, three girls got 29 out of 30 in last week's spelling test. All very fascinating for him, but a bit of a bore for us after the umpteenth, "How big a coincidence is that?"

I could hear him now. Literally. He was obviously in the open square of playground which 'belonged' to this block. Okay, so it was bare, without a seat or a blade of grass, but it was big enough for football or marbles or hopscotch.

"It's the wrong place. The wrong place."

I ran through the flat and out of the front door to peer over the top of the shared balcony. Douggie was standing, rooted to the spot, resisting Dad's attempts to move him. He was shaking his head firmly, his dark curls bouncing around.

Oh dear. Dad and I had seen this coming, so we'd brought Douggie for quite a few visits before moving day to get him used to the idea. We'd even shown him the flat when it was empty last week, let him choose his room, which he'd done quickly and with little interest. Obviously he hadn't understood what we'd been saying. That this was going to be home.

14

I put the door on the latch and went down the two flights of stairs to help Dad. "This is our new home, Douggie. It's bigger, it's warmer, it's got an inside toilet. An *inside* toilet. And a bath. Remember you chose your bedroom? Your very own bedroom?"

"It's the wrong place."

This was so embarrassing. A couple of people had come out onto the balconies that stretched from one side to the other of each floor of the eight storey block. A few net curtains were pushed to one side, revealing curious faces, one of which looked just like Cassius Clay. A couple of boys around Douggie's age, sharing a bicycle, stopped to watch the fun, smirking knowingly at each other. Not that they knew anything. But I could imagine what they were thinking.

All the names that Douggie had been called over the years had meant nothing to him. But they meant a lot to me and to Dad, although we never talked about it. 'Spaz', 'soft brain', 'idiot', 'retard', 'imbecile', 'mental case'. Yes, I knew exactly what they were thinking.

At first I used to answer back. Even swear, though I tried not to, for Douggie's sake. While he ignored what strangers might say, he latched on to what I said, often repeating it in front of Dad. So, nowadays I usually just raised two fingers in silence, avoiding Douggie's line of vision. I would never get used to it, but now I realised that they just didn't understand; they didn't know what they were saying. Their problem, not Douggie's. But it was still hard. And still embarrassing.

We had to half carry and half encourage Douggie up the stairs. Not easy, because he was nearly as big as me. His body didn't have the problems that his brain had. But we did it. We were in. Once I'd persuaded him to sit on his bed and given him some of his lists and his favourite custard creams, he seemed much happier, although I had to leave the door open when I left the room.

"Well done, Lin." Dad sounded genuinely pleased. "What shall we tackle next? The rest of the kitchen stuff, or shall we plug in the gramophone and see if we can find your Beatles records?"

No contest.

It was nearly as embarrassing to have a dad that liked the Beatles as to have a brother like Douggie. Dad liked them because they were 'clean', whereas he thought the Rolling Stones were 'dirty'. I don't know where he got that idea from. Ugly – yes. But dirty?

Luckily for me, Dad criticised most of the other groups I liked, especially in front of my friends – he didn't like to agree with us about anything if he could help it. There'd be no generation gap then, would there? And then where would we be?

Singing *She Loves You* (with lots of *yeah yeah yeahs*) seemed to help us empty another three packing cases. Then Douggie came to see what we were up to. He wasn't used to being ignored.

He made his way over to Dad's pride and joy, the gramophone player, smiling widely. "Oh no." We said it together but neither of us got there in time. Up went the volume to the maximum level.

Almost immediately, there was the sound of banging from below and a yell from someone next door at number twenty-four, followed by the sound of a crying baby. Oh no.

"Schmuck."

"Linda! Don't call him that."

"Why not?" It was one of Mr Cohen's favourite words, after all.

Dad hadn't just turned the record down; he'd turned it off. I was not happy but he wasn't interested in how I felt, only in Douggie.

He knelt and held on to Douggie's arms tightly, looking into his face, staying serious in spite of Douggie's ear-to-ear grin. "Listen to me, son. Are you listening? Because the people who live upstairs and the people next door and the people downstairs – all these new people, they don't want to hear us. They don't want to hear us shouting. They don't want to hear our wireless and they don't want to hear our gramophone player. It's too many noises coming from too many different directions."

He let go of Douggie's arms, but immediately my predictable brother reached for the controls again.

I butted in before Dad started losing his temper. "Nice try, Dad. Let me."

It was no good telling Douggie not to upset other people. He didn't care about other people.

I took over Dad's position and made sure Douggie was looking at me (or nearly looking at me). "Douggie. If you turn the music up too loudly, your hair will fall out."

"What the...?"

"Ssshh. I know what I'm doing, Dad." I picked a stray curled hair from Douggie's shoulder. "Look."

Douggie looked. He fingered the stray hair. He put both his hands up to his head. "No. No. Not hair fall out. Not Douggie's hair. No."

"This is what will happen." I stood holding up the hair as my evidence. "Look."

"Take off uniform now."

I heard Dad breathe out. Crisis over. "Thanks, girl," he said putting a hand on my shoulder.

As I hunted out the box with Douggie's clothes in it, I thought about Dad's attempt to reason with Douggie. Of course I spent a lot more time with Douggie than anyone. Since Mum left, that is. And I'd found out long ago that reasoning didn't seem to work. I'd also found out that Douggie always took everyone literally. So when Auntie Ivy told him that carrots would help him to see in the dark, and they didn't, eating the carrots he detested was no longer an option.

"What did you do at school today?" An automatic question, but not one that usually produced an answer.

"Forty six divided by two."

"Dividing?"

"Thirty take away seven."

I had to think about it for a minute before the penny dropped. "Oh, twenty-three. Yes, that's our new house number. Or flat number, I should say. 23 Whitechapel House." The move was occupying his thoughts more than answering my question.

"Eleven and a half times two."

"Look out of the window, Douggie. See how high up we are."

"Fifteen plus eight."

This could obviously keep him amused for hours. I left him to it for a while after checking the windows were secured. Not that he was unaware of the danger everywhere around him, which was a blessing according to Doctor Gillespie, our G.P., a man who thought of Douggie as an 'unlocked genius'. Nice idea but I had yet to see it. Good at maths and spelling and anything that could be learned by rote, yes, including French and German vocabularies, but genius…

Dad was still unpacking and unwrapping pots and plates in the kitchen.

"Have a break, Dad. Go on. I'll make us a fresh brew. Try out that new armchair that Mr Cohen put on the van for you."

He rubbed his eyes and then his back. "Yes, girl. I will. That was decent of the old boy, weren't it?"

"Well, like he said, the bungalow that he and Mrs Cohen are going to is so tiny, he had to get rid of some of his stuff. How did he put it? Better you have it than the dustmen?"

"I still think it was bloody generous."

I followed him into our living room, still awash with boxes, the velvety plum chair with its high back just waiting for an occupier.

Dad eased himself down, making the most of the moment. After a quick adjustment to retrieve the comb – or quiff teaser – from his back pocket with an exaggerated, "Ouch," he leaned back and closed his eyes. "This is the life, Linda. I could get used to this."

"Why didn't we ever use the living room in Globe Street, Dad?"

He didn't open his eyes but he smiled. "Ideas above our station, girl. A room for parties, for knees-ups, funerals, family get togethers, for celebrating. But…"

"We never did much celebrating."

"You got it. Well, she, your mum, lost interest in partying… after…" He didn't like to talk about Mum, and we'd all got used to being without her.

"After Douggie was born, I suppose."

Dad opened his eyes. "Yes, you're right. But there were other things, Lin. It would have crucified our heating bill for starters. Do you know, the rent we paid for those couple of bloody rooms was as much as we're paying for this whole flat. But now they're knocking down the whole street and building a whole row of, what are they called…?"

"Maisonettes?"

"Something like that. Well, it meant the council had to see us right, so here we are. Sitting pretty."

"Four times three plus eleven." Douggie had come in wearing his p.t. kit.

"Sorry, Douggie. I didn't finish unpacking your clothes." And this, of course, was my job, not Dad's.

He looked down at his outfit. "It's fine."

"I suppose so. But come on, let's sort out as much as we can."

"Clock."

"Yes, we'll find that too."

"Time for milk drink."

"Could be. I'm sure I packed your clock with your clothes. Come on."

Yes, there was his prized clock. The hands and numbers were luminous and he liked to be able to see it without getting out of bed. "There you are."

Douggie spent a good twenty minutes winding it up, manoeuvring it into exactly the right position on the solitary bookshelf, and testing it by lying on his bed to check its visibility. By the time he was happy, I'd unpacked his clothes and put them into the chest of drawers, including the large size nappies that he still wore at night but which remained our – Douggie's, mine and Dad's – secret.

Dad had the only wardrobe and I'd been promised a dress rail by Mrs Gibson from Globe Street who had a stall down the Roman, although she hadn't turned up with it yet. So, in the meantime, I took my clothes into my very own bedroom and lay them across some of the empty boxes.

I was lucky, really, when I thought about it. Dad was very generous with money. Although we didn't talk about how much he earned, it seemed that he handed over just about every penny to me after paying rent, his bus fares to work and for his Old Holborn and football pools. There were none of the visits to the bookmaker I remembered from the days before Mum left, or visits to Leyton Orient on a Saturday afternoon. But I always had money left over after buying food.

There was enough to buy *Jackie*, and to collect the essential mod uniform, piece by piece: blue nylon mac, hush puppies with coloured laces, a sweater with three stripes around the hem. And even enough to go clubbing in the West End a few nights a week: the Marquee and the Scene had free entry nights. True, I could only afford to drink coca-cola but it didn't matter. The music and dance were more important than the drink.

"Are you out tonight, girl?"

"Dad, you made me jump. I was just thinking about going out. Can you trim up my fringe for me? Would you mind? I know there's a lot to do…"

He patted me on the shoulder. "There's no hurry. And your fringe will only take ten minutes. You go and enjoy yourself. You need a break too. This will be your only chance this week, because I'll be doing some overtime to make up for having today off."

"Won't you be paid? I thought you got two weeks holiday a year?"

"I do, girl. I do. And I will be paid. But that don't get the work done that I didn't do today – and the extra always comes in 'andy."

"Are we all right, Dad? For money I mean?"

Another pat. "Course we are. Do you realise how cheap Douggie is to run?"

"What?" What? I sat down on my unmade bed and looked up at him. "What are you on about?"

It was good to see him laugh out loud. "When I picked him up from school, I couldn't help but notice how many of the boys have bikes, one even had roller skates, and I heard a couple of mums talking about taking their kids on holiday – to Butlins. Butlins! Whereas you, God bless yer, and Douggie, who doesn't really like going anywhere, wouldn't dream… well, you know what I mean."

"Butlins, eh? Blimey, we really are missing out." But I laughed, too, to reassure him that he was right. We were okay. Who needed flash holidays? I had happy memories of holidays in the Ramsgate B&B, though perhaps it would be nice to have a change. I know some of my friends from school, those who were working, had talked about going on holiday next year without their parents, but I couldn't see that happening.

"What's Blimey?" Douggie and his timing!

"Er, it means what a shame," I explained.

"What's a shame?"

"Not going to Butlins."

"What's Butlins?"

"A holiday camp near Clacton-on-Sea. A special place for holidays with lots of things to do."

Douggie looked at me and Dad in turn. "No holidays. Douggie doesn't like holidays. Douggie stay at home."

"See what I mean, girl. Cheap to run. You gotta look on the bright side."

"Time for milk drink."

"Okay." I pointed towards the door. "What's everyone doing in my room? Did you hear that? *My room?* Blimey."

"Is it a shame?"

"No, Douggie, it's not, not at all."

Chapter Three

1970

I swear to God, or I would if I believed in the bugger, that I will never ever forget that attempted abortion. Nothing to do with pain, because I'd only got as far as a local anaesthetic and a kind of fumbling... no, I don't want to go there. But I know I will remember what I tried to do every time the word is mentioned, every time my baby looks at me.

Oh, well, better get it over with. Rick had a right to know. "Can I use the phone?"

"Yes, of course you can, darling. I'll bring the trolley." The nurse winked at me like we were some kind of conspirators. I suppose we were. Certainly Dad didn't know what I was up to, he just thought I was with Rick. Because I was always with Rick. That's how I'd ended up here. At twenty-three, I was a good few years older than some of the teenagers in here, though; at least I'd managed a bit of a life before a baby. Well, a bit.

The white trolley arrived at my elbow. White uniforms, white walls, white bedding. Everything looked very professional, and I was grateful Rick had found the money to pay for the real McCoy. It wasn't his fault that I'd seriously miscalculated and the abortion had been called off before it had even started, as soon as the doctor put his hand inside me.

"This baby is more like a twenty nine week gestation than a ten week. We cannot proceed. Your G.P. ought to be shot." Least, I think that's what he said – he had a very strong Indian accent – and he'd whipped off his gloves and walked away, shouting at everyone around him. Of course my G.P. hadn't been involved. That was the last thing I would have wanted. This had been a private arrangement.

"Hello, darling. Yes. I'm fine. But I've got some news... bad news, I suppose... seems I'm well over six months gone... well, it means it's too late... yes, there's nothing they can do... what can I say? It's my fault. I never was any good at maths." I tried to laugh, but I didn't do a very good job and he wasn't laughing either.

"Rick, I'm so sorry... I know... it's a bit late for that... yes, me too... no, it was okay, really... legs up in the air, lots of people peering at you, that kind of thing... and then being told... well, it was disappointing... although... oh, I don't know... I'm a bit mixed up about it all... I do love ya... I do... lots and lots... I know... don't rush over... No, I'd rather you didn't... most of the girls here don't seem to have visitors... it's all very clean and crisp... yes, I'm sure... I'll be fine... just pick me up as soon as you can. I expect they need the bed."

The nurse was hovering, signing that she wanted the telephone trolley for someone else, cheeky whatsaname, and she nodded briskly at the words "need the bed". It was a real conveyor belt, this place. "Yes, of course after work. Half past five is just fine... I think we may have saved some of your money, at least, so we can have a slap up meal. What do you think? Oh, yes, spag bol sounds just perfect... no, I told Auntie Ivy I'd be late back... well, that's what I thought... Dad will just think we've been clubbing again... she came over as soon as he went out this morning... to take Douggie to the day centre... no, of course I didn't... well, she has been eyeing my waistline recently... but I told her I was going to spend the day with you... I told her you had tickets for the *Jesus Christ Superstar* matinée... no, I haven't, but I know someone who has, so I'll ask her... got to go, nursey is drumming her fingers... don't say that... you'll make me cry... we'll just have to face the music... best not talk about it now... I'll see you later."

Funny, really. I think he sounded just a bit pleased. Not that I was devastated myself, just a bit numb perhaps. One of the other nurses, a Jamaican cow, had told me the baby was a girl, after I'd asked not to be told. If you don't know, then it's not a person somehow. But the cow had told me it was a girl. A little girl. Our little girl. And I was glad she was still there. I was glad I hadn't lost her. We'd be all right. If Dad didn't kill me.

I pulled myself into a sitting position and put my hand on my swollen tummy. She'd kicked me. Sorry, Poppet. I'll make it up to you. I promise.

One of the doctors was making a bee-line for me. "Mrs Fletcher?"

"Miss."

"Quite. I'm Doctor Richards. What an unpleasant experience."

"Oh, well, my own fault I suppose."

He looked genuinely concerned and he was playing with his hair just like Douggie did in times of crisis. "Do you understand what happened, why we couldn't proceed?"

"Yes." I leaned back, emotions beginning to surface. "Yes. The nurse explained."

"I'm sure your baby will be fine."

That woke me up. "What do you mean? Why shouldn't she be?"

He put up a neatly manicured hand as if to hold me off. "No reason. A bit intrusive for her, that's all. Have you been aware of her moving since… since?"

"She's kicking, if that's what you mean."

"Just perfect. Perfect. Would you like to see our psychiatrist at all?"

"What the hell for?"

"There's no need to be offensive, Mrs Fletcher."

Did he have a problem with his hearing? "Miss."

"Just trying to help. Did you want to talk about adoption, perhaps?"

"No, I don't want to talk about adoption. I'm stuck with her, and she's stuck with me. So that's it. Nothing more to say. We'll be just fine."

"I don't suppose you've been going to ante-natal classes."

"You suppose right. There wouldn't have been any point if… well, if…"

"Quite. Well, we'll let your G.P. know and he will contact you about classes and about arrangements for the birth. Perhaps a little talk about contraception, hmm?"

Condescending bastard. "Please. I'll contact him. I don't want him writing home. He might write before my family know, well, everything there is to know."

He put that soft hand on my shoulder but I shook him off. Silly, really. I knew in my heart of hearts that he was only trying to be kind. "If you promise," he said gently.

"'Onest injun. No, seriously, I will. I want to. I have to." I felt the tears welling. Do me a favour. Not in front of his nibs. And what was there to cry about, anyway? I'd probably been saved from doing something I might have regretted for the rest of my days. If it hadn't been for the prospect of facing Dad, I might almost have felt relieved.

"Good. Excellent. How about some food? You're probably starving."

"Sounds good. Though I'll be eating soon after my boyfriend picks me up."

"Cucumber sandwiches, perhaps? Our kitchens do a mean cucumber sandwich."

"What, cucumber on its own?"

Dr Richards seemed to find that amusing and he patted me on the shoulder again. "Priceless."

He toddled off, flanked by nurses, and one came over just moments later to see if I wanted anything to drink with my cucumber sandwiches. I think she was a bit surprised when I asked for Tizer. But who needed sophistication. I picked up my Agatha Christie. This was turning into a happier experience than I had imagined.

Rick duly arrived - with an engagement ring. Unbelievable. In just a matter of a very few hours since my phone call, he'd been into Ratner's and picked out a Victorian style ruby and diamond ring. Not only that, but it fitted. I confused him, of course, by bursting into tears all over the spaghetti bolognese, but I think the other diners thought I was just happy. They didn't realise what an emotional day it had been; how a life had been saved, and all our futures changed absolutely.

It took me a while to regain my speech faculty. "Rick, you don't have to do this."

"I know, baby doll. But I want you to bloody show your dad the ring before you tell him about the baby. And I want you to tell him that we're not going to rush into a nasty little wedding, we're going to have the total bloody works after the baby is born."

"You're assuming I'll marry you, of course."

His mouth opened but no words came out.

"I'm only joking. I knew I was never going to get a down-on-your-knees proposal."

There was no answer to that.

"And Rick. This baby. I haven't told you. It's not an it any more. It's a girl. And she'll be here in just a couple of months."

He kissed my hand, the one sporting the obviously new ring.

"Two girls to look after. I'm looking forward to it. I'll take my H.G.V. test, so I can do better paid work than just driving a bloody van. And I'll start looking for a place for us."

"There's room in Whitechapel House, you know."

"Not for all of us. And anyway, I was thinking of buying a place. Getting a bloody mortgage."

Well, you could have knocked me down with just the tiniest touch of the tiniest feather – if I hadn't been heavier than usual. "A mortgage! What do you know about mortgages?"

"My dad. He works for Lloyds, remember? Knows how I can get a hundred per cent mortgage. It's the way forward, Linda. It's the future. If we move out a little bit, Essex or Middlesex, we can buy something for around four thousand."

"Four thousand! It'll take forever to pay that back."

He kissed my hand again. "Trust me, angel."

Such a lovely bloke. I had thought he would be angry that things hadn't gone according to plan, but he was already planning a very different future for us. I used a Dolce Vita serviette to mop up bolognese sauce and smudged mascara from my face.

"Who'd ever have thought that just a few years after you followed me home from the Flamingo, that we'd be sitting here talking about babies and mortgages. Can you really believe it?"

"The bloody Flamingo. Georgie Fame. Rod Stewart. Yes, those were the days."

I giggled, and it had nothing to do with alcohol, because I was definitely on the wagon until my baby was weaned. Dr Richards had re-visited me and replaced my Agatha Christie with a book about pregnancy advice, and that was one of the first things I'd read: about the effects of smoke and alcohol. I'd never been that keen on drinking, to be honest. I hadn't acquired the knack for it that my dad had. And, although I did smoke ten No. 6 a day, even that was all a bit of showmanship, because I didn't breathe the smoke into my lungs. It made me cough my guts up if I did.

I let Rick light up, though. There was a limit to how much he would be prepared to do for me and for our baby. And I knew that giving up smoking for him would be as impossible as giving up football or driving his rusty bucket MG just that bit too fast.

"Linda. Do you miss it?"

"What?"

He blew a smoke ring at me. "The Flamingo."

"No. I loved it, but I don't miss it."

"We've become very bloody boring and domestic, Linda, don't you think? When was the last time we went clubbing?"

"But isn't clubbing just for pulling?"

"Not really. Would you mind if I went out one night a week with the boys after we're married?"

"What a silly question. Of course not. I'd be able to wash my hair and do all those boring girly things. And you'll need time away from a screaming baby and smelly nappies and…"

"You paint such a rosy bloody picture. And the other thing we need to talk about is …" He hesitated.

"Is what?" Where was he going now?

He twisted the new ring on my left hand. "Douggie."

Douggie. He was right. We needed to talk about Douggie.

"Douggie." We looked at each other, thinking our own thoughts. He was probably thinking 'bloody nuisance' but there again, he'd always got on with Douggie; one of the few, and perhaps I wasn't being fair. "You mean I won't be able to look after him and the baby?"

"And your dad. And me."

"And you. Yeah. Of course. I see."

I thought about it. He was right. "As it happens, I'm sure I could manage. People do. But no, I see your point. And I think there is a way round... there is a possible solution."

"Oh yeah? Then I'd like to hear it. You've been looking after Douggie ever since I met you, since before I met you. Good on yer. But that hasn't left you with much of a bloody life, let's face it."

"Now, Rick, that's not fair. I had a few part time jobs when he was at school, a few holidays when Auntie Ivy has taken over. I've had time to go to college and get myself a few A-levels, which I probably wouldn't have done if I'd worked full time. It's not been that bad. Really."

"Whatever. So, go on then. The solution is..."

"Dad has been thinking about taking voluntary redundancy. He's been with the brewery for thirty years, since he was a lad, so he'll get a fair bit of compensation, if that's the right word. And he's been coming out with the same sort of stuff as you just did – oh, about me not having much of a life, and about feeling guilty, about taking his turn before he's too old, about getting Douggie settled with some kind of a future."

Rick lifted his glass of lager and clicked it against my glass of bitter lemon. "Here's to Frank Fletcher. He's a good man. A bloody good man."

I reined him back in a little. "Well, I'm not sure he's made up his mind. Not finally."

"But when he hears the news. About Poppet." I smiled at his unthinking use of the name I was using as a stop-gap. "About the wedding. About moving out..."

"About moving out."

"What about it?"

"Let me tell him, Rick. In my own time. In my own way. Better still, he might even suggest it himself. Which would be just perfect."

"So why the long face?"

My glass was blurred as was Rick's face and our empty bowls. "I'm going to miss them."

Rick was stopped from grabbing my hand again by a brisk waiter who was trying to persuade us to have a knickerbocker glory. "Not very bloody Italian is it?" he growled.

"Rick! Ice cream *is* very Italian." I smiled at the baffled looking Latin. "Yes, I'll have one."

"Two spoons, pal."

"Rick!"

"What? I know you, eyes bigger than your b... well, perhaps not, not at this very moment."

That made us both laugh. Poppet kicked again. "Rick. How will they manage?"

"They'll manage. You're going to have a baby. And me, too. I want you to look after us properly. No farming our kid out while you go to work. Oh, no, don't look at me like that. I want you fresh and ready when I get home. Ready and willing and..."

The knickerbocker glory arrived before he could finish the sentence, sparing my blushes, and we scooped in unison, playing footsie beneath the long tablecloth. My pregnancy had not affected my desire for Rick and his thrusting body. Our sex life was fantastic and, although he looked like a rough diamond with his coarse skin and thick neck, he was very, very gentle – at least with me. I had never asked him about anyone else. I didn't want to know. Not now, not ever.

To his macho pals, I was his 'crumpet', his 'old lady'. When we were alone, I was his 'angel', his 'virgin' (as was), his 'sexpot' or his 'baby doll'. Not that we managed to be alone very often, as we both lived at home still. Our sessions were in his very cramped car, his firm's van, or – most comfortably – his best friend's bedroom: Tony turned up the volume on his record player and left us to it. There had been a few steamy sessions on my sofa when Dad was working late, but I was always aware that Douggie could come wandering in at any moment, and so those were less successful. I had been such a fool to rely on withdrawal for birth control. But the thought of discussing anything with the doctor who'd known me since I was a tot… that was something else I would have to contend with.

"Penny for them, angel."

"Oh, I was thinking. About you. About…" I lowered my voice, "… sex."

"You are insatiable." The words seemed very loud to me, and I suspect that was deliberate, with Rick amused by my discomfiture as a few people glanced in our direction.

But, to be fair, he lowered his voice before going on. "I love you, angel. Come on, I'm throbbing. I've got the van outside. If it's all right…" That was my Rick. Crude, tender, mouthy, romantic, sexy, considerate.

"Of course it's all right. I asked before you picked me up. And it wasn't easy."

"What wasn't easy?"

"Asking."

We literally ran out of the restaurant. Although running in platform shoes and with all that extra weight I was carrying wasn't easy. I had to sort out what was going to happen with Dad and Douggie. But that could wait till later.

I should have known not to worry. Dad restrained any anger he felt, although I saw a vein throbbing in his temple that I'd never noticed before. He was happy about the wedding, happy about the baby, a bit concerned about my reputation, I think, but I only cared about what Rick felt and Rick was there for me. To be honest, I think it helped Dad make up his mind about the redundancy. Forced his hand, even.

"Dad, I feel guilty about lumbering you with Douggie."

"Now, you listen here, girl." He sat me down next to him on our dralon sofa, as if I was a child again. Still the same Dad, if I ignored the paunchy waistline and the greying hair, the quiff long gone. "I am not being *lumbered*. Don't you use that kind of word. Douggie is my son. He is a wonderful, special boy. Okay, so he needs 'elp to do all those things me and you take for granted – crossing the road, queuing, cooking, shopping. And 'e gets cross if his timetable is altered. And we can't have a proper chat. Well, not one that makes much sense. But he's 'appy, he don't stay out late, he's not going to get himself pregnant, he don't have wild friends – or any friends come to that. And 'e needs me.

"I'll tell you somethin', girl. Being needed is a good feeling. Maybe when I'm old and grey… okay, greyer… it won't seem so important. But I'm a few years off fifty still. I can't just sit with my roll-ups and my slippers in front of the telly. Looking after Douggie will give me a reason for getting up in the morning. What else am I gonna do all day?"

"Dad." I didn't know what to say. So I kissed him and he rubbed his cheek like a schoolboy who had been zapped by his least favourite aunt.

"Dad. I need to know something." Something I'd been thinking about. Could be a touchy subject. Best to just go for it. "About Douggie's… problems. Is there a chance that my baby…?"

He stopped me by putting a nicotine stained finger on my 'satin coral' lips. "Lightning does not strike twice, young lady."

"You don't mind if I check that out in the library, do you?"

That got me a welcome hug. I thought, out of the blue, that my mother had been a damn fool to leave this lovely man, even if he did give her the occasional slap. But the subject was taboo, so I just grinned at him.

"Pity we can't call her Frank."

"No. A nice thought, though, girl. How about Georgina?"

"Where did that come from?"

"Oh, I dunno. I've always liked the name. And your granddad was called George. You never met him of course."

"He was called George? I never knew that." There was a lot I never knew. "Georgina." I said the name slowly. "Yes, I like it. It's a possible."

"Toilet paper." Douggie had appeared in the doorway holding the cardboard innards of a toilet roll, and with his trousers around his ankles.

"Okay, son. I'm coming." Dad pushed me back down onto the sofa. "You're going to have to start taking it easy, girl. I'll do it."

"Toilet paper."

"Yes, Douggie, I'm getting it."

Six feet two, his dark curls cropped short and shiny, he could have been a male model. Or a matinée idol.

Dad led my beautiful little brother back into the toilet. "Come on, sunshine. Let's sort you out."

I could hear Douggie's voice counting out the sheets of paper: "Seven, eight. That's it. No, no, eight. It should be eight."

"Schmuck."

Douggie repeated it. "Schmuck." And then I could hear them laughing.

Seemed Dad had already taken over. Douggie didn't seem to mind. As long as someone was there. Someone familiar and reliable. Whether it was me, Dad, or whoever. He'd be fine. Both of them. All of us. I patted my tummy happily.

One of those days for the journal. The only other day this year worth writing about had been the day Paul McCartney had decided to split from the Beatles. And there was still a wedding – a very important wedding – and Poppet's – or Georgina's – birth to come. Quite a year.

Chapter Four

1975

"It's not fair. I wanna berfday."

"You will have. In November. You'll be three." Stephanie was proving a handful; jealous, I guess, of all the planning involved for Georgina's fifth birthday party. We were really going to town this year, with pizzas from the new place in Enfield town centre, as well as the cake, candles, balloons and goodie bags that every five year-old at Georgie's school had started to incorporate into their birthday bash. The jellies hadn't set, the magician hadn't turned up yet and the rain was chucking it down but, fingers crossed, everything would turn out okay.

"I wanna blow candles."

"They're my candles. They're mine, ain't they, mum? They're mine."

"Yes, George. And you'll be blowing them out later."

"It's not fair." Stephanie's new phrase, often repeated. I looked down at the top of her head with its shining chestnut ringlets, so reminiscent of Douggie and Mum.

The more Stephanie complained, the more Georgina got bossy. She stood now, arms akimbo, my sturdy no nonsense little girl, her much straighter hair pulled tightly back into a pony tail. "You're just a baby. When you're five you can have a party – can't she Mum?"

"Of course. It's only fair."

"See? It *is* fair."

"Want a party now."

"Tell you what. You two go and get changed. Mr Magic will be here soon, I'm sure, and then your friends will be arriving. I've still got lots to do here. If you need any help, just yell."

"I don't need any help," Georgie announced proudly, dragging Stephanie behind her as they climbed the narrow stairs up to the bedroom they shared. We'd thought about looking for a bigger house now that Stephanie was getting older, but Rick just wasn't in work often enough for us to commit to any more borrowing. There were no problems at the moment, because when he did work, he earned a cracking wage, but he didn't seem motivated, somehow. And every time he had a few days off without a sick note, that was it. He lost his job. Let's face it, there was always someone else willing and able to take over. But Rick didn't care. As far as he was concerned, there was always another job around the corner. But one day he'd come unstuck. He'd suddenly find himself unemployable, with his track record.

"Don't worry, sexpot. There's always work for H.G.V. drivers."

"Not unreliable ones."

That would be his excuse to put a hand up my skirt and caress the flesh between my stocking tops and knickers. "Give me a break, sexpot. I'm doing my best for you and the girls. And I'm keeping you satisfied."

Yes, that was something he was good at. Ten out of ten. Every time I brought up the subject of money, he would just take me to bed.

The bell of the telephone made me jump. It was him. "I was just thinking about you." And it was true.

"That's what I like to hear. Look, I'm on the way home."

"But it's only two o'clock."

"You didn't think I'd miss Georgina's birthday, did you?"

"I thought you said you were going to Wales today."

"Nah. I got Dave to cover and I did a few local drops instead."

"But the extra money…"

"Oh, don't start, Linda. If we're short of anything, there's always H.P. for Chrissake. And I'm bringing Georgie's trike with me."

"You got it? Oh, well done." He was a good man where the family were concerned.

"When did I ever let you down? Or my girls? I'll see you soon. Luv ya."

There was a tearful yelp from upstairs and I put the phone down in a hurry.

It was Stephanie. She hadn't yet mastered the skill required by hooks and eyes or sash-tying. It didn't take long to sort her out and the mint green lace looked stunning. Georgina, ever more conservative, was in white satin adorned only by an appliquéd black cat. It was the more babyish of the two outfits and didn't suit her, but I'd let her have a free hand on such a special occasion. Thank goodness her interest in the Bay City Rollers didn't yet extend to wanting to dress like them...

The doorbell heralded the first arrival. "That must be Mr Magic. Come on."

I would have to find time to change out of my grubby jeans in the next ten minutes, perhaps while Mr Magic was setting up. My little black number would be fine, and my Barbra Streisand hairstyle was extra blonde, thanks to the spray-on bleach I'd managed to apply before the girls woke up that morning.

The doorbell kept going as Georgina's friends arrived, all carrying girly gifts which she didn't seem to appreciate. She certainly didn't say thank you very convincingly and discarded the Ballerina Barbie, the tiara, something that was presumably a Womble, and the Snow White money box as energetically as she discarded the wrapping.

I'd managed to pull on my dress before the first one arrived, although her mum looked at me as if I was something that had crawled out from under a stone. Too blonde perhaps? Or too voluptuous? Well, there was nothing I could do about the latter. Rick liked it, and that was all that mattered.

"Don't worry, Mrs... Carey? Moira will be in safe hands."

"I'm sure."

Less disapproval from the rest. Or perhaps I just didn't notice. Let's face it. We had moved to our little – heavily mortgaged – terraced house in Enfield while many of our friends were still in council flats in Stepney and Bethnal Green. So there was nothing for me to be ashamed of. I had two great girls, a husband who couldn't keep his hands off me, clean net curtains, a Fanny Craddock cookbook – which I used all the time – and imitation Clarice Cliff china. What more could a girl want?

Mr Magic had just started his stuff when Rick arrived with the trike. Silly bugger, he'd wrapped it. As if you could disguise its shape. We left it in the pint-sized porch until Mr M. had finished. He was a real 'life and soul' type and got the girls happily yelling out and choosing cards and oohing and aahhing all over the place. He finished off by retrieving some fizzing sparklers from under his top hat.

"How did he do that?" I whispered in Rick's ear. We were as entertained as the kids. Rick shook his head and grabbed my bum simultaneously, momentarily forgetting why he was home so early.

But not for long. "Where's the birthday girl?"

Georgie put her hand up.

"Are you ready to eat now?"

"Yes, please."

Mr Magic winked at me. "Please? Did you hear that? You've got her well trained. I'll leave you to it, shall I?"

"Would you like a drink before you go? Some sandwiches?"

"That's nice of you. But I've got another party, believe it or not. It's all go on Saturdays and Sundays for me and then I get to twiddle my thumbs for a few days."

"Sounds like my kind of job," laughed Rick, helping him pack away as the girls argued over who was sitting next to who.

"Girls. Perlease. You can't all sit next to Georgina."

"She's my best friend," said the tallest girl. Lucy, I think.

"No, she's mine," said Stephanie.

"She's your sister, silly," laughed Carol and Holly, the twins.

Stephanie looked as if tears were about to flow again, so I sat her on one side of Georgie and the Lucy girl on the other. Georgina started protesting – she wanted to sit next to Gwen, our next door neighbour

– until I said she could have her surprise present now if everyone would just please sit down.

Her "Sit down, all of you" was pure Peggy Mount. And, amazingly, they did.

Rick carried in the trike and placed it reverently in the empty centre of the room which had been quickly vacated by Mr Magic. "Bet you can't guess what this is."

"Don't be silly." Yes, siree, that was my daughter. "Thanks, Daddy." "And Mummy."

"Yes." She jumped up and ripped off the crepe paper. "Red and white. It's beautiful."

"Manchester United."

"Rick!"

"Only joking. You like red and white, don't you, George?"

"Did Uncle Douggie tell you?"

Rick looked bemused, but I couldn't help him. "Er, perhaps he did. Do you know, I can't remember."

"Uncle Douggie always remembers."

"Yes, Georgie." I was touched by her positive approach towards her – let's face it – odd uncle. "I think you'd better start eating, or there won't be much left."

"Oy. Don't eat all the pizza." Bossy rushed back to the table, diverted.

Rick kissed me, asking the question with his eyes.

"Douggie? He sent a card. Or rather Dad enclosed a card from Douggie with his. They're coming over later, after the party. I thought it best."

"Of course. And my folks? Too busy I suppose."

He was trying to sound flippant, but I knew that he was disappointed at what he perceived as their general lack of interest in their grandchildren. "I think it was the journey. A train to Fenchurch Street, the tube, and a bus."

"It's not exactly the bloody Hebrides, is it? Your dad didn't complain, did he?"

"My dad's different."

He changed direction. "How is he?"

I didn't answer, feeling the party spirit recede, and Rick squeezed my hand.

"Sorry, sexpot. Wrong time, wrong place. And bloody silly question."

"No. Don't apologise. His luck's holding, if you can call it luck."

The thought of Dad's stomach cancer brought mixed feelings. Memories of the overwhelming sense of disaster at the diagnosis, and then the sheer joy of the news that he and the surgeon had won the battle. I was still worried about the war, of course, but Dad was proud of beating what he called the 'Big C' and had been in remission for over two years. "I'll make sure I'm ready to hold that new baby of yours," he'd promised me. And, although my pregnancy had been burdened by his burden, he'd done me – all of us – proud. Stephanie's birth had been even more special, given the dual nature of the celebration.

I got involved again in the squabbling over the last few sausage rolls before I got maudlin. Rick, on my okay, went to get the birthday cake from the kitchen. He lit the candles before bringing it in and carried it proudly to the table with cries of: "Make way, make way," to imaginary hordes, like a Roman Emperor.

Georgina was so excited, it took three puffs before the five candles were well and truly gutted. Whether her gesture in giving Stephanie the first slice, expertly cut by Rick, was out of generosity or convenience because Stephanie was nearest, I don't know, but it was good to see. I'd always wondered what it would be like to have a sister and, through them, I was finding out.

Dad and Douggie arrived as the last child, Moira Carey as it happened, was leaving. Her mum looked at my black number, now smeared with icing sugar and pizza topping, and at the young man who was telling anyone interested that, "Douggie has two hundred thousand hairs. Linda has one hundred and ten thousand."

She didn't say anything apart from a muttered, "Thank you," for the goodie bag, but I heard her questioning Moira as they walked away:

"Who *was* that man? What *have* you been eating?" Oh, well, it didn't matter.

Dad looked old, I thought. He was so much greyer, even his skin seemed more grey, and he had a stoop that I'd not noticed before. In fact, it seemed to me as if he had shrunk a bit. Although I still saw him – and Douggie – regularly, it wasn't often enough. I wouldn't have noticed his ageing if I saw him more often.

The frilly bouncy bundles that were Georgina and Stephanie made a difference to Dad's demeanour immediately. Their sticky faces and sticky smiles had the effect that no anti-ageing cream could achieve. There was even a discernible smile on Douggie's face, although he, predictably, ignored them. They understood. They didn't think of it as being ignored. That was Uncle Douggie. That was the way he was. So be it. Oh, to be able to teach that level of acceptance.

"Sit down, Dad. Georgina's saved you some birthday cake."

"I should hope so too. It's not every day my big girl is five." He looked so proud. Faded, frail, but so proud.

"Douggie likes candles."

"Yes, I know. Rick is going to re-light them for you – aren't you Rick?"

Rick had obviously completely forgotten, but he jumped up gamely. "Of course. I'll put them on your very own slice, Douggie."

Douggie followed him into the kitchen while Georgina showed her grandfather the treasured tricycle. "Wow. That's really something. Is there enough room in your garden to ride it around?"

"Dad said I could go on the pavements."

"Did he now?" Dad looked at me and I shrugged. Rick and George had obviously been making plans behind my back. The pavements worried me, I must say, but I suppose if one of us was with her…

"Happy birthday to you!" Rick was reprising the earlier event, but Douggie cut him short.

"Don't like singing."

"Sorry. I forgot."

We watched Douggie blow out the five candles again and he didn't want me to remove them. He wanted to sit watching the smoke spiral up.

"We did that already." That was Georgie, scornful.

"It's not fair." That was Stephanie, out of sorts again.

"What's not fair?" That was dad, placatory as always.

"It's over."

"What's over?" Dad lifted her onto a bony knee.

"Georgie's birthday."

"It's not over till bed-time. Is it, Mum?"

"No, Georgie, but I think the eating is. You must be bursting. Show Granddad your other presents."

Georgina looked around her. "Oh. Yeah."

Dad removed Stephanie, wincing as if with some discomfort. "Let me look at you."

"Dad?"

"She's beautiful. They are both beautiful. I'm so glad I came."

"Dad? Are you okay?"

He leaned back and closed his eyes. "Just a bit tired. It's a hell of a journey."

I got busy making tea and clearing away the leftovers and the mess while Georgina showed Douggie her other presents, chattering away, oblivious to his lack of interest. Except in Barbie's hair. "How many hairs?"

"You can count them if you like," Georgina suggested. And he did.

Stephanie was preening herself in the lace dress in front of Rick. "Is it pretty?"

"Yes, it is. Perhaps you should take it off now that the party's over."

"No. More pretty than Barbeee or Shnow White."

Rick laughed loudly. "She's getting competitive already."

I smiled but sat at Dad's feet, concerned by his appearance. He didn't open his eyes, but he put his hand on my head. "I'm fine, girl. Fine. Really."

The ambulance took him an hour later. His breathing had got louder and louder and then, I couldn't wake him. Rick stayed with the girls and Douggie, reassuring them that Granddad needed some special medicine from the hospital, keeping the birthday going. I held up well until I was in the ambulance, then I fell apart. He'd lied to me. I knew it. He was dying. I just knew it.

"You silly old bugger. Why didn't you tell me? There are so many things I haven't said, Dad. Not today. It's Georgina's birthday for Chrissake."

I was babbling and the paramedic put his hand on my shoulder. "I want to give him some oxygen. He's hanging on in there. Can you tell me about his medical history?"

There wasn't much to tell. Leastways, not much that he'd told me. Why didn't he tell me everything?

He pushed the mask away for a moment and opened his eyes. "Douggie. The Miltons. Margate."

Those were his last words. He held on for two days, so at least he didn't die on Georgina's birthday. That could have been so difficult for her, and for me, as she grew older. I hadn't left his side and Rick had taken time off work – not an issue for him – to be with the girls, with Douggie on our camp bed, asking constantly about his dad. But I didn't want Douggie to come to the hospital. I didn't want him to see his dad slipping away. It was bad enough for me. But for Douggie… He showed an interest in life expectancy, and often asked when he was going to die, when all of us were going to die. Because "no-one knows" was not acceptable, I'd given him guesswork dates, around eighty years from our birth dates – but Dad was only forty-nine.

Auntie Ivy, still upright, still hennaed, was there for me. She agreed to stay in the flat in Whitechapel with Douggie as soon as I phoned her to tell her that I felt he should be in familiar surroundings while I sorted out his life, all our lives. She was the only one in the family with a car and she came to pick him up. He hadn't reacted when I told him Dad wasn't coming home. I don't think he really believed me.

"I think you may have some explaining to do when you get him home," I confessed to her.

She smiled. "You mean he may be expecting to see his dad. Yes. I see."

"Here's the key. I've got things to do here for a few days. And I'll arrange the funeral at St. John's. But I don't think Douggie should come."

"No. I agree. And after the funeral?"

"Can you stay till then?"

"Yes. Of course."

"Oh, thanks, Auntie Ivy. That will be such a great help. Afterwards? Well, Dad said something about The Miltons. In Margate. I need to check his paperwork, but I'm pretty sure it's a home of some kind. He seems to have known this was going to happen. He's probably made some kind of plan."

"Yes. Frank phoned me a week ago. He didn't want to bother you because you were busy with Georgina's birthday party. But I'm only his sister-in-law. His ex-sister-in-law. You're his daughter. He should have told you. Still, he meant well. A good man."

She knew. About Dad being so ill. About The Miltons.

"Frank arranged everything, Linda."

"You mean for Douggie? He's arranged everything for Douggie?"

"Of course. He didn't give up smoking, you know. And he knew it was only a matter of time. And he knew you had your own life. So he had to sort out Douggie."

She took the key. Douggie was waiting patiently in the passenger seat, but he wouldn't be patient for much longer.

"After the funeral, go and see the place. Take Douggie with you. Just for a visit. Then we'll pack his things and get him ready for his new life. You'll see. Your dad chose carefully. He took his time."

I wanted to sob. To sob and sob. Because he hadn't told me. And because he had relieved me of the biggest decision that he knew I would have to make: Douggie.

I was kept busy for quite a few days. And there was a lot to do. The funeral, visiting the flat in Whitechapel to sort out Dad's belongings and finances, talking to the council, the neighbours, the G.P.

The Miltons was a huge 19th century pile on the outskirts of Margate. It was home to just twenty people with learning difficulties, and they all had their own en-suite rooms. More like a hotel than a home. There were sea glimpses from most of the upper rooms, but Douggie wasn't interested in the view, only in the facilities. There had to be room for his television, his digital clock, his beloved – if bulky – video recorder. Our first visit had been brief, because that was all he wanted to establish at that stage.

I had been so worried about trying to talk to Douggie about Dad, about trying to explain. But Dad was already very much a feature of Douggie's past, not his present. "Dad gone to see Jesus and the Angels." The acceptance was almost scary.

"Yes, Douggie."

"How many millions of light years away?"

"Too many to count."

"Will he be a skeleton?"

"Not if he's with Jesus."

"Will he be dust?"

"Not if he's with Jesus."

"When will Douggie go to see Jesus?"

"No one knows."

"Is it a big mystery?"

"Yes." I could taste the salt of my tears as they reached my mouth, but Douggie didn't notice. "A big mystery."

"Guess a date. Go on. Guess."

"Guess? 2032."

"2032. Douggie will be eighty."

"Yes."

"Linda will be eighty-five."

"And still plodding on, I expect." I'd often thought that I'd like to outlive Douggie, but it felt a bit mean to give it voice.

Ivy and I were helping him to unpack. This was it. The big move. I didn't want to say goodbye. He knew no one here. No one. If he felt abandoned, he couldn't explain the feeling. If he was scared – of being alone, of being without Dad, of being in a new place, in a strange place – he couldn't find the right words. How would I know?

I hugged him tightly and looked him in the face. He looked over my shoulder as usual. "Look at me."

It was a struggle.

"Are you going to be okay?"

"What day is Georgina coming?"

I told him. And I told him what day Rick and Stephanie were coming. I told him when I was coming back and when Auntie Ivy was going to visit. We put all the dates on his calendar.

There didn't seem to be anything else I could do. I just had to let go. I had to trust that Dad had chosen wisely.

The Matron, as she called herself, accompanied us to Ivy's prized Beetle. She was ideal: mumsy, gentle, softly spoken, experienced. "Don't worry, Mrs North. We'll ring you with any queries during this settling in period."

"However trivial?"

"However trivial."

What more could I ask?

Dad had sorted out Douggie's future, literally – the paperwork had revealed assessments, negotiations, visits to several potential homes, meetings with Social Services in London, Social Services in Margate, endless correspondence, none of which I knew about. None of which Dad had ever mentioned – although Douggie wasn't quite as surprised as I'd expected, so some conversations must have taken place between the two of them. I'd asked Douggie what Dad had told him about The Miltons, but he said he couldn't remember. Maybe that was the truth. Maybe not.

We sat in the car for quite a few minutes. I needed to make sure he didn't come running out, calling me. I just needed a bit of time. Ivy understood.

"Do you think I should have tried to contact Mum?"

"No." I didn't think she was going to say any more but then she added: "I expect she knows."

"What do you mean?"

"She keeps in touch with… people."

"What people?"

"Nobody you know."

"You're telling me she probably knew about the funeral."

"Probably."

"But she didn't come."

"No." She patted my hand and then started up the car. "She doesn't deserve you. Any of you."

I thought about my daughters. About sisters.

"Were you close as children?"

"I hated her then. And I hate her now." She spoke calmly and we pulled out of the grounds of Milton House, heading for the seafront and a cup of tea.

"Do you want to tell me why?" I don't know why I'd asked that. I wasn't really curious about my mother. I didn't know, or care, where she was, or even *if* she was. She was part of my past, not my present or my future. It just seemed the right thing to say.

"No."

"Good."

Ivy laughed.

As she drove, I sat back, thinking of a myriad of different things. Perhaps Margate might be a good place to move to? Before the girls got settled at schools. Something to think about. Something to discuss with Rick.

Chapter Five

1980

Margate wasn't for Rick. He didn't like the whole 'kiss-me-quick', Dreamland image of the place. A shame. I liked the idea of living at the seaside and Georgina and Stephanie would have loved the beach on those few days that the weather encouraged a prolonged visit.

But we did move: to Ilford in Essex. It kind of combined elements of the ethnicity of the East End that we both remembered from our youth (Rick was a Hackney lad) with the elements of suburbia that we had got used to in Enfield: department stores, big gardens, good range of transport links, and decent schools for the girls. "And it isn't as far from London as Margate." Why that was an issue for Rick, I'm not sure – he did very little work in London and I had no ties in the capital and no time or money to visit, apart from an occasional trip to see Auntie Ivy, who lived in a high-rise council flat in Bethnal Green.

It wasn't exactly easy to get to Margate from Ilford. It involved a long tube journey to Victoria, changing at Mile End, and another train to Margate. And Rick didn't relish the driving option either, via the Dartford Tunnel; his pet hate.

For Rick, visiting Douggie was never going to be something on his 'have to do' agenda. Okay, so they had problems communicating, I knew that. And I had to agree with him that it was 'difficult'. Of course it was. It didn't help that he took Douggie's 'how many minutes?' questions regarding his departure personally, however many times I told him he always asked that of everyone who visited, including me. On our last visit, he'd mentioned that he didn't feel it was a good idea to take the girls next time, although I hadn't seen a problem. They were far more accepting than Rick was, and were used to Uncle Douggie as part of the family; eccentric, odd even, but just Uncle Douggie. For Rick, it was something more, something unnerving, something he couldn't put into words. It seemed to be a situation that provoked issues he didn't want to face.

I remembered the application form Rick had to fill in for his last job – the jobs still kept coming and going. The application had asked about his family medical history, probing into such issues as epilepsy and diabetes. And he'd asked me if he ought to mention Douggie.

"Of course not. He's not your family, not directly. He's mine."

The look of relief on his face was understandable, but not nice. Not nice at all.

And now this, with the girls. What it boiled down to was that I would have to go alone, on a day when he wasn't working, so that he could stay with the girls. And he knew about the horrendous journey, but just shrugged.

"I could take the girls to the seafront, I suppose," he offered grudgingly, "while you visit."

"But that's ridiculous. What will you tell them? Uncle Douggie bites?"

"No." He wriggled uncomfortably, the conversation at an end. And I let him win. Our visits as a family faded, and my visits alone became more and more difficult. Not just the transport issues, but the fact that even if Rick wasn't working, he always seemed to have a reason why he couldn't look after the girls on any date I thought of going – an important snooker match, tickets for West Ham, helping brother Larry out behind the bar of the Rooster, an interview for the next job. Always something.

The Matron at the Miltons had changed a few times in the last few years. The latest didn't seem so keen on visitors and, I am ashamed to say, I let her influence me too. "It's a bit disruptive, dear," she said to me. Mrs Sutton, that was her name. "A bit disruptive. Not just for Douglas. Oh, no. But for everyone else, too. You see…" She looked around conspiratorially, although we were alone in her modern office.

"So many of our residents don't see anyone. Not anyone. Not a single visitor from one month, one season, to the next."

"Surely that's their problem." I had made a feeble attempt to remonstrate.

An unmanicured finger waggled at me. "They see Douggie getting a regular visitor, and they ask questions. Unanswerable questions. Disturbing questions. You do see my point?"

"Yes, I do. But…"

"Disruptive, you see. Unsettling."

"Well, perhaps if I took him out. I could meet him in the reception. They wouldn't need to know."

"There are windows." She was smiling at me as if I was one of her 'residents'. "And don't forget that all our residents go out regularly – oh, yes, with appropriate staff, there's always someone out along the seafront, in the arcades, at the shops, in one of the cafés. Oh, yes. And you would bump into them."

"For goodness sake. Are you asking me not to come?"

"Not at all. You can come as much as you like. I'm just asking you to think of the consequences, Mrs North."

"But if I don't come, the main consequence would be that I am abandoning my brother."

That didn't please her at all. Her face stiffened and she stood up to assert her authority. "And do you think he cares?"

"How dare you?"

"Mrs North. He has his own little world here. His own little life. He is happy. He doesn't need anyone in particular, as long as someone is looking after him."

"I'm sorry. There may be an element of truth in what you say. But he's my… my little brother." Damn. I hadn't meant her to see me get upset.

She sat down again and burrowed for a tissue. "Here. Please. Go and see him now. He'll be expecting you."

"Yes. Exactly."

"And if he wasn't expecting you…"

"He just needs to know."

"Yes. Exactly. That's all he needs. I agree. He needs to know when you are coming. Whether he needs the level of frequency that *you* feel is appropriate is something else."

Damn the woman. Did she have a point? I stood up to leave.

"Oh, I nearly forgot. He had a visit from your mother."

I changed my mind about leaving and leaned against her door instead.

"What?"

"Yes. A bit of a turn up for the books. I meant to tell you earlier."

"He had a visit from, from…" I couldn't say the word. "She came here? She saw him? You let her see him?"

She gave me an odd look. "She's his mother. How could I stop her? She phoned first, to make an appointment, as it were, so he was expecting her. I gather she has no plans to return."

"I bet she bloody hasn't."

"Please."

"Is that it? Did you leave them alone?"

"Not as such. Mrs Fletcher wanted to see the gardens. Said she liked gardens. So, they spent time looking around outside. It was a lovely day, and other people had the same idea."

"So, when was this then?"

"Oh, a fortnight ago or so. It will be in the visitors' book if you want verification."

"Yes. I'll look for myself. And what was his, Douggie's, reaction?"

She shrugged her plump shoulders. "I'm not sure he understood that she was his mother. I heard him say, 'Goodbye Audrey'."

I wanted to know what she looked like. Was she still glamorous as a pensioner? But I didn't want this woman to know that I hadn't seen her, *we* hadn't seen her, since 1957. Twenty-three years. Where had she been? Why had she come? What had been said? What the hell did she think she was playing at?

Mrs Sutton was watching me curiously. "Are you okay? I didn't realise it would be quite such a shock."

"I'm fine. But I would like to see the visitors' book before I see Douggie, if that's all right."

I wouldn't recognise her writing if I saw it, so it meant nothing to me. But it made her real. April 20th. And there was an address in Kent. So she wasn't that far away.

Mrs Sutton closed the book. "What would you like me to do if she should come back?"

"You say you can't stop her visiting?"

"No. She produced a copy of his birth certificate, a few photos... And he didn't seem upset by her visit. So, no, I have no reason to stop her. I meant, would you like me to pass on a message or something?"

"Oh. No. I can do that myself perfectly well. But thanks."

I shook her hand. "Just one question. Did she arrive alone – in a car? Did you have much of a conversation? Did she say much – about why she'd come?"

"Rather more than one question." She smiled and smoothed the damson coloured folds of her cord skirt. "But she arrived alone, yes, in a Mercedes. Just exchanged pleasantries about the weather. Said she'd lost contact and wanted to see him once before she moved abroad."

"Abroad?"

"Yes. Did you not know she was planning a move?"

"I knew something was up, yes," I lied. "I see. Thank you. And I'll think about what you said."

Douggie pointed at the clock as soon as he'd opened his door.

"Yes, Douggie. I know. I've been talking to Mrs Sutton."

"Linda late. How many verys of unusual is that?"

"A hundred." I kissed him but he didn't respond. He never did. Unless I asked him to. "Give us a hug."

I clung on to him for a moment before presenting him with the double pack of videos I had brought: *Planet of the Apes* and *Star Wars*.

"Monsters?"

"Yes."

He trotted off to get his box of index cards so the tapes could be entered and logged into his system with no delay. It kept him occupied for several minutes while I watched him. This was his world. He had everything around him he needed. He didn't ask about me, about Rick, or the girls…

"I've got some photos for you."

"Douggie likes photos."

"Yes, I know. Of Georgina and Stephanie."

"Douggie's friends."

"Yes."

He looked long and hard at the snapshots. Ten year old Georgina was sporting a new page-boy hairstyle, having at long last tired of the ponytail, and Stephanie's curls, so like his own, were as unruly as ever.

"Sisters."

"Yes."

"Linda is a sister."

"Yes, I'm your sister."

"Straight hair and curly hair. Not the same."

"No, they are very different. You're right."

Douggie put a hand up to my hair, purely for research reasons rather than in a gesture of affection. "Linda curly hair, Stephanie curly hair, Douggie curly hair."

"Yes, but mine's not very curly naturally. The hairdresser puts in rollers."

He looked at the photo again. "Take Georgina to the hairdresser. Needs to be curly."

I laughed. "Georgina wouldn't be too happy about that. A bit too girly for her, I expect."

'Girly' didn't register. I tried to think of another word. "Feminine." No, that didn't work either.

"Needs to be the same. Like Audrey."

Aaahh. He'd saved me the trouble of bringing up the subject.

"Do you mean Mum?"

Something snapped. "Not Mum. Not Mum. No Mummy any more. Where's Mummy? Audrey's not Mummy. Audrey." He was shouting, flailing around the room.

I spoke calmly. "Okay. I made a mistake. Audrey. Not Mummy."

"How many verys of a big mistake?"

"Two thousand." Funny, I didn't like denying her existence, even though she'd effectively denied ours for so many years. It seemed, what was the word... blasphemous almost.

"So. Audrey. Did you show her the gardens?"

"Audrey likes gardens. Likes roses. Douggie likes roses." He put his hand up to his own hair and changed the subject. "Same hair. Curly. Brown. Twelve inches."

I brought him back to the visit. "Isn't April a bit early for roses?"

"Some roses in April. Look."

He pointed to a small vase I hadn't seen before, with half a dozen jaded-looking yellow roses in an inch of water. "Oh. They need some fresh water."

I got busy with the water while he watched me. "Did Audrey give you these?"

"Yes. Not from Milton House."

"No. She must have brought them with her."

"It's a coincidence."

"What is?"

"Audrey likes roses. Douggie likes roses. And same hair. And same name."

"Fletcher. Yes."

"How many verys of a big huge coincidence is it?"

"A million at least."

As I filled the kettle, I wondered how to get him to tell me what they'd talked about. 'What did you talk about?' would, I suspected, get me the response he used to give on being asked 'What did you do at school today?' namely, 'Nothing'.

"Did you talk about Dad?"

"No."

"Did you talk about hair?"

"No."

"Did you talk about Milton House."

"Roses."

"Only roses?"

"Roses. Tea now."

Oh, well. Perhaps it didn't matter. If he didn't want to talk about it, it couldn't have been an issue. If something had been worrying him, something about the visit, I would have picked up on it. There would have been some kind of vibe. Something. But he was slurping his tea, standing up, shifting from one foot to another, looking out of the window, smiling, fingering the new videos. Perfectly normal Douggie behaviour.

And if she came again? Would it worry me? No. Perhaps she was going abroad. Good riddance. Perhaps not. I could find out. I had an address, although of course it could be fake. I hadn't written it down but I could remember it. 24 Acacia Drive, Welling.

Rick felt rather differently, predictably. "What about you? What about her grandchildren? Bloody woman. Appearing out of the blue. Out of the bloody wide blue yonder like some, some… Bloody woman."

"Think about Douggie, not her. Do you think I should encourage him to maintain contact? Write her a letter – from him, not from me? Or do you think I should just not mention it again? Treat it as a one off. He certainly was adamant that she wasn't his mother. Got quite angry. I don't know if he really believes that, or just doesn't want to believe the truth. It's impossible to say. I should have asked Dad what he'd told Douggie about her."

"I bet he said nothing at all."

"She always had a soft spot for Douggie."

"Oh, yeah. Some soft spot. Probably wanted to see how he'd turned out. Or after his benefits or some such."

"Rick. You don't know that."

"And you do, I suppose? What do you know?"

"What are you arguing about *now?*"

Georgie came in to the kitchen where we were, on the surface anyway, washing up.

"You make it sound like we're always arguing, kid."

"Well, you are. At least…"

"What does 'at least' mean?"

"When Mum comes home from visiting Uncle Douggie. That's when you argue."

Rick looked at me, rubbing vigorously at the mug in his hands, a triumphant grin on his face. An 'I told you so' grin.

"That's not true. It was nothing to do with Douggie."

"I don't believe you. Can Stephanie stay up a bit longer? She wants me to paint her nails."

"I don't think so. It's after eight. And I don't want her nails painted, anyway. She's too young."

Georgie pouted. "It was her idea."

"I daresay it was. I'm not blaming you. Come on, let's go sort her out. Daddy can finish in here."

"Oh, great."

"You know the deal. If you're not working…"

"Okay. I know the deal. No need to remind me." He hummed under his breath. Domesticity quite suited him. Perhaps it should be me looking for work and not him. Role reversal. Why not? I wouldn't be the first.

We could talk about it when the girls were in bed.

Stephanie didn't put up a lot of resistance to the ban on nail polish. I suspect she was just wanting Georgie to wait on her as usual, little minx. Memories of Mum's manipulative skills surfaced from somewhere, freshly stirred. Are these things in your genes? Or is that what Rick would call 'bullshit'.

"Why don't we visit Uncle Douggie any more?" Stephanie suddenly asked, out of the blue.

"Would you like to?"

"Don't know."

I turned to Georgie. "What about you?"

"I don't mind. But I would like to go to Margate."

"That settles it. Next time, we'll all go."

"When will that be?" Georgie wanted something a bit more definite.

"I'm not sure. I'll have to see if I can persuade Daddy to take us. Perhaps in the summer holidays. What do you think, Stephanie?"

"Yeah. Beach. Can I have a new swimsuit Mummy? A red one."

"Why not?" Rick would find it very hard to say 'no' to his youngest daughter, when she told him she wanted to show off her new swimsuit on Margate beach. And I would feel doubly guilty if I cut Douggie totally out of their lives. They had already lost both my parents, and Rick's parents had eleven other grandchildren from his three prolific brothers. I was convinced that they sometimes forgot the girls' names when we did visit their little bungalow in Barking, and we never seemed to be the only ones visiting. What with a resident poodle, two budgies, and the Meals on Wheels lady, our last visit – just three days ago – had been like a madhouse. Funny, really. 'Like a madhouse'. Whereas Douggie's home was quiet and tidy…

"And can I have a beach ball – in West Ham colours?" Trust Georgie to be different.

"If we can find one."

We hugged each other as if it was all settled. Rick would probably be cross, but for me to take matters into my own hands didn't happen that often. And why not? He could indulge in his favourite food – fish and chips – with seagulls overhead and the smell of the salt water.

But when the girls were in bed, I would first need to tackle the issue of me working. I had a feeling he might like the idea, even if only for a few years. I decided to wait until we were in bed. The crotchless knickers I'd bought in that new boutique in Ilford High Street would come in very handy.

Chapter Six

1985

The girls hadn't really decided whether they liked our role reversal. The idea wasn't that widespread, certainly not in Ilford. So it had a novelty value, kind of trendy. But at the same time, I think they found it a bit embarrassing when it was Rick who went to the school sports day or parent event rather than me. He was often the only man, and he didn't mind at all. I asked him once if he felt a bit isolated, surrounded by mums, and he said, "I bloody love it. I love standing out in the crowd. I love the way the single mums – and not just the single mums come to think of it – flirt with me, presumably because they assume I'm in the same boat as they are."

"Why couldn't it be that you're an attractive man?" I couldn't help feeling just a tad jealous. Although he was already grey, he was attractive in a boyish blue eyed way, his broken nose a minor blemish compared to his wide shoulders and his ultra-white teeth.

I was actually quite lucky. He had turned into a perfectly adequate cook over the last few years, since I'd started working in London, and he knew his way around a washing machine and was happy to do the weekly family shop. The time he spent in the Sainsbury's near Ilford station was a bit over the top, because it seemed he liked to stand and read most of the sports pages, followed by a spot of male bonding in the betting shop across the road. But he never spent more than a few quid. So I couldn't, and didn't, complain.

We had the best of both worlds. I had worked on the limited typing and shorthand skills I had acquired at school, and had found myself a plum job in Berwick Street, near Soho Market. My boss, John Riddell, was the Company Secretary of a big ad agency, Beavers, and he kept me busy and buzzing. I loved it. So much better than doing what Rick now did. And I was now earning more than Rick earned when he was driving six days a week, so it was a real turnaround for us. I felt more useful; somehow, more important. And Macho Rick obviously didn't feel in the least diminished by me being the breadwinner – far from it. It was more "About time too" – although he drew the line at ironing and hoovering. But that wasn't a problem. I had the weekends, and the girls were of an age where they could help out, given an appropriate bribe.

Not that it was perfect. I hated the commute on the central line from Gants Hill to Tottenham Court Road. Rick didn't like me spending so many hours with John. They hadn't met, but they'd spoken a few times on the phone, and Rick had taken an instinctive dislike to John's cultured tones.

"I suppose he wears designer clothes."

"Not at all. Very conservative three piece suits with a watch chain."

"And I suppose his wife doesn't understand him."

"She understands him well enough to work for Beavers. She's the Repeat Fees Manager."

He found that rather reassuring. Of course I didn't tell him about John's roving, if ageing, hands, and his tendency to come up behind me if I was bending over a filing cabinet or stretching up to open a window.

"Here. Let me help you." And he'd push his manhood hard against me, so I could make no mistake as to what he was offering. But it was all a game. It came with the territory. A giggle meant another thousand pounds a year if you were lucky; a "fuck off" meant the sack. I'd seen other girls come and go, and I knew just how to handle him. Well, not literally. I wouldn't go that far.

John's wife wriggled in a few times a day for his signature on cheques or authorisations and she always winked at me. Conspiratorially. Kind of: "You're years younger than me, but look what he's got at home". As far as I was concerned, she could do a lot better. She had a huge, unnatural bust but she was sweet and smiley, whereas he was moody, always beaded with sweat, and with thick lensed glasses slipping off his nose. The unnatural bust was probably his idea.

"I'm a boob man," he'd proclaimed at my interview. So I knew where I stood from the start. And I'd survived over four years, inching my way up the corporate ladder from Shorthand Typist (one of several rusty mums as we were called) to P.A., promising everything, delivering nothing. I'd have to leave eventually, when John had had enough of the waiting game. But till then, the situation was idyllic. He spent a lot of time away from his desk (i.e. away from me), he bought me outrageously expensive perfume, he praised my work in front of colleagues, including the Managing Director, and he was happy to let me leave early if one of the girls was a bit poorly or if I had to make a visit to their school for some reason.

"Can you work late tomorrow to make up the time?"

"Sorry, John, you know I have to get home to my family."

"Why not come in early then – it will be just you and me."

"Sounds tempting, but I have to get the girls ready for school."

"Always some excuse. You spoil that family of yours. Well, think about what kind of reward I can have if I let you go at three."

"I will think about it. I'm sure I can come up with something. In the meantime, three o'clock?"

"I suppose so."

Thank goodness I shared an open plan office with all the other P.A.s and secretaries, who often had similar conversations with their own bosses. And John's office was a glass box so he couldn't come on strong there, either. It just meant I had to avoid the lift, where he'd followed me once, when I was a lot less aware. Luckily for me, the doors had opened to let in the tea lady with her trolley just as he'd managed to unfasten my bra, and I'd fled to the Ladies, leaving him talking calmly about doughnuts.

Most of the men flirted. And the women. It was part of life there. I rather liked the underlying sense of temptation – not that I was tempted by John, far from it, but there were others… And I loved the gossip with the girls in the canteen at lunchtime. Who was doing it with who, who was getting divorced or engaged, who'd had a blazing row, who had been sacked, who fancied who. There were always clients coming and going: artists, celebrities, city slickers and effete cravat wearers. All human life was there. Very different from Rick and his lorry driver pals, and very different from the atmosphere at the rather sedate girls' school that Georgie and Stephanie attended.

I think Stephanie would have liked a mixed school, but Georgie was approaching the age when boys would have been a distraction. So I was pleased with my choice. For me at their age, the distractions had been different: keeping warm, knitting scarves or – trickier – gloves to put aside for Christmas presents, keeping Douggie amused.

Douggie. Mum.

I hadn't thought about them for weeks.

Visiting Douggie had become more and more difficult since I had been working full time. There were weekends, but there was much more to fit in now, plus Rick sometimes went fishing; his way of changing his day-to-day routine. I think I'd persuaded him to take the three of us to Margate just three times in the last year, and I had taken the girls on a couple of Saturdays on the train.

But they were becoming more and more aware of Douggie's difference. On our last visit, without Rick, they had helped him cut out pictures of Godzilla, Quasimodo, and The Elephant Man from the comics Ivy had spent hours searching out for him. He had always been interested in monsters, and seemed to be moving on to an – unhealthy? – interest in disability. But, watching him sticking the pictures into his scrapbook made the girls uncomfortable – something about the intensity of his concentration perhaps, or the precise nature of his placement, or just about this man in his thirties being so preoccupied with fantasy.

On the way back to Victoria station, Georgie brought up the subject. "Mum. What is wrong with Uncle Douggie exactly?"

"Well, the staff at Milton are all convinced he is autistic, but he's never been diagnosed. It never seemed important."

"What is autistic?" asked Stephanie, although it seemed more of an automatic response than from an interest in the subject. She had looked up from *How to Survive Summer Camp* and obviously wanted a quick answer so she could carry on reading.

"Oh. It comes from the Greek word for selfish. Not interested in other people particularly. Not good at communicating. But quite happy to be isolated."

"Humph." She went back to her Jacqueline Wilson.

But Georgie wanted to know a bit more. "Has he, has Douggie always been, well, whatever it is?"

"Yes. Always."

"Was he bullied?"

"Why do you ask?"

"Oh, no special reason. Just something in Dad's *Mirror* the other day. About some kid being bullied because he was… not autistic… something else. But different."

"No. There were a few children like Douggie at his school. I mean, a few that were different, with different disabilities. The teachers were kind. And a lot of the children were quite caring, really, although some were obviously curious. I do remember a few things that happened out of school, though, involving able-bodied children…" There was that example of the day we moved into Whitechapel House and the boys with their bike. "But… no, I don't think it was an issue. A bit of name-calling, perhaps, which didn't seem to affect him. No more than that."

But it made me think. There was a lot I didn't know. Mainly about how he thought, about what he thought.

"When are we going again?"

"I'm not sure. Do you like going?"

Georgie thought about it. "I don't think so. Not really. He doesn't seem to care if we go or not, does he? But if we didn't go, no one would, would they?"

"I like Uncle Douggie." Stephanie's attention had been diverted again. "He doesn't treat me like an idiot. And he has great videos. And hair just like John McEnroe could have if he tried. And he doesn't say "Don't do that," and he doesn't tell us off for not going more often. Like Auntie Ivy."

"Auntie Ivy is getting old. And she's right, we don't see that much of her."

"I don't like her flat. The furniture is too big and dark. It smells of polish. And the lift is always breaking down."

"Some people like the smell of polish," I said mildly, impressed by Stephanie's attention to detail. She was a quiet child, but naturally observant. She'd make a good journalist: her current precocious ambition. Although last year's was nursing, the year before it was ballet, and who could tell what it would be next year. Never mind, there was plenty of time.

For Georgie, the tomboy, the ambition was very different. Lots of children. She hadn't deviated from her plans since first formulating them a few years ago. I was surprised then, and continued to be surprised every time the subject came up. She would almost certainly do well with her O-levels, then there could be A-levels, then uni, all the things I'd not managed. But for Georgie, it was all pointless. "Unless I do a bit of nursery nursing. That could be useful."

"Well, let's wait and see how you feel next year."

Which had come and gone. As had the next. She was already earning pocket money from babysitting a few of the neighbouring children and, I have to say, the parents had, without exception, been delighted with her maturity and attitude.

Oh, well, at least it was an ambition, of sorts. For me and my school pals, it was just 'get a job' – in the baby boom years, any job would do. For me, the family situation had dictated that I do something rather different. For them, some ended up in shops and stores, some in factories, others in offices. The important thing was to get a job, to be seen to be working and earning, to have a disposable income ready to spend, and to pay your 'old lady' something for your food and keep. No one could afford to live independently of their parents until they got married and, even then, it wasn't always possible.

Times they were a changing. Bob Dylan? Probably twenty years ago? He was right. Slowly, but changing.

"So we might not go again, then?"

"Sorry? Oh, to see Uncle Douggie? Oh, I think that we should. As you said, we're his only family. I'm sure he likes to see you growing up, even though he doesn't say anything."

"Do you think so, Mummy? But anyways, I like Margate. We did a poem at school about blowing away cobwebs, and that's what Margate feels like. Blowing away cobwebs." That was my journalist-to-be daughter speaking – in clichés, but it was early days.

"You mean it's bloody windy."

"George. Don't say 'bloody'. And don't tell me your dad does. It doesn't mean you can."

"Tell you when I like going, Mummy."

"Okay, Stephanie. Let's hear it."

"On Uncle Douggie's birthday. Remember those photos we've got at home of him blowing out the candles on his cake? And he really enjoys it. His face is just full of smiles. It reminds me of Christmas when we were young, me and Georgie, and we believed in Santa, and we ripped open our presents, and helped to stir the pudding and ice the cake. We don't do that any more." She sounded wistful and she'd put her book down.

"Because I'm working now. There's not so much time. And Daddy can cook dinners, but cakes and puddings… That's something else."

"I suppose so." She didn't sound convinced.

"Why don't we have a go this year? At the cake and the pudding?"

Georgie was less than impressed. "Well, I suppose so. Although, what was wrong with the Marks and Spencer cake we had last year?"

"Nothing. It was stunning. But we'd like to, wouldn't we, Steph?"

"Yeah. Why not? And mince pies? It would be good fun. We should have made a cake for Uncle's birthday – with a monster on it. He'd have liked that, wouldn't he, Mum?"

"It's a nice thought, Stephanie. We can make it up to him at Christmas, though why we're talking about Christmas in September, I don't know, I'm sure."

"Did you know all the magazines have probably put their Christmas issues to bed by now?"

"To bed?" Was that the right term?

"Yeah. Finished. Ts dotted and Is crossed."

"I think you mean the other way round, Steph." Georgie was laughing, and Stephanie, briefly annoyed, soon joined in.

"Perhaps Dad would help," I suggested, unconvinced.

"We don't need him. We just need a couple of Sundays and we can do it all."

"Plus the shopping."

"You can give Dad a list, can't you, Mum?" Stephanie had got a bee under her bonnet now.

"Yes. Of course. Sounds like an excellent idea. I didn't think you were the domestic type."

"I'm not. Nor is George. But we're both the Christmas type."

They started laughing again, Uncle Douggie forgotten.

I looked out of the train window. Nearly back in London on another grey autumn day. I wondered if Douggie thought about us when we were not there. I wondered what he thought about, period. And I thought about Mum, about Audrey Fletcher.

I hadn't followed up on the Welling address. If she wanted to find me, I was easy to find. And if not, that was fine by me. I was curious, I had to admit, but I was angry – with the way she had treated us, all three of us. And I was also proud. I convinced myself that she had probably gone abroad anyway. She had certainly not repeated her visit to The Miltons. I sneaked a look at the visitors' book occasionally to reassure myself. Mrs Sutton's replacement, effusive Ms Delaney, a fan of martial arts and psychology, would have told me in any case, I was sure. She told me everything else, from the minutiae of Douggie's diet to her plans for a computerised accounting system.

"Is he going to get better?" Georgie read my thoughts – or some of them.

"No, Georgie."

"And will he always live alone?"

"He doesn't… well, there are other people there. Carers, staff. Most of the residents are long term, too."

"Does he talk to them?"

"No. I don't think so."

I glanced at Stephanie who was curled up with her book, one ringlet falling down unnoticed across her face. In repose, she looked just like Douggie. Just like him. I wondered if Georgie noticed, if she shared her sister's observational skills.

"How come we never see him at Christmas?"

"Douggie doesn't really like leaving his home, or at least only briefly. Not overnight or anything. And if we go to see him, Christmas transport is a bit of an issue. Don't suggest Dad drives; you know he's not keen, especially at Christmas when he likes a drink. But I know they do a lot of things at Milton House."

"Such as?"

"Why are you suddenly so interested?"

"Don't know, really. I always feel a bit sad when we leave."

Was it my imagination or was that a tear in Georgina's eye? Could this be the daughter who didn't cry during *The Way We Were* or *The Sound of Music?*

Stephanie looked up. "Moron."

"I'm not a moron."

"Don't call her that."

We were back to normal.

Chapter Seven

1990

Thirty three years on and it was my turn for a note. From Rick. Following another spat over my late arrival home, thanks to London Underground. I looked at it and thought of my own parents.

Georgina and Stephanie were sitting at our dining room table in silence. The note was in the middle. They didn't look at me when I picked it up and took it into the kitchen. They knew. I knew.

> *You're probably wondering where I am. Don't wonder. Just get on with your hot-shot life without me. The girls know where I am. I had to tell them because I want them to come and see me. Maybe they will. Maybe not. I hope so. It's been fun.*

"Fun!" I threw the piece of paper in the bin. I had seen it coming. Of course I had. But it didn't make it any easier. I took a couple of deep breaths and put the kettle on before facing the girls.

They hadn't moved. They didn't speak. It was surreal. They looked like bronze carvings, their suntans the result of a family holiday in Spain. There was a crumpled tissue stuffed in Stephanie's diaphanous sleeve, perhaps the sign of an earlier weep, confirmed by a few smudges of mascara beneath her eyes. Georgina was staring at her bitten fingernails.

"When did he go? Where? He says you know."

They looked at me then, wary, still not speaking.

"Well? Let's hear it. Don't worry. I'm not going to break down." I was a big girl, after all, with my next big milestone – fifty – only seven short years away. And this situation wasn't that unexpected.

"Is that it?" Stephanie looked, what, horrified?

"What do you mean?"

"Shouldn't you be smashing things, swearing, sobbing, screaming like a banshee, rushing upstairs to see what he's taken? Oh, I don't know, just… just reacting, for Christ's sake."

"You read too much Jackie Collins."

"Tea?" Georgina was more practical.

"Yes, love. Tea." I sat down and patted Stephanie on the shoulder, seeing the anger in her beautiful face.

"Bloody tea?" Her eyes began to fill, the curls around her face trembled and a red stain spread up from her neck

"Stephanie. It will be okay. What are you so angry about? These things happen. Often. Didn't you suspect?"

The tears spilled then and I hugged her as Georgie got busy in the kitchen. "Baby. We'll be fine. You're both working. You're building your own lives now. I can build a new life too. You'll see."

Georgie had made extra strong tea and when I sipped it, I could taste the extra sugar too. It made me smile. "Are we in shock?"

She shook her head. "Not me."

Stephanie pulled back, sniffing. "Well, I am. I never thought he'd do it. Not go. Not just go." She gulped down a mouthful of Georgie's brew and then protested. "Shit. It's hot."

Georgie smiled at me. "Are you okay?"

"Of course I am. Is Mark coming over?"

"No. I phoned him. I thought you might need me." She twirled the solitaire engagement ring she was so proud of. "Oh, Mum."

"Now, don't you start. Just tell me. Tell me what happened. What he said."

Stephanie started the ball rolling. "I came home first. The temp job was ultra boring and they obviously didn't have enough work for me, so what's the point? I left."

"The money's the point," interrupted Georgie mildly.

"Don't start. When I came in, he was carrying a couple of cases down the stairs."

"What time was this?"

"Oh, half three. Something like that. He stopped on the stairs and looked a bit sheepish, and I asked him what he was doing. Silly question. It was bloody obvious what he was doing."

"And what did he say?"

"He just said 'I'm going'."

"That was it?"

"That was it. He brought the suitcases down and tried to hug me but I wasn't having any. Then he only asked me if I would like to go with him. As if."

"How did you react?"

"I asked him if he was going to her." She glanced at me quickly. "And he said of course. He said he loved her and she... she needed him." She bit her lip.

"I see."

"Can you believe he asked her if she'd like to go with him? The bloody cheek of it. To that awful woman. That two faced, bandy legged, cow."

"Please, Georgie. It doesn't help. In fact, it makes it worse. When your husband leaves you for a stunner it's rather different to when he leaves you for..."

We both laughed, a tad hysterical I guess.

Stephanie joined in. "A bandy legged cow."

The hysteria increased. "We'll have to find a new hairdresser," Georgie gasped.

"Perhaps she'll leave," I said, although I didn't believe that. She would enjoy her victory, which would be less effective if she moved away.

We were talking about Janine. Our hairdresser. She did Rick's hair as well, and I'd noticed early on how she always asked about him when one of us went. She always showed such an interest, which suddenly stopped about two years ago. That was when Rick started going out fishing more and more and coming back with less and less.

Since then, there had been an occasional long blonde hair on his shoulder, a trace of unfamiliar perfume, a diminishing of sexual interest, odd purchases cropping up on the credit card bill, an extra interest in his grooming.

It wasn't difficult to piece it together:-

Me: "I tried to phone you a few times today."

Him: "I was out."

Me: "Obviously. Where?"

Him: "What is this? Since when do I have to answer to you? I went over to help Larry for a few hours."

Me: "That was a bit sudden wasn't it?"

Him: "Oh, give me a break."

Me: "Tell me, Rick. Is it Janine Taylor?"

Him: "Is what Janine Taylor?"

Me: "The affair."

Him: "I don't know what you're talking about."

Me: "It's the way she purrs 'How's that drop dead gorgeous husband of yours?' every time I have a blow dry and yet she can't look at me in the mirror."

Him: "You're imagining things."

Me: "And then there's the gossip."

Him: "Don't listen to it."

Me: "I can't help it. She's actually been seen coming here, into my house, presumably into my bed. What the hell are you doing?"

But he denied everything. Always. And every time I passed her shop, I looked in at that lithe young body with its armful of ethnic bracelets and the long hair that touched her pert bum, and I thought about them together. I suppose I assumed it would blow over. She was about twenty years younger than him and he wasn't exactly a catch financially, only working intermittently in recent years as the girls grew up – driving a mini cab, a bit of decorating. I hadn't put him under any pressure as I earned enough for all of us.

Three years ago, my Managing Director had promoted me to Account Executive, and I'd escaped John Riddell's clutches. The M.D. was younger, single, and had been having a steamy affair with his married secretary for years, so he left everyone else alone. Occasionally, he remarked to me how attractive he found older women, but that was as far as he went. The promotion, thank goodness, was on merit.

I'm not sure Rick believed me, though. He had met Andrew Marriott, the M.D., and seen just how young and sexy he was, and he'd got quite a surprise when I'd been singled out for attention.

"Why you?"

"Why not? I work hard, I know the clients really well and can make the right decisions for them and I don't spend as much on business lunches as the men who applied. In fact, I expect I'm cheaper all round. The Equal Pay Act is taking one hell of a long time to kick in, let's face it."

"So you didn't drop your knickers."

"Don't be so crude."

The idea seemed to turn him on. And, in fact, that was probably our last really lusty night before his attentions were diverted by a younger model. He had occasionally asked me about Andrew over the last couple of years, but in the same crude terms: "Still giving the boss one?"

But we'd kept our mutual suspicions from the girls. Or we thought we had. But then there was that odd conversation I'd had with Georgie the day she got engaged.

"Mum, is there any point?"

"In what, love, getting engaged?"

"No. Getting married."

"Of course there is. Just don't set your expectations too high."

"But isn't it about expectations?"

"What are you expecting?"

"Fidelity. Commitment. Affection."

"Well, you may be lucky."

"Luck? Is that it?"

"Partly."

"And have you been lucky, Mum?"

"Mostly."

I wondered how long they'd known about Janine. And why they hadn't said anything to me. We decided to order a take-away curry – Rick's pet hate – and talk it through.

It arrived in under twenty minutes. Seriously impressive timing. The Maharajah was aiming for the *Guinness Book of Records*.

"You saw him kissing her?" I queried mildly. "A real, proper kiss?"

Stephanie nodded and she swallowed a mouthful of chicken madras before giving me the gory details. "Full on, mouth and tongue, clutching and groping. In the salon. So anyone passing, like me, could see through the plate glass window. I wanted to rush in and beat her over the head with her curling tongs."

"And you didn't say anything? I can't believe you'd do that."

"I didn't want to upset you. I thought he might be drunk. I thought perhaps she'd made a pass. Oh, I don't know what I thought. But I told Georgie."

"Yeah. Thanks. As if I hadn't already worked it out for myself."

"You mean you saw them too?"

Georgie licked her lips, and grabbed the last onion bhajee before I could get there. "It was an evening when Dad was mini-cabbing. I was parked up with Mark in Seven Kings Park."

"Doing what?"

"Perlease. Give me a break. Dad arrived, with her. They were all over each other. I just wanted to get away, so Mark drove me back to his place. In fact, that was the first time we, we... And he kept saying, 'Are you sure,' and I kept saying, 'Yes, I'm sure.' I was so mixed up. I thought, well, everyone else is doing it."

"Did that include me?" My vegetable curry was coagulating. I had lost my appetite.

"I wasn't including you, no. Although I'd heard you arguing once, about Andrew, was it? I told you. I was confused. I thought, what the hell, just live for the moment."

"And was it worth it?"

"Of course it wasn't. But we've improved." She grinned at me. "I'm sorry, Mum. I should have told you what we'd seen. But I couldn't. If I'd known that you wanted to know – if you'd asked me. Well, perhaps then. But I thought you'd be hurt, upset. And I didn't think it was anything more than a bit of romping. I thought she'd soon get fed up with him. She can't be that much older than me, can she?"

"Twenty five," said Stephanie knowledgeably, the only one still eating.

I had a thought. "So Mark knew?"

"Yes." Georgie nodded.

"Is that why he has been so unpleasant to Rick?"

"He's not been unpleasant."

"Okay, Georgie, let's call it distant then."

"Yeah. All right then. Distant. To use his phrase 'Not much of a role model there then'."

"Quite. I don't know what to say. This has been an evening of revelations."

Georgie stood up. "How about some wine?"

"Good idea. I'll go. You two tidy up this smelly mess."

"Didn't you enjoy it? We did, didn't we, Steph?"

I had to admit it. "It was fabulous. It made a real change just to eat for once without thinking about fats and calories. They are the bane of my life. And, what's even worse, I'm sure they will continue to dominate my thinking for many years to come."

"Don't get alcohol free or low calorie wine, Mum," said Georgie. "It's disgusting."

"No, don't worry. We'll continue in purely diet-busting vein."

"And don't forget me," Stephanie grinned.

"Of course. The magic eighteen … though I'm sure you've indulged in a bit of under-age drinking with your friends; I know I did…"

"Of course."

"This really is confessional time." Georgie curled up. "Come on, Stephanie, let's hear about you losing your virginity."

She coloured up. "Georgie. No way. There's no-one special."

"Since when has that stopped you?"

I left them arguing sociably. Talking about their sex lives. To think that even at Georgie's age, I was still a virgin. Hard to credit it in the swinging sixties, but there were more of us about than the media credited. Although I had succumbed to Rick before our wedding night, that in itself was really an irrevocable commitment, not entered into lightly. And, of course, a girl had to be sure in that department before committing to one man, leastways that had been my thinking then.

I wondered how many partners Stephanie had had. Already. Perhaps Georgie was just teasing. Although there had been at least one partner, as Stephanie left her birth control pills around openly. When I'd mentioned them, trying to be casual about it in this very different world, she said she wanted to make sure she didn't suffer the consequences of a one night stand. "And do you have many of those?"

"Of course not. Do I look like an idiot?"

The phone was ringing as I got back with the wine. Stephanie answered it, as it was usually for her, but it was Ms Delaney from the Miltons.

The hair on the back of my neck prickled as I pushed the bottle into Georgie's arms. "Nothing wrong, Mrs North. Don't worry."

"Oh, thank goodness."

"No. Just to let you know that I'll be leaving at the end of the week. There's been quite a lot of changes here recently, and Mr Devereux is taking over."

"Mr Devereux? Do I know him?"

"He was the Senior Care Worker, but has been wanting to move into administration for a while, it seems. So all very convenient."

"Devereux. Devereux. I don't think…"

"Not to worry. Perhaps you'll be able to get to meet him in the near future. It's been a while."

Was there just a tiny bit of criticism or was it my imagination? "How's Douggie?"

"Absolutely excellent. He has been going to computing classes."

"Has he? Well, that's good to hear. And how is he getting on? What is he doing exactly?"

"Oh, it's early stages. Computer games, Clip Art... oh, and he's learning how to input names and addresses for labels for Christmas cards and such. He's doing very well, Mrs North. Very well."

"But does he have access to a computer at The Miltons?"

"Oh, yes. We have two small PCs in our Leisure Room now. You really must come and see us."

This time there was no mistaking the critique. And quite right too. How long had it been? Six months?

I suddenly felt guilty about everything, about everyone. It really hit me that I was a complete failure in so many areas of my little life. I'd built a successful career, but in everything that counted... "Ms Delaney. You're right. I'll come tomorrow. I'd like to say my goodbyes. You've been good to Douggie."

"Oh, there's no need. I didn't mean for you to jump on the next train or anything." It was obviously her turn to feel guilty.

"Please. I'll drive down." Something else I'd achieved: a driving licence and a company car. It wouldn't be easy to take a day off just like that, but I knew that I only had to mention my disabled brother to Andrew and he would succumb without protest. He was a man who supported every charity that crossed his path, except animal charities, where he drew the line. Plus I had a client in Rochester, so I could probably kill, or at least see off, two proverbial birds.

"So the old bat's leaving, is she?"

"Georgie, that's not very generous. She's been fine."

"All those books on Taekwondo," chipped in Stephanie. "It's not natural."

"You're both very unkind. Any volunteers for a trip to Margate tomorrow?"

Silence.

"Stephanie?"

"Do I have to? I've got to make some phone calls to get myself another temp job. And if not, I've got to find a new hairdresser. I fancy a change of colour. As everything else is changing. You don't need me, do you?"

"Well, no."

"Good."

"And what kind of colour exactly?"

Stephanie waved a vague, red taloned hand. "Oh, nothing too drastic."

"Change for change's sake is not a good idea."

"Try telling that to Dad," Georgie muttered.

"Georgie!"

"Would you take him back, Mum?"

I had to think about that one. "I suppose I would. I'm not sure. It's too early to say."

Georgie kissed me unexpectedly, quickly. "Who needs him, eh?"

"Suppose you can't get a day off tomorrow?"

"No. The nursery is short staffed this week as it is. And I'd rather not. The Miltons is a bit depressing."

"You think so?"

"Perhaps not for Uncle. But for anyone in the real world. Don't you think so?"

"Too many questions. Now, who's for wine?"

I had a nagging pain above my eyebrows when I started the drive to Margate next morning. It was a bright, dry Friday in June. Perfect seaside weather.

Last night was the first night I'd slept alone for over twenty years. It had felt odd. But I hadn't missed the snoring. And I'd appreciated the extra space. And I could hardly miss the sex. How long had it been – close to a year? We should have discussed it, I suppose, but life got in the way.

No good thinking about what we should have done. I had revised my answer to Georgie's question. No, I wouldn't take him back. Not because of Janine. She was the result, not the reason, of our drift apart.

The result of his lack of interest in me, in Linda North. In my job, my ambitions, my needs and in my little brother. It was as if Douggie didn't exist. As if he was something I should write off. And I very nearly had. Not because of Rick. But through my own selfishness.

Thank goodness Ms Delaney had phoned. *Ms*. I hate that word. How are you supposed to say it for Chrissake?

At the next traffic lights, I flexed my padded shoulders and thrust out my breasts as I caught the man in the car next to me checking me out. Just because my husband didn't want me, didn't mean that I was undesirable. I glanced across and put my index finger in my mouth, licking it gratuitously and he shot away as fast as if I had grabbed his testicles.

The game amused me and I played it a few more times when I came off the A2 but I knew I was playing with fire and I soon got bored with it. Grow up, girl. You don't need reassurance on that level, surely.

Ms Delaney looked pleased to see me. I had flowers for her as well as a world clock for Douggie. I'd bought it months ago in Dixon's and had been looking forward to giving it to him because I knew Douggie would love it, given his interest in time. You just had to press a number to check the time in over a dozen different countries. And there was a built in stop watch, too. Perfect. But I should have brought it sooner. There was no excuse.

"Douggie. You've put on weight. Too many chips, I expect."

Douggie looked down at his expanding waistline in surprise. Obviously he hadn't noticed. He had made no comment about my lack of visits, but I hadn't expected him to. He probably hadn't noticed that either. And, even if he had, that didn't mean I was important in his life. No one was. Only Douggie. That was Douggie.

"Have you had to buy new trousers?"

"New trousers. Tesco's."

"Oh, right. I didn't know they sold clothes."

"Tesco's sells everything. Tesco's is Douggie's favourite place."

"I didn't think you liked shopping."

"Not shopping. Hot chocolate. Comics. Custard creams."

"Oh. Sounds good. And who do you go to Tesco's with, then?"

"Debbie. Steve."

"Are they your friends?"

"Debbie. Steve."

I made a mental note to check with Ms Delaney before I left – not that it mattered whether Debbie or Steve were staff or residents. Either way, I was glad he wasn't left stuck in front of one screen or another for hours, even days, on end. I showed him the clock and, as I suspected, it was a huge success. It also reminded him that he hadn't asked me, "How many minutes?"

"Oh, I thought I might stay a bit longer this time, Douggie. I haven't seen you for a while, have I?"

"How many minutes?"

"How about two hundred?"

"One hundred and eighty."

"Three hours? Okay, then. Three hours it is."

After all, I didn't want to outstay my welcome.

Chapter Eight

1995

Mr Devereux had turned out to be quiet, quick to laugh, with Ken Dodd hair and a Scottish accent, at odds with his name. Although he didn't have to, he showed a genuine interest in Douggie's – and no doubt others' – personal lives, sending birthday cards, dropping in for a chat, taking photos of him engrossed in front of the computer or enjoying a knickerbocker glory on the seafront. I liked him, and I think he was pleased that my visits had gradually increased to the level they were twenty years ago. He probably thought he had something to do with that and I didn't disillusion him.

He really came through on February 14th – I didn't need to refer to my journal to remember the date. I had gone to Margate with a Valentine's Day cake for Douggie – although Mr Devereux arranged for every resident to get a card, which was so sweet, even if it meant nothing at all to some of them, Douggie included. As it was a Tuesday, I'd had to ask Andrew for another day off, but he'd not even hesitated to agree. And why not? I was making a fortune for him and for Beavers.

Mr Devereux opened the front door himself. Not the usual form. He ushered me into his office for a wee word.

"Douggie's in bed, Mrs North."

I looked at my watch. It was eleven o'clock. "In bed?"

"Yes. It's the second day he hasn't wanted to get up for breakfast. He's not complaining of pain or discomfort, but I think I'd like to get the doctor in to look at him, perhaps today, while you're here. What do you think?"

"Of course. If he doesn't adhere to his routine, then you can bet something is wrong. Though it could be psychological or something other than a medical reason. Can I see him now and I'll give you the nod before you contact the doctor?"

"Fine."

Douggie's door was locked and he didn't answer when I tapped and called his name. I dropped the cake-box and ran back down the stairs so that Mr Devereux could unlock the door. I pushed it open gently, although I wanted to rush in at full tilt, and peeped round quietly in case he was asleep. Douggie was sitting up in bed, looking fixedly at the poster of the Moscow State Circus on the opposite wall.

"Douggie?"

He looked round. "Linda opened the door."

That was a good sign. I picked up the box and shooed Mr Devereux away. "I'll report back."

"Yes, because you didn't answer," I explained as I closed the door behind me, my mouth a little less dry, the sense of relief virtually tangible.

"Douggie's in bed."

"Yes, so I see. You missed breakfast. Aren't you hungry?"

He shook his head.

"That's a shame. I brought you a Valentine Cake. Look."

Although he didn't reach out the way he usually did for presents of any kind, he did look. "Valentine."

"Did I hear 'thank you Linda'?"

"Thank you Linda."

I approached warily, still concerned. "What time are you getting up today?"

"Can't do it. Douggie can't do it today."

As I sat on the edge of the bed, he winced. There was no mistaking it. My mouth dried again.

"Does something hurt?"

"Too difficult to get up."

"What's happened? What's changed? Is there a pain?" I struggled to find the words he could relate to.

He threw back the duvet and pointed to his left hip. "Not working properly."

"Show me."

"Too difficult."

"Right. I'm going to ask the Miltons' doctor to take a look."

"No."

"Douggie. If you can't get out of bed, there must be something wrong. And the doctor can put it right."

"Yes. Put it right. Fix it. Today, please."

I hugged him, gingerly. "We'll do our best. Can I have a quick look myself first?"

He made no protest but I could see nothing obvious, perhaps a little reddening. Nevertheless, he'd winced again when I'd moved his pyjama bottoms to have a look.

"Haven't you been out of bed to use the toilet?"

"Can't do it."

"I'll get someone to help you."

I moved as fast as my heels would allow to ask Mr Devereux to phone the doctor and to 'lend' me a pair of hands to get Douggie to the toilet. He did better than that; he called out to the receptionist to make the phone call, and he matched my speed back up the stairs.

"Let's be 'avin' you then, young Douggie." For a big man, he was very gentle, and we half carried, half cajoled my not so little 43-year-old brother through to his personal en-suite, luckily with plenty of room for all of us as it was built to accommodate a wheelchair. I left Douggie briefly with Mr Devereux, thinking of his dignity, although this was unlikely to be something that Douggie himself would be aware of.

We'd had to help him swivel his body around so that he could get out of bed, and this had obviously been painful for him. On the short journey across the room, he had yelped a few times, but he seemed able to move his leg without any problem, although not able to put any weight on it.

Douggie didn't want to get back in bed, although this seemed to be the easiest place for the doctor to examine him. "Sit here." 'Here' was the wing chair by the window. We lowered him into it gently.

"No breakfast. No lunch. No wash and clean teeth. Toilet at..." He looked at the clock. "... Twenty-five past eleven."

"We can bring some lunch up to you," offered Mr Devereux.

"How many veries of mixed up is it?"

"At least a hundred," I told him.

"More."

"A thousand."

"Doctor make it better."

"Does it hurt all the time?"

"No."

"Does it hurt only when you move?"

"Yes."

"I'm glad you're here, Mrs North. You have managed to get a lot more out of Douggie than I could. Can you stay until after Doctor Kowalski has left?"

"Of course."

"How many minutes before doctor comes?"

"I'll find out." Mr Devereux addressed Douggie but smiled at me reassuringly. "And I'll get someone to bring you up some tea, Mrs North."

"Thank you."

"Douggie wants tea."

"I'll be right back." And he was. "Doctor Kowalski will be here by one. But he suggested no lunch or tea for your brother till he gets here, sorry. Just in case."

"Oh, yes. In that case, I'll wait, too."

Inflamed hip joint: it could have been a lot worse. The doctor was prompt, brisk, intense, and confident. "Anti-inflammatory tablets should eliminate the pain as well as the problem. And promptly. But make sure that Mr Fletcher completes the two-week course, or he could find himself back at square one."

He was in and out in fifteen minutes.

I heard his parting remark to Mr Devereux in the downstairs hall. "If there's still pain three days from now, I'll come back. Let me know."

"Right, folks. Tea for two. And lunch on trays at one o'clock."

"Ten minutes."

"Yes. I'll make sure it's on time."

When he'd closed the door, I thought it best to tackle the situation, without high expectations. "Douggie, you should have told someone about the pain yesterday."

"Talk to Linda."

"I know, pet, but this is important. It could have been append… it could have been something very very serious. Now listen. The tablets should stop the pain soon, but if it comes back you must tell someone. How about I make you a sign with PAIN on it and you can hang it on the door?"

"When will the pain be gone?"

"Three days maximum, the doctor said."

"How many days minimum?"

"Perhaps two."

"One day?"

"If you're lucky."

"Is Douggie lucky?"

I kissed him. "Not as lucky as me."

My Valentine's Day at the Miltons had made a much bigger impact than I'd expected. I couldn't stop thinking about it. Not just the situation with Douggie and what might have happened if the cause of the pain had been something very different, but about all the people in his situation. Especially about the ones without families. Without people to care unless they were getting paid to do it.

Stephanie and latest flame Orlando – Orlando! – and Georgina and her husband took me out to lunch on Mother's Day a few weeks later.

"This is nice." The carvery was new, with lavish soft furnishings. "Very nice. You can bring me here again."

"Mother." Stephanie called me that in front of Orlando for some reason. "You make it sound as if we never take you out."

"You do. Of course you do. My daughters are very good to me, Orlando. And since Stephanie started earning more than me, well, she has been very generous." I smiled at him and he winked. He was absolutely drop dead gorgeous. On our first meeting, I thought his blond hair just that bit too long, but I had seen how he used it, like a girl, flicking it backwards with plumped up pursed lips, or tucking it behind one ear where it was just too glossy to want to remain in that position. It was no wonder Stephanie seemed to spend more time with this one than with any other, but she was adamant that he was not 'the one'.

"Who wants one when you can have twenty?"

"Hussy."

I grinned at her, thinking about our oft-repeated conversation. She always laughed when I called her a hussy. "Leave it out, Mum. That's what this body's for, apart from Page Three."

Oh, well. The money she earned from modelling was certainly unprecedented in our family.

Georgina actually approved, to my surprise. Although I could see why. "Did Stephanie tell you that she'd bought me a new car?" she asked me now as we drooled over the roast lamb.

"No, she didn't. You see what I mean, Orlando? There aren't many girls around like her, you know."

"Oh, I know, Linda, I know." It made my toes curl when he called me Linda. Sexy little devil.

"Georgie. I told you. Someone gave it to me. It didn't cost me a penny."

"That's not the point. Is it, Mum?"

"Of course not. Er, who gave it to you?"

"Oh, some fruitcake. He gave me this, too." She indicated the ornate crucifix around her neck, and Orlando fingered it delicately, making her nipples stand erect through the satin dress she was wearing.

"Luckily I'm not jealous, sweet pea."

"Mrs North?"

Mark had trouble calling me Linda, even though he'd been married to Georgina for three years now. "Linda, please," I said automatically anyway.

"Linda." It didn't sound the same as when Orlando said it. Not that Mark wasn't good looking, but he was more the Barry Manilow type. Less conventional looking, and possibly the jealous type. I could see that he was disapproving, and jealous by proxy. He obviously felt that Orlando should not be tolerating Stephanie's references to another admirer – or even lover. Mark was apologising. "We're going to have to break up the party a little early as we're going off to see my mother."

"Of course. I understand."

"Will you be okay here with these two?" he asked.

"Of course I will. I don't think Orlando's actually going to ravage her here and now, are you Orlando?"

"That comes later, Linda."

"Only if I say so," grinned Stephanie.

Georgina laughed messily, food in mouth, but Mark still looked disapproving. I decided to change the subject before they left.

"I've something to tell you. Well, Stephanie and Georgina."

"It's a man."

"No, Stephanie. It's not a man. It's me. I'm getting out of advertising. I'm giving in my notice."

"To the lovely Andrew?"

"Stop it, Stephanie."

"And if he gets down on his knees and kisses your toes…"

"I said stop it."

"What will you do, Mum?" Georgina's question was much more sensible.

"Well. I've been talking to the local Mencap."

Silence. Four pairs of eyes looked at me.

"And they are looking for advocates. To help those who can't help themselves."

"But…" Georgie swallowed hastily.

"Mencap?"

Understandably, my girls looked sceptical. It must have been quite a surprise for them. I'd told them about the Valentine's Day drama, but I hadn't mentioned the direction in which it had pointed me.

"Is this paid work, Mrs... Linda?"

"Oh, yes, yes, it is. I have to pay my way."

"Good on you, Linda. You're just the sort I would turn to for help." Orlando, of course.

Stephanie glared at him. "For God's sake, Mother. How depressing."

"Not at all. It's a very positive thing. And far more rewarding than the mercenary existence the rest of us inhabit."

"Speak for yourself, Mark. You may regard selling computer software as mercenary, but I love those kids at the nursery. I don't work there for the money. Never have, and never would. It's pure job satisfaction. The smiles on those little faces." Georgina had strong feelings, obviously.

"Yuk." Not a lot of common ground these days between my daughters. "And all for a pittance. Oh, well, Mother. If that's what you want. I can always help you out financially."

"Stephanie, I'm touched. No, Orlando, I mean it. It's a wonderful offer. I hope I won't need it. But I couldn't ask for a better Mother's Day present than the support of my family."

"I can only give you moral support, I'm afraid."

"That's all I need, Georgie."

They jumped up as one and gave me very different kisses, one dry and soft, the other wet and sticky.

"Thank you, girls."

Mark raised his glass. "Here's a toast. To... er... Linda."

"To the lovely Linda." I wondered briefly what Orlando's kisses were like. It was very brief but I felt immediately ashamed of myself. Stephanie was watching me with a grin on her face. I was sure she knew.

"And there's more."

Georgina raised an eyebrow. "Blimey, Mum. What have you been doing, saving it up?"

"No. But it is kind of linked. New life. New start." I raised my wine glass again.

Georgie looked at Stephanie. "I think I know what's coming."

"Divorce. I saw my solicitor this morning."

The other glasses clinked mine. They all looked pleased.

"Go girl," breathed Orlando.

"For God's sake, Orlando, stop flirting with my mother. You are just insatiable. As for you," she grinned at me, "about bloody time."

"Well said." My daughters were right behind me, and it made me feel even more emotional than I was already feeling.

"Is it what you were expecting?"

"The news about your divorce? Absolutely. I'm dying to see if Dad actually marries the cow. And now I'll find out."

"Georgina!" I'm not sure I'd intended any of our grubby laundry to be aired in front of my son-in-law and potential – if unlikely – son-in-law.

"Now you can see who the real bitch is in the family, Mother."

Mark seemed to take more offence than Georgina. "I think you've had enough, Stephanie."

"Why? I'm not driving. He is. Aren't you poppet?" Her right hand disappeared under the table, but Orlando casually retrieved it and gave it an affectionate pat.

"Anything you say, darling girl. Especially as I think Mark may be right."

Mark looked pleased with himself. "Well, thank you, kind sir. But we really do have to be going. I am sorry, Mrs North. And I do hope you are making the right decisions. I'm confident you are, but only you know the reasons, and the reasons are sometimes more important than the decisions."

"Very profound, Mister Baker." He grinned at me. "But I appreciate your concerns. Come and give me a hug."

Stephanie giggled. "The only thing that worries me is that you'll be back on the market, mother. I'm not sure I can handle the competition."

"Goodbye, Mum. I'll give you a ring tomorrow to find out Andrew's reaction. Have you actually had a written offer from Mencap?"

Georgina had brought me back down to earth. "Yes. I'm hoping he'll let me go in a month, although it should be three."

"Course he will. He's always had a soft spot for you. Dad used to think – well, you know what Dad used to think."

"You mean he actually discussed Andrew with you?"

"Not discussed. More like pumping sessions actually. I'm glad about the divorce, Mum. Although that may be what Janine is waiting for before, well, before…"

"Before what, Georgina?"

"Getting pregnant. How would you feel?"

"Distanced. It's all right, Georgie. I've given it a lot of thought. I'm not doing it for Janine. It's the best thing for me, for Rick, and for you, so you don't hold out false hopes."

"You mean of a reconciliation? It never crossed our minds, did it George?"

Georgina ignored Stephanie and looked at me. "No. Never. Speak to you tomorrow."

When they'd gone, Stephanie picked at her food. "Georgina always thinks that everyone is desperate for kids. Is that because she is?"

"Don't you talk about these things? Sister to sister?"

"No. Probably because she thinks I'm, well, not interested."

"Are you?"

She glanced at Orlando. "That would be telling." Orlando excused himself and disappeared in the direction of the Gents. "I just think Georgina would be upset if Janine gets pregnant before she does."

"Or you."

"Not me. I like kids, don't get me wrong. I've helped Georgina out in the nursery sometimes, did she tell you?"

"No. I'm surprised."

She shrugged. "Why not? I don't work every day, and there's only so much shag… sorry." Her next question was unexpected and abrupt: "Do you think he likes me?"

"Orlando? Yes, I do."

"He's gorgeous, isn't he? I just want to eat him."

"He's gorgeous, yes. Remind me, I can't keep up. Is he a model?"

"No, a photographer. And a lech."

"I see."

"Anyone and everyone. It's disgusting."

"But you like him."

She nodded, looking suddenly bereft. I wanted to cuddle my little girl, stroke her over-bleached hair, and kiss it all better. But Orlando was on his way back. And there was nothing I could do. Nothing I could say.

Until this moment, I'd never considered that she might be envious of Georgina. I'd always figured it was the other way round. Now I wasn't so sure.

"Stephanie tells me that you have a mother somewhere. Don't you ever think of a reconciliation on days like these?"

"Well, well, you know quite a lot about us all, don't you, Orlando?"

"I'm sorry, I just…"

"It's okay. The answer is absolutely not. Although Stephanie may be interested to know that Douggie apparently sent his mother a Mother's Day card. Mr Devereux thought it would be a good idea. Not sure that I agree."

"So who's Douggie?"

"Ah. So, you haven't told him everything."

I felt a bit mean. But if she cared about him, she needed to know how much he could handle, in every sense of the word.

I changed the subject. "Well, I don't know about you two. But I am having the lemon sorbet."

Stephanie could tell him about Douggie in her own words. She knew what I was doing, but I'm not sure she was grateful. Her choice of chocolate profiteroles – she always indulged when she had something on her mind – told me that she was worried about Orlando, worried as to whether he was interested in her or her perfect body. But I couldn't see anything more than admiration in his eyes or his attitude, and I didn't want her to get hurt if I could avoid it.

I tried not to feel guilty. It was the story of my life so far.

Chapter Nine
2000

Advocacy had turned out to be more difficult than I'd thought, and so more of a challenge. In some ways it had turned out to be unexpectedly soul-destroying, largely because of the way money drove so many decisions which should have been driven by need, and because of the general incapacity of so many suited types to understand the problems of the less articulate that make up a fair sized sector of our society. But – nevertheless – still rewarding on a one-to-one basis. It felt as if I was doing too little too late, but at least I was doing something.

When I say 'too little', though, I'm talking about results. I don't mean in terms of the hours I was putting in. My nine to five existence had gone out of the window. I ran a literacy group once a week on Tuesday evenings, and afternoon meetings with social workers, care workers, family members, or whoever, could often be protracted in an attempt to reach a decision rather than a postponement. People with learning disabilities found it hard to understand why a meeting to sort out their accommodation, their family contact, their finances, or a more specific problem – like their diet – did not actually sort it out. Often as not, it just left lots of questions, requests for reports, and plans for further meetings because someone had not turned up or had not brought the relevant information. Frustrating? Very. But I felt very needed, very useful, and that made a refreshing change.

For years, I had always thought that if I had a day off, no one would really miss me, no one would actually care very much, and it would make no difference to the organisation I worked for. As a result, I often did have days off – a sneeze would become flu, a short-lived headache would be a migraine, a mild period pain would be 'doubled up with stomach cramps'. Since hitting fifty, three years ago, I could count my absences on the fingers of one hand. And I felt better for it. A bit poorer, but enriched and valued. It was nice to be needed again in the way I'd felt needed when the girls were young.

The financial issue had been addressed by moving to a small modern flat near Barking station. The equity from the house Rick and I had been buying in Ilford had given us both a hefty deposit, and enabled us to move on.

Today's meeting had run on as usual and I'd stopped off at Sainsbury's, which had made me even later. So I was surprised to see Stephanie sitting in her car outside my flat, obviously waiting for me in the gloom. She waved when she saw me and came over to help me with my carrier bags, her face hidden by that thick blonde mane.

"What are you doing here, darling?"

"Honestly, Mum. I don't know why I bother. You asked me to cut your hair, remember? And I've been sitting smoking myself to death for well over an hour."

"Oh, God. Was it today? I'm so sorry."

"You're bloody hopeless."

Stephanie's husband, Peter, had insisted she give up modelling when they married so she'd spent the last two years training as a hairdresser. Both professions were worlds away from her childhood ambitions but I often wondered if Janine had been some sort of secret role model.

As if reading my mind, she shot a question at me as we climbed to the first floor. "Did you know Janine's pregnant again?"

"Oh? No, I didn't. I haven't spoken to Rick in months."

"He phoned and told me."

"So that you'd tell me?"

"Not necessarily."

I tried to see the expression in her eyes but she was bending down, her hair flopping forward.

"Is he pleased?" I asked her.

"So he says. Another boy apparently."

"He always wanted boys."

I was in front of her, putting my key in the door, but she didn't say anything.

We dropped the bags onto the kitchen worktop, and I turned on the light, thinking that perhaps that had been the wrong thing to say. "I didn't mean…" I broke off as she pushed her hair back from her face. "Stephanie, what happened this time?"

She smiled, a little crookedly as a result of her split lip and blackened eye. "An argument with our microwave door. You know it's fitted high into the units? I just can't get used to it."

I stared at her. It sounded convincing enough, but then there had been the golf ball in the face just a few months ago, the drunken trip onto the bath taps before that. I hadn't believed any of them, but I wanted to. Oh, yes, I wanted to.

"Stephanie. You never used to be… accident prone."

"Before I met Pete, you mean?"

"Well, before you married Pete."

"I know what you're thinking."

"I'm not going to deny it."

Our voices were gradually getting louder and she put her hands on her hips, pushing her damaged face close to mine. "I didn't come here for an argument. Do you want your bloody hair cut or not?"

"Oh, Stephanie. We used to talk."

The hands moved up to her face to smother her gut wrenching sobs. What had happened to my beautiful little girl?

"I'll kill the bastard."

"No, you won't." There was a hiccup but the sobs continued. I put my arm around her shaking shoulders and manoeuvred her onto my minuscule sofa in my minuscule lounge.

"No tears on my faux suede upholstery, please. I'll make tea and then you can tell me why I can't kill him."

By the time I'd produced mugs and digestives, she was standing up, peering in the mirror over the fake modern fireplace. "Look at the state of me."

"So. What is it that provokes him?"

She looked at me in the mirror, composing herself. "I never said it was Pete."

"Now don't start that again."

Taking a deep breath, she turned to face me. "He loves me."

"Do me a favour."

"Mum. You don't understand. That's why I never said anything. I knew you wouldn't understand. I knew no one would."

"Sit down."

She kicked off her shoes and huddled up in the corner of the sofa, keeping me at a distance. She looked terrified.

"Drink your tea."

She drank.

"Stephanie." I didn't know what to say. I wanted to cry myself. Seeing her so vulnerable. I wanted to hug her. I wanted to shake her. I wanted to tell her what a fool she was. I wanted to kill him. I think it showed. Perhaps that was why she was scared. I took a deep breath. "What are you going to do?"

"There's nothing I can do."

"Leave him."

"Don't be bloody silly."

"Silly? There's only one idiot round here."

"Now you're starting on me. I suppose you think it's my fault."

"You haven't told me what it is that provokes him."

She lit a cigarette, and for once I didn't object. "Anything. Everything. The last time was because I answered the door to the postman in my dressing gown."

"You mean he's jealous."

"Ouch. My lip. Don't make me laugh."

"What then?"

"Well, yes, he's jealous. But it's more than that. Remember, I'm jealous, too. But for him, I only have to speak to a man, even look at him. Any man. A supermarket assistant, a customer, a newspaper seller, my accountant, our next door neighbour. Any age. However unattractive. Anything with a cock."

"Please."

"Sorry. But don't you see? It's because he loves me. He loves me so much that he thinks that any and every other man wants me. And because I can't get enough of him, he thinks I need more sex than he can give me. So when I'm not with him, he imagines that I …" She broke off, floundering.

"Stephanie. It's horrible. He needs help."

"I know what he needs. He needs me. That's all."

"Stephanie. Marriage is not about slavery."

"You've found the word. For Pete, that's exactly what it's about."

"And are you faithful?"

"Yes. Ridiculous isn't it? But I owe him that. Mum, he's the only one who wanted to marry me. All the others. They just wanted a shag. Or a lot of shags. Do you realise how much I've been hurt? And I don't mean just an occasional black eye. I mean let down, dumped, like a piece of meat."

"Are you talking about Orlando?"

"Yes. And not just him. But Pete, he kept proposing. He wouldn't give up. Imagine how that made me feel. He loves me."

"He wants to own you."

"Perhaps. But because he loves me, I love him too. I love being so important in his life."

"You love being beaten up regularly?"

She put a hand back up to her face. "He just lashes out. He doesn't mean to hurt me. He's always so apologetic afterwards. Sometimes he cries."

I nearly spilt my tea. Apologetic for Chrissake. "Oh, well, that's fine then."

"Look, this is getting us nowhere. I knew I shouldn't have told you. Let's just get your hair cut, and then I can go. He knows where I am and I don't want to get back late, or…" She didn't have to finish the sentence. I didn't want her to go. And I didn't want ever to set eyes on him again.

Once more, she knew what I was thinking. "Perhaps we'll cancel Sunday lunch. Give you time to get used to… things."

"You can take it from me, I'll never get used to it. But okay. Probably a good idea." I stood up and brushed digestive crumbs away, wondering if I should do something. Go behind her back. But if I did… and if I didn't… There was no way out.

"Time I went to see Douggie anyway. It's been a few weeks. Mr Devereux is leaving, and I gather there are going to be some changes."

"So." She retrieved her cutting scissors from her carpet bag. "Okay then. How short?"

While Stephanie snipped and shaped, we went back to the subject of Janine's pregnancy. Because of the effect it might have on Georgina.

It didn't bother me because Rick, for me, was history, but for Georgie… "Poor Georgie. She's thirty and it's a big issue for her."

"Last time the subject came up, I gathered that Mark's not too bothered, is he?"

"Probably not." She was right. My other son-in-law was so laid back that it meant the two of them were at odds about the whole issue of parenthood. "But he is bothered by Georgie's unhappiness. If she's not careful, she'll drive a wedge between them."

"She doesn't know how lucky she is, having Mark."

We were heading towards dangerous ground again. "It's a pity she keeps postponing the possibility of I.V.F. or adoption. The more she postpones the options, the less viable they become. But she won't listen."

"Mum. I'm coming off the pill," she said suddenly.

"What?"

"Pete asked me to."

"But you. What about you?"

"I'm cool. Perhaps it will help."

I wanted to scream *"No. No. No."* The world I moved in during my working hours was populated in part by people who confused violence with love. And the thought of Pete with my grandchildren… But she was my baby. "I hope so, darling. But I'm not convinced it's the answer."

She made it plain that she had no more to say on that particular subject, so I changed it again. We talked about Douggie.

"Mum. About Douggie."

"What about him?"

"Is it… Is his condition… genetic?"

"Not to my knowledge."

"But it could be?"

"I don't think so." I could see that wasn't enough. "I looked into it when I was pregnant. And everyone pooh-poohed the idea."

"But things have moved on," she said vaguely. "Perhaps you could check. I can't imagine Pete's reaction if we had a child, well, with a problem."

This could be a way out. "There's always that chance. Leave Douggie out of the equation and there's still always that chance. At any age."

"Give me a break. I wasn't thinking about age. One of my clients is in her forties, and she's just had an eight pounder, and Georgina always tells me about the older mums at her nursery – because she's interested, not me. I'm young, healthy and fit. And I see no reason why… but if you could just double check?"

"Yes. Okay."

I thought about the conversation with Stephanie on my way to Margate. There was plenty of time to think. In an odd way, although I didn't like admitting it to myself, I would actually be happy to find that some kind of genetic link had been discovered. Because that would sway Stephanie's decision to try for a family, though hopefully not

Georgie's. But Pete? He was an unknown quantity, obviously. A powder keg just biding his time till the next explosion. How would he react?

I thought back to the mild mannered quiet bookseller Stephanie had introduced me to a couple of years ago. The first time we met, he had told me he wanted to marry her, and I'd thought how sweet it was. And what a relief, because I knew Stephanie, then 25, was already getting worried, although she put up an admirable façade of a footloose bachelor girl.

Perhaps his taste in books should have told me something. He collected true life crime. But, no doubt, lots of people collected true life crime. In itself, it meant nothing. "I've got a degree in psychology, Mrs North." That was where his interest lay.

It amused me that someone had come along who admired Stephanie for something other than her enormous breasts and her willing libido. Around the time she met Pete, she had been talking about totally unnecessary breast implants, but he had talked her out of it. He hated what she did for a living, so it came as no surprise when Stephanie gave up modelling for hairdressing. "He wants to look after me. Financially. So why not?" Why not? The modelling wouldn't last for ever. Should warning bells have rung then?

I closed the magazine that I wasn't reading. There was no point beating myself up about it. A degree in psychology. I wondered if Pete was into self analysis.

My thoughts spiralled in the way that thoughts do. Such a qualification could be useful to me in my job, and would probably advance my career if I wanted it to. I made a mental note to contact the Open University. I had already come a long way academically during my professional career. In fact, it was one of the reasons Rick and I had grown apart, I could see that. But I'd only touched the surface. The more I learned – from books, from evening classes – the more I realised there was to learn.

I had bought Douggie a couple of new games for his Game Boy.

"Play now."

"Yes, fine."

The Game Boy had been such a successful birthday present. He absolutely loved it. He wasn't that interested in achieving different levels, although he liked to see his score climbing and could always remember his previous results. As a family, we were planning on buying him his own P.C. for Christmas. Primarily for the games, of course, but who could tell what he might move on to? Mark had offered to spend time with Douggie showing him how to load C.D.s, how to use the mouse, how to save. He was a good son-in-law.

I avoided the obvious mental side track.

"Have you had any visitors, Douggie?"

"No visitors."

"Have you been out?"

"Too busy doing this."

Translated as: 'mind your own business,' or: 'I can't be bothered to think at the moment.'

"Would you like me to make you some tea?"

"Blackcurrant drink, please."

"Blackcurrant? Okay, fine."

I made myself a mug of the same. I hadn't had Ribena for years. Ideal, with winter looming.

"Not hot. Cold drink."

"Oh, sorry. But it's even more delicious when it's hot."

"Burns. Wait for the steam to go."

"Okay. You can wait. I like the steam. Who bought the Ribena?"

"Don't know."

"Did you buy it?"

"Not Douggie."

"Mr Devereux?"

"No. Don't know her name. Number Twelve."

Another resident. It occurred to me that I knew nothing about the social mix in Douggie's home. The other residents. The staff other than

Mr Devereux and the receptionist. He had a whole life really that I knew nothing about. I should be ashamed of myself, getting busy helping perfect strangers when there could be areas in Douggie's life that were not being fully developed.

"I'm just going to have a word with Mr Devereux."

He looked up from the tiny darting Tom and Jerry figures on his screen. "Linda going now."

"No. I'll be back soon."

"How many minutes?"

"Oh, no more than ten."

"Ten maximum?"

"Yes. Ten maximum."

There were more issues connected with a change of management at the Miltons than the mere fact of Mr Devereux's departure. He explained to me that they were changing 'the make up of residents' and that I might no longer think of the home as suitable for Douggie.

"In what way?"

"The Miltons will be offering a home and a safe environment to people with mental health problems as well as those with learning disabilities."

"I see. Though they do share some common ground."

"Some. But if Douggie were a member of my family, I would have some minor concerns." He was smiling but there was something behind his words.

"Can you be more specific?"

"I'm afraid I can't. The new management will not want me to encourage anyone to leave, but they are planning on extending the premises and taking in another dozen residents."

"I see. And these extra people will have mental health problems?"

"Yes."

"So they will need different levels of care and expertise?"

"Yes."

"And they will make different demands on staff?"

"Yes." His smile was widening, and I sensed I was getting to the point.

"And present different, er, challenges, to the other residents?"

"Exactly."

"And you think Douggie might have a problem with that?"

"I didn't say that, Mrs North."

"No. Thank you. You didn't."

I thought about it for a moment. Oh, damn it. Douggie had been settled here for years. "Do you have any suggestions, Mr Devereux?"

"Your turn to be more specific."

This was hard work. But I appreciated that he was in a difficult position. "Okay. Would you recommend another home for Douggie?"

"I couldn't recommend one as such."

"Help me out here. Where are you going, for instance?"

"Sadly, the Isle of Wight. Even further from Essex."

"Is there somewhere in Essex?"

"Aaahh." He leaned back in his chair. Now he could tell me. "I used to work with a real wee charmer. Moira Paul. We were in Exeter together years ago. And I heard only recently that she's taken over an establishment in Southend on Sea. How would that be?"

"As far as location is concerned, terrific. But what about the home?"

"Learning disabled. Fifteen residents, ten in shared rooms, five in singles. Many, like the ones with Down's Syndrome, are happy to share, but not those with autism. Like Douggie."

"And might there be a single room available?"

He put a stubby finger to his stubby nose. "There just might be."

"Can I use your phone?"

"Feel free." He left the room after opening his Filofax to reveal the address and phone number of Dunkirk House, Southend on Sea. What a star.

Moira Paul sounded fine. The place sounded fine. The move from one Social Services Provider to another was, of course, complex but she assured me that she would look after that side of it. I would just have to meet up with Douggie's social worker, clear a move date with

Mr Devereux, and bingo. It sounded amazingly simple, but, given the job I now did, I had my doubts. Still, it was certainly worth a try.

"Oh, and you may also be asked to take Douggie to see a psychologist."

"What for?"

"To ensure there's no trauma, that kind of thing. Nothing to worry about."

Psychologists. They were suddenly everywhere.

Mr Devereux didn't need to knock on the door of his own office, but he did. Sweet. "Douggie's on the landing, looking for you. Something about ten minutes."

"Yes. I'm going straight up, thanks. I'll be going to see Dunkirk House next weekend, with Douggie, if that's all right. And we'll need to get the social worker involved."

"Of course. I'll liaise with Moira. Good. I'm pleased."

"Thanks again," I called down the stairwell as I caught sight of Douggie. He had left his room door wide open and still had the Game Boy in his hand.

"Douggie. I've got some good news." I ushered him back into his room. "Would you like me to visit more often?"

"Don't know."

"Would you like more presents?"

"More presents. Douggie likes presents."

"Well, next Sunday we're going to visit a house in Southend on Sea. Another seaside place. Much closer to Barking."

"Barking?"

"You remember that's where I've got my flat?" Although I'd been there several years, I hadn't yet taken Douggie there for a visit. Not even once.

"Because soon The Miltons is going to have too many people. And you will need a new home."

"Douggie likes The Miltons."

"I know. I know, darling. But you don't like places with lots of people, and soon The Miltons will be a lot more crowded."

"How many people?"

"Oh, about thirty extra." The white lie was justified in my eyes.

"Too many people."

"Exactly. But the home in Southend on Sea is much smaller. And much closer to me."

"How many miles?"

"About thirty instead of about seventy five."

"Nearer to Linda."

"Yes, darling."

"Seaside."

"Yes."

"Blackcurrant drink now. No steam."

Bless.

Chapter Ten

January 2004

Visiting Dunkirk House when the sun shone was always a more pleasant experience than in the middle of winter or on bleaker days. The home was no more than, what, half a mile from the seafront. And some of the upper rooms had sea views. Not Douglas's, though. Not that Douglas cared.

I spoke into the entry phone and eventually found my way through the security systems to where he was sitting, laptop in front of him as usual. It had been the best present yet. He probably spent, if anything, too much time on it. But the pleasure he derived from it helped allay some of the guilt that I might otherwise have felt at what could be seen as an encouragement to be inactive.

"Hello, Douggie. How are you?" I put a bag of marshmallows beside him. They were his favourites, but he didn't react. Only when I put my face right in front of the laptop did he acknowledge me, grumpily.

"Hello, hello, hello. Move it."

I got out of his way. No point trying to talk to him until he'd finished what he was doing. I looked at the cover of the P.C. game: *The Italian Job*. It was easy to see where every penny of his pocket money went.

Funny really. He was fifty-one, but it was still pocket money.

Whenever I visited him, every month, I thought about the past. Natural enough. But, unlike most people it seems, the past for me was always about the rotten things, not the nice things. I never seemed to acquire the use of rose tinted specs, and that worried me. Why could I remember the day Mum left, the day I was caned across my palm at school, the day Douggie was so ill when he had his tonsils out at age ten, Dad's funeral... times of crying, pain, sadness. It would be nice to get rid of those memories and replace them with memories of cosy Christmases, or happy rainy holidays in Ramsgate, or getting a gold star for a school essay, but the happier the memory, the more difficult I found it to access.

"Marshmallows."

Right. Game over. I turned my attention back to Douglas, who was ripping open the packet.

"Are you going to give me one of those?"

"Douggie's marshmallows. Not Linda's."

I know that sounds as if my young brother has grown up to be a selfish adult, but no, that's not the case. Douglas has never recognised the needs of other people. Dad described Mum as selfish – rightly? Who knows. It was just too long ago – but that was a very different scenario to Douglas's situation. It was only in the last – what – ten years that the word 'autistic' had been more widely used to describe the Douglases of this world and only sixteen since *Rain Man*.

"So what have you been doing, apart from playing computer games?"

"Internet."

"Okay. What have you been doing apart from using the computer?"

"Can't remember." He had got halfway through the bag of marshmallows, and dropped them on the floor. I could help myself now if I wanted to, with no objections, but I was more of a chocolate person.

For "can't remember" read "don't want to talk about it" or "it's too boring to discuss". So I progressed to the best way to get some interaction – I should have known better than to start any other way.

"Okay. Have you been to the beach?"

"No."

"The pier?"

"No."

"The park?"

A hesitation. "Southchurch Park."

"Good. I'm glad you haven't been stuck indoors. It's been decent weather for January. Did you feed the ducks?"

He started fiddling with his hair, a sure sign of boredom setting in. "Yes."

We worked our way through a list of other possible activities and it turned out that he had been ten-pin bowling and to Roots Hall market and the gym during the last month. So, not too bad. I hated the idea that he just sat in his room with his solitary pursuits, day in, day out. Not that he minded. All he seemed to need was his "screens" as he called them, and the usual basic necessities of food and drink. Clothes didn't interest him, nor did other people.

Was it my imagination, or was he making even less eye contact than usual?

"Look at me." I had to repeat it before he did as I asked. "Is everything okay?"

Another hesitation?

"Has anything happened that you don't like?"

He looked away again and went back to hair fiddling.

As I struggled to find the words to ask the right question, he suddenly said: "Don't want to see the book man. Not the book man."

"Who?" I glanced at the pile of reference books on the table. This was Douggie's preferred reading when he wasn't glued to a screen. Atlases, books of lists, books about the weird and the wonderful, and especially about the disabled – not that there were many of those. I opened one up. "Oh, the mobile library? I thought you went to the library in the town centre."

But that was all I could get out of him. "Linda go now."

"You sure know how to make a girl feel welcome." The sarcasm was, of course, wasted.

"How many minutes?" He was looking longingly at his laptop.

"Only five minutes. Do you want me to bring anything next time?"

"Candles."

Here we go again. "Sorry, Douggie, but you know you're not allowed candles. They are too dangerous, too risky, they could cause a fire too easily." He looked disappointed, and I wished I hadn't asked. If I hadn't asked, he wouldn't have mentioned them. He was allowed candles on his – or anyone else's – birthday, and everyone at Dunkirk House, staff and 'clients', allowed Douggie to blow out the candles on their birthday cake. It was worth it to see the joy on his face, and they could always re-light them if they wanted to have a go themselves.

I didn't outstay my welcome. The sea front was calling, and it was a chance for me to catch a bit of ozone before returning to the suburbs of East London that I called home.

Before I left, though, I sought out the home's manager. Moira Paul. From the time we had met, we'd never really hit it off. I don't know why. I think I couldn't understand her, couldn't understand why anyone would do such a job year on year, even had it been well paid, which I'm sure it wasn't. I'd had some experience myself now of her world. The mostly hidden underbelly of British life. There again, where would I – and people like me – be without people like Moira Paul? Okay, so she was a bit withdrawn, a bit evasive, but on the plus side, always smiling, and the smiles seemed genuine enough. Perhaps that was just a professional façade? That was something else I knew all about.

"Mrs North, isn't it? Douglas's sister. Nice to see you again. Would that all our residents were like Douglas – and all our relatives like you, eh? eh?" She pumped my hand jovially. "Nothing wrong, I hope?"

"Probably not. Just something he said about the book man… is he getting his books from a mobile library now?"

"Let me think. Come in to the office for a minute while I rev up the memory cells. Mobile library, mobile library…" She sat down in her untidy office and pursed her lips. "Got it. Sit down, sit down, Mrs North."

I moved a file from the only other chair in the room, revealing threadbare upholstery. So décor and equipment was not a financial priority, then. That was good news. It meant money was being spent, hopefully, on improving the quality of the lives she was controlling, rather than on their surroundings.

She leaned forward, revealing a cleavage which must have been a bit tempting for some of the male residents, though not Douglas. "Yes. Did Douglas tell you? How interesting. He doesn't say much here at all, as you know. Yes. The mobile library has started coming, initially for old Mrs Newley. Know her? Wheelchair bound. Great Mills and Boon fan. We couldn't keep up with her insatiable reading appetite, because she was running out of reading material at times when we didn't have a carer available to take her to the town centre library, so the mobile library tops up her supply, and the service can also be utilised by our other residents, so everyone is happy.

"The book man? Yes, indeed. Robert. Thirties. Very quiet. You say Douglas doesn't like him?"

"I didn't say that exactly. But that could be the case."

"Hmm." She frowned. "I wonder why? We can keep him away from Douggie easily enough. If that's what you'd like."

"Has he been alone with Douggie at all?"

She looked a little more wary and leaned back again. "Highly unlikely. Not something we would advocate. Is that what Douggie said?"

"No. It's just that… I don't know. He doesn't often take a dislike to people. Doesn't take an interest in them at all, really. So…" I wanted to ask her if Robert was gay, but I knew I was being ridiculous. "Would he have had all the usual police checks and such?"

"Mrs North!" She was beginning to look concerned. "What exactly did Douglas say? Perhaps you should tell me."

"Oh, nothing really. Nothing specific. It's just me. I'm a bit paranoid, I'm sorry. Just keep him away from Douggie and, yes, that will be fine."

She stood up and held out a highly be-ringed hand. "Well, that was an easy problem to solve. Would that all our problems could be resolved as simply."

I returned her smile at last.

On the way out, I looked up at Douggie's window on the second floor, automatically lifting a hand. For the first time ever, he was looking out and I stopped and waved more vigorously. No response. He was mouthing something. Could it be "book man"?

Get a grip. Paranoia with knobs on.

Douggie was still on my mind when I got home, so I phoned Rick. It was months since we'd spoken, but he was one of the few people who had spent time with Douggie and I felt I needed his impartial advice for once. I phoned both of my daughters as a bit of an afterthought, just to see if they thought I was being over-sensitive. That paranoia word came up several times.

"Linda, he can communicate. Okay, it's not his forte, but he can do it if he needs to or wants to. So, if it was a problem, he'd keep on. That's my over-riding memory of your brother. Persistence, oh, and repetition." That was sensible Rick. And, of course, Rick was always right. Always bloody right. According to Rick, anyway.

"Do you remember when he took a dislike to the caravan man?" Georgina reminded me. "And it turned out to be that golf cart thing he rode about in that Douggie really disliked."

Yes, I did remember. It was, what, twenty years ago? Amazing that Georgina had retained the image of Douggie wailing non stop, spoiling our holiday in the Dorset caravan park and constantly talking about, "no more caravan man."

"Oh, for God's sake, Mum. You've done your bit. The boss lady says she'll keep them apart. End of story." The impatient, staccato Stephanie, unchanged by recent motherhood.

I knew I was not being logical. But I couldn't get the image of Douggie in the window out of my head. Although my family were Douggie's family, too, they had never been that keen on maintaining contact, no doubt for a variety of reasons. And they rarely visited. Their lives got in the way.

Admittedly, Georgina had started sending him e-mails but he didn't reply, although Moira Paul confirmed that he could and did access them, so Georgie wouldn't keep that up indefinitely. Phone calls were not an option, of course, because he didn't like talking on the telephone, or, more accurately, he wasn't sufficiently interested in talking to whoever was on the other end.

I wondered if I should unload my concerns on Jeff. As the thought crossed my mind, I realised how important he was becoming in my life. A complication I didn't need right now. My job was sometimes on the verge of depressing and I was finding it more difficult than I thought I would to get used to the idea that Rick's young sons were far more important to him than his daughters – he forgot an occasional birthday now, saw them far less often… Then there was Stephanie's marriage, still potentially shaky, despite the arrival of Ronan…

I couldn't make up my mind whether to phone Jeff or not. I looked at my watch. He was probably sitting in a traffic jam about now, after what he regarded as another hard day at the office, and what I regarded as a jammy day playing with other people's money.

What the hell? I dialled his mobile and left a message on his voicemail inviting him over for spaghetti bolognese and red wine – if he didn't come, it would be pasta and stir-in-sauce – even easier.

But he did come. He phoned first, enthusiastic and happy. That was his greatest asset in my eyes. That gift for happiness. "There must be more to this accountancy work than is apparent to the outside world," I'd told him when we met just a couple of months ago at Spanish for Beginners evening classes. He had given me a lift home from the first class, and that was it. That indefinable spark that brings two people into the same orbit.

He arrived with flowers. I didn't have the heart to tell him that I had never been a fan of real flowers: I didn't even have a vase. "Oh, thanks, Jeff. You shouldn't have." I had no idea what they were called but enthused suitably.

"Freesias. It means sweetness."

"You're full of surprises." I put them in the sink and found he'd followed me into the kitchen.

"So. See how I dropped everything to be here, just like that. At your beck and call. Am I invited for my body, my superior knowledge of Spanish, or…?"

"At my age, bodies are not an issue, and as for your Spanish…"

He was even nearer. "Don't keep on about that 'a' word."

"A?"

"Age. I have always fancied older women. Did I tell you that?" I could smell his aftershave, which he must have in his car as he hadn't had time to go home first. Applied in my honour. I was flattered. Especially by his obvious interest. He was a beautiful male specimen, blond, toned, early forties... and I wanted him, and he knew it. But it just wasn't right.

"When will your wife be back?"

He retreated to the doorway immediately. "Okay. Okay. I get it."

"No, really. When is she back?" I kept any emotion out of my voice. "Saturday."

"And remind me, where she's gone this time?"

"Are you really interested, Linda?"

"Probably not, but tell me anyway. It'll keep you focused."

He smiled his perfect-toothed smile. "A little bit of flirting never hurt anyone. Okay. Okay. A seminar in Lincoln. Entitled *Recruitment as a Partnership in the Twenty First Century*. There, are you any the wiser? And can we talk about us now?" He was getting closer again, moving sideways along the kitchen units.

I tossed him the bottle opener. "Jeff, there is no 'us'."

"So what am I doing here?"

"Company for dinner. But if I've misjudged the situation..."

"No, I can handle it." He removed the cork from the Cabernet Sauvignon effortlessly and looked around for wine glasses.

"Over the sink." I turned my back and concentrated on the bolognese sauce. I liked the danger, the palpable effort involved in resisting. It made me feel like I was back in the race. It made me feel desirable again. "I wanted to talk to you about Douggie."

"Little brother? Fire away. I'm all yours. In every way." I shot a warning look at him and he held up a hand. "Sorry, shoot."

Unlike my family, he listened, he asked questions, he didn't accuse me of paranoia or pooh-pooh my concerns. I think I'd known that. That's why I'd called him. He was becoming just too damn perfect. Damn his perfections. And damn his perfect wife, Julia, the overworked, overpaid, over-groomed managing director of Extremis Recruitment in Bond Street – where else?

We'd finished our spaghetti before I'd poured out my concerns and filled in some of the background.

"When are you going to see him again?"

"I thought I'd go next week. Why?"

"Would you like me to come?"

I thought about it. It was so sweet of Jeff, so typical. Although, there again, I hardly knew him. Perhaps he thought by taking a hands-on interest in Douggie, that would speed up the process of getting me into bed. I poured myself the last of the wine, feeling mean spirited. "I don't think so."

"What then?"

He was gently stroking my hand on the table and the tiny movements were intensely pleasurable. I could feel myself weakening. This was not a good idea. Especially the red wine.

His mobile rang. It was her. "I'm en route... Can't talk. I'm driving...Talk to you when I get back. Yeah... Yeah."

I withdrew my hand.

"Sorry."

"At least you didn't call her darling, and make kissing noises. Someone did that to me once, and then do you know what he said? 'It doesn't mean anything'."

"I don't want to hear about other men." He sounded jealous. Jealous, I ask you! "Except Douggie. I'd like to help. To set your mind at rest. But what can I do?"

"Okay, then. Why not? Douggie can be uncomfortable around strangers, but if you take him some marshmallows, or better still a computer game... I don't suppose he'll talk to you, but if he was to say he didn't want you to come again, say, and I knew it was for no good reason, perhaps that would help." I was clutching at straws.

"And if he liked me?"

I shrugged. "I'd know a bit more about you, if nothing else." I was testing him, and he knew it.

"That's settled then." He leaned over and I let him kiss me. This wasn't the first time I'd cooked for him when his wife was away and certainly not our first kiss. But it was the first time I'd let his kiss linger. I felt the probe of his tongue, very gentle, hardly penetrating. Somebody moaned. "Linda."

I stood up. "Jeff, please. Julia. I can't do this. I'm not used to it. If you were... were..."

"Okay." He wiped his mouth with the heel of his hand. "I've told you. I'm not leaving her, if that's what you want."

"I didn't say that. How could you think that of me?"

"No. You think I'm not being fair on her? On you? Probably not. I want it all. But you deserve some pleasure, too. What the hell's wrong with a bit of no strings pleasure? You can have it all, too, Linda. When you're ready. I can wait. In the meantime, I'll help you with Douggie, if I can. I'll do anything – well, nearly anything." He was grinning and I couldn't resist planting another kiss on his upturned face.

"Begone, temptation. Hasta la vista."

He stood up, still smiling, stretching slowly. "Until Thursday's Spanish class then. Wonder what the Spanish is for 'lust'?"

"I dare you to ask Antonia." We both laughed at the prospect, thinking of her little Edith Piaf body.

He kissed me on the tip of my nose before disappearing into the cold night. "You know what they say about books and covers."

Chapter Eleven

February 2004

"You know, this looks pretty decent." Jeff was looking admiringly up at the façade of Dunkirk House.

"So, what were you expecting?" I tried to look at it objectively, through a stranger's eyes. Four storeys, big modern windows, stained glass entrance doors.

"Oh, I don't know. Something more… grim, I suppose. Come on, it's freezing out here."

He needed to give his address when signing in and I could see him hesitate momentarily before reverting to his what-the-hell bravado. One hand clutched marshmallows AND a computer game and the other clutched my arm, wanting to lead but disadvantaged by his surroundings.

We ran up the stairs to warm ourselves up a bit, although the central heating was on full blast, even in the communal areas. "Must be expensive to run," Jeff muttered as we tapped on Douggie's door.

"Typical accountant's comment," I laughed as we waited. Douggie wouldn't rush. He would open it when he was good and ready.

"It's me, Linda. And a surprise."

"What surprise?" he said as he finally opened the door. He didn't walk away as he usually did to leave me to follow him, and he didn't look at Jeff, either. He just waited for an explanation.

"Hi, Douggie. I'm Jeff. I'm Linda's friend. Can we come in?"

"It's who?"

"Jeff. His name's Jeff."

"How many minutes?"

"Perhaps twenty."

"Less."

"Perhaps eighteen."

"Less."

"Look, Douggie, let us in and we'll decide how long we'll be staying, okay."

He turned away and Jeff glanced at me, raising both eyebrows, removing his leather jacket as we closed the door behind us. But I had warned him, told him that he wouldn't be well received.

Douggie went into his mini kitchen where he'd obviously been making himself tea, and took the cup to his favourite seat by the window, moving the mantel clock an inch en-route to ensure he could see that we didn't outstay our welcome.

"I'll make some tea, too. For me and Jeff. Is that okay Douggie?"

He ignored me, slurping a little too loudly. I knew he wouldn't put the cup down until he'd drained it, so I made myself busy with cups and teabags, and left Jeff to it.

"So, I hear you like computers, Douggie."

Slurp.

"I've brought you a new game. I hope you like it. It's called the Dam Busters. Aeroplanes fighting, manoeuvring... er... moving around, dropping bombs... er... It's exciting. Fast."

Douggie drained his cup. "How many miles an hour?"

"Sorry?" Jeff looked at me for help as I handed him tea.

"You said 'fast'. He's asking you how fast."

"Oh, right. I'm not absolutely sure."

"That's not an answer. Not for Douggie, anyway." I rescued him. "Five hundred miles an hour, Douggie."

Douggie got up and rinsed out his cup before unceremoniously grabbing the Virgin bag at Jeff's feet. I grabbed his arm before he sat down again. "Say thank you." Grunt. "No, say thank you properly."

"Thank you."

Then he spotted the bag of marshmallows. "Douggie's marshmallows." It wasn't a question.

Jeff picked them up from the floor and handed them over. "Yes. Douggie's."

"Presents. Douggie likes presents. More presents." He was looking at me. Interesting that he could make excellent eye contact when he wanted to.

"I don't know if you deserve presents. Have you been looking after yourself properly? Your hair needs cutting."

"Hairdresser Monday February 17th at two o'clock. Claire's, Hairdresser to the Stars. More presents."

"Next Monday. Good. Okay, then, I've brought you some teabags."

The teabags were vehemently ignored. Not at all in the same league as computer games and marshmallows.

"Books."

I felt myself tense, and Jeff too. "What do you mean, books?"

"Presents. Books. Magazines. Take A Break Street Where Everyone's Friendly."

Jeff looked at me, but now I was lost too.

"Douggie, I don't know what you mean," I said gently, knowing that his inability to convey what he wanted to say was often a source of frustration for him, with the potential to fracture his normally placid temperament. "Tell me about Take a Break Street…"

"Where Everyone's Friendly." He got up and rifled through a pile of papers and magazines on his coffee table. "This one." He handed me a copy of *Take A Break*, and I flipped through it.

"Oh, right." I showed Jeff the Letters page, headed up *Take a Break Street Where Everyone's Friendly*. "You'd like some more of these?"

"More. Every Thursday, please."

"I'm sure that can be arranged. I'll talk to Moira Paul."

"Don't tell her."

"Don't tell her what?"

"Don't tell her about the talking."

I got up and ruffled his curls affectionately. "Silly billy. She knows you can talk. In fact, she'd like it if you spoke to her more often."

"Don't want to." He was beginning to look a tad concerned.

"Okay. Okay. And did you say you want some books? What about the mobile library?" I had to know.

Douggie put a marshmallow in his mouth, obviating the need to reply.

Jeff squeezed my arm and stood up so that he could see out of the window. "Nice view. You can just about see the sea until the trees leaf up again."

I looked at his back. Was he saying that I should change the subject? But this was my brother, not his.

"Douggie. Does the mobile library still come?"

"Don't see the book man." He was fiddling with his hair.

"Has he stopped coming?"

"Don't know. Don't see him. Linda buy books."

"Tell you what. Why don't we go to the library?"

Douggie looked at the clock. "Lunch half past twelve."

"That's no problem. We could stay for an hour, if that's okay, and it's only a ten minute walk."

"It's too many minutes."

"What is? Our visit? It's about eighteen minutes in the flat. And an hour altogether for a visit to the library."

"Douggie and Linda. Not Jeff." Jeff turned around, but Douggie was smiling. "Jeff wait outside."

He smiled back, not taking offence. "In this weather? I don't think so."

"There's a café in the library. Perhaps if you wait there."

Douggie made no objections to my idea. A very good sign. I gave Jeff the thumbs up.

"How very civilised. A café in the library. Do they sell bacon sandwiches?"

"Doubt it. Can't imagine librarians tolerating the smell, somehow."

"True. Oh, well, it's more tea then."

Douggie had been listening while he painstakingly fastened his favoured duffle coat. "Bacon comes from pigs."

"What?"

"Bacon. From pigs."

Comprehension dawned on Jeff's face. "Oh. Yes. Indeed. From pigs. Don't you like pigs?"

"Not pigs. Not animals."

I thought about his visits to the park. "But you like ducks, don't you? You feed the ducks."

Douggie looked at me with something approaching scorn. "Ducks not animals."

"Oh, no. Sorry." I spoke seriously, studiously avoiding Jeff's eyes.

The visit to the library went smoothly. As always, we got some odd looks from some of the people who overheard any of our conversation, but I was used to that. Douggie often chose books as a result of their size rather than their content, so a fat encyclopaedia was of more interest to him than the very thin book about the planets that I picked up. He also chose a book about candle making, which was harmless because I knew the home wouldn't let him have the materials to make his own. Then there was *Brewer's Dictionary of Phrase and Fable*, *The Timetables of History*, a book of facsimiles of old maps of London, *The Book of British Lists*, and a massive tome about *The Galaxy Unravelled*. Should keep him away from his laptop for a while.

"Home now."

Jeff hadn't finished his tea, but didn't seem too perturbed at having to leave it. "No worries. My taste buds have been well and truly serviced."

"Crap."

Douggie's remark broke into one of those real old fashioned library type silences.

"Are you talking about the tea?" Jeff was obviously trying very hard not to laugh.

I explained to him quickly and quietly: "He's heard me call it that. Sorry, I should have warned you."

"Crap."

"Okay, okay, Douggie. You don't need to say it any more, thank you. We're going home now."

We giggled our way back to Douggie's cosy flat, with Douggie laughing too, and saying "Crap" at intervals. I don't know if he was laughing at us or at himself but I enjoyed seeing him laugh. It was like being kids together again.

I realised with a bit of a jolt that I didn't see him laugh much at all. I wondered if he was happy. Okay, so his happiness was measured by different standards, but I really wanted to find out, and I didn't know how. Was it partly because of the years we had lost contact, those lost years? There had been reasons, perhaps good ones, but that was not the point.

Our time was definitely up, according to Douggie and his clock, so we didn't even shed our outer clothes. Just a few hugs − from us, not from him − and we were back in the cold air. "I think I should talk to Moira Paul again before I go."

Jeff shrugged. "Up to you. But remember he said he hadn't seen the book man and there were no books from the mobile library in his room that we could find, were there?"

"No, it's not just that. It's…" No, it was pointless. She couldn't offer me any of the reassurance I was looking for. I took a few steps and looked up at Douggie's window. Nothing.

I kissed Jeff on the mouth. His lips were cold. The weather, no doubt, rather than lack of emotion. "Thank you."

He shrugged again. "I did nothing. In fact, I felt completely useless. Out of my depth. Like some sort of intruder."

I kissed him again. "You were wonderful. You didn't talk down to him. You didn't treat him like an idiot. You didn't ignore him or avoid him. All the things that I've seen so many people do over the years: family, friends, strangers, even professionals. You weren't offended by his indifference. You were perfect. Thank you."

It was his turn to kiss me. "You are one hell of a sister. Douggie is lucky. And as for me, I can't believe how lucky I am. You know what you did by bringing me here? You showed me that I count in your life. That I'm a part of it." He kissed me again, oblivious to people coming and going around us. "I love you. Don't say anything. I know what you're thinking. But you have to know. Come on, I'll buy you a high calorie winter's day lunch."

"Bacon sandwiches?" I murmured into his muffled-up neck.

"Why not?"

I had been nervous about today, but it was turning out to be one of my better ideas. Jeff didn't just like me. He loved me. Well, me and bacon sandwiches.

One of the few places still open at this time of year along the sea front specialised in all-day English breakfasts. So we enjoyed our treat. Plus brown sauce for me and tomato ketchup for him. Wonderful stuff. We grinned at each other inanely, our chins shining with grease.

I couldn't help thinking that I should tell him how I felt. But I couldn't do it. I wasn't even sure how I felt. Did I love him? He was very comfortable in his marriage, but he didn't want children to spoil his – and Julia's, no doubt – lifestyle. And he was ambitious. A professional, beautiful wife suited him just fine, fitted in with his plans. As for me, he didn't know what to do about me. I knew that, I could sense the struggle.

"One new penny for them."

"I think you'd regard them as a lot more valuable than that. Because I was thinking about you. No. I was actually thinking about us."

He put down the remains of his sandwich, very slowly, keeping his blue eyes firmly fixed on my face. "Tell me more."

"Do you know what I wanted to achieve by bringing you here?"

"No. Tell me."

"I wanted meeting Douggie to put you off. I wanted you to be disgusted, embarrassed, appalled, horrified, unable to cope, to think 'what am I doing here', to look for excuses to leave, to be free of me and my… my responsibilities." I felt my throat beginning to close up.

"Bad luck. It didn't work. I love you. Meeting your brother helped me to realise that. Now I want to meet your daughters. I want to be a part of everything."

"But Jeff, it's impossible."

"Ridiculous." He read my thoughts. "Julia? She's hardly ever at home. When she is, we have glorious sex. No, don't look away. I screwed Julia five minutes after I met her, and every man I know, every man I've ever known, has screwed her too. And you know what I think about these days when we are rolling around in bed? I think about you. I wish it was you. But Julia is my wife.

"She proposed to me. Did I tell you that? No, she *told* me I was going to marry her. I wasn't used to being bossed around, especially by a woman. And I rather liked it. A beautiful, desirable woman. Why hadn't she been snapped up years ago? But you should have heard my friends laugh when I told them – they were all pissing themselves. They called her Martini, apparently. Something to do with anytime, anywhere... Can you imagine how I felt? But I was committed. And I thought she'd do. I thought she'd be enough. It turned me on that all my friends fancied her, if I'm honest. Though I soon realised that they also hated her. And I learnt to hate her too. But Julia and I, we... we deserve each other. We're a shallow pair. She waxes my legs. She's my slave, my woman."

"You Tarzan, she Jane."

"If you like."

"And me?"

"You are everything she's not." He finished his sandwich and licked his lips. "There. Something to chew over."

"I don't know what to say. I don't know what to do."

"Don't say anything. Don't do anything. What will be, will be. Julia has gained such confidence by our marriage that I suspect she's moved on to someone else, someone at work probably, someone who's becoming more than just another shag. And if I'm right, then she'll abandon me without a look backwards. A boring accountant for the rest of her life? I don't think so."

"And you? How will you feel if she abandons you?"

"Just that. Abandoned. Don't you see? She's my pet. Thanks to her, I don't have to live alone. I hated living alone. She was there. Right place, right time. You are shit timing. Where were you ten years ago? But you must wait, Linda. You must."

"I can wait." The conversation was surreal. We were talking in hushed tones, with greasy fingers, looking out of murky windows at a murky sky and a murky sea with stalwart dog walkers braving the chill winds. And we were talking about his life and his future, and perhaps our future. He never even invited me to bed any more. He genuinely seemed content to wait. Perhaps more content even than me.

"What you have is so different from what I had when I was married. Me and Rick loved each other. Oh, yes, make no mistake about it. And we enjoyed exclusive sex. And we enjoyed raising our family, and building a life. So I don't understand your marriage. But it doesn't matter. I actually feel a bit sorry for you."

He stood up and brushed crumbs from his jeans. "Do me a favour. Remember, you are not old enough to be my mother. So don't try and behave as if you are."

We braved the cold again. "Darling, I have to go. I'm supposed to be seeing a potential client. And I wouldn't be spending this much time with a client unless they had handed over their account for me to look after."

"I know. Okay. Listen. Douggie."

"Do you want me to come with you to visit him again?"

"That would be nice. I've been neglecting him a bit lately. Not for the first time. Even though he's only a half hour or so away. I've just been so busy. But I thought I'd step up my visits a bit."

"You think it matters?"

"For him? Maybe not. But for me, yes. Call it guilt if you like."

"What will your family say? Do they visit much?"

"They'll probably think I'm overdoing it and, no, they don't visit much at all. Hardly ever. But I have an idea."

"What kind of idea?"

"A holiday. Perhaps Easter. Me, Douggie, my grandson, my girls and their husbands. Somewhere warm. A chance for me to practise my Spanish. Do you know, Douggie's in his fifties and he's never been abroad. He doesn't even possess a passport."

Jeff looked horrified. "You must be barking. Absolutely barking."

"It's only a holiday. A family holiday."

"Look, you're talking dysfunctional family here, right? You've got Stephanie who's been married, how long…?"

"Over five years."

"And you tell me you think her husband knocks her about a bit and it seems to be getting worse, but she won't talk about it. And who had a baby a year and a half ago to – how did you put it – cement her marriage, but it doesn't seem to have worked."

"Right."

"And you've got Georgina, who's been married, what, ten years, and who is desperate for children, and gets tearful at the very sight of a baby, any baby, including her nephew."

"Ronan. His name's Ronan. Yes, excellent summation."

"And you want to take the whole happy bunch on holiday – with Douggie."

"Right."

"Abso-bloody-lutely barking."

"You say the nicest things." I kissed his eyelids, his nose, his ear lobes. "Perhaps the next holiday could be you and I?"

"Tease. But I won't forget you said that. Am I, perhaps, making inroads?"

"I think you could be. I appreciate your honesty, Jeff. It's what I adore about you. I'll see you on Thursday. Have you done your homework?"

He groaned. "No. I only go there to see you. What are we supposed to be doing?"

"Families and relationships." We laughed and kissed all the way back to our respective modes of transport.

I drove back in silence, avoiding the radio. Not that it worked very well – nothing much worked well in my old Metro, but I wasn't in the company car league any more. I poodled along, taking time to think about Jeff. I hated admitting it, but having a man in my life was something I hadn't realised I'd needed. And I felt that I did need him.

The realisation was that it wasn't that I needed a man. I just needed Jeff. There was a difference. His being married was a huge barrier for me, however, although I knew that was a dated viewpoint.

My job had filled a huge gap. But all this involvement in other people's lives had taught me the importance of becoming more involved with my own family. And my own happiness. I needed time to think, perhaps make a few decisions. I still thought about the Open University on occasion, but had never done anything about it. Time was my excuse, no, my reason. But now I was edging towards retirement, for Christ's sake, and I wanted to indulge myself a little. Or a lot.

A holiday would do me good. I hadn't had one for a few years. Nor had Stephanie, not since she reluctantly gave up her lucrative modelling career. Georgina and Mark were the only ones who made it to exotic climes on a regular basis and Georgina often joked – painfully – about conceiving somewhere exotic, but it didn't happen.

I still kept a journal and I just had a feeling that this year, anything could happen.

Chapter Twelve

April 2004

Of course, arranging a holiday to suit all seven of us didn't prove that easy. In the end, Stephanie's husband, Pete, opted out, claiming he was too busy at work.

"I thought bookshops were only busy at Christmas," I challenged him but he just shrugged, emphasising muscle bound shoulders through a tight t-shirt; a physique unmatched by the average bookseller, which he achieved with a lot of effort at the gym.

"That's what everyone thinks. But when there are staff shortages, agreeing holiday dates becomes a problem. See?"

Aggressive bugger.

"You'll lose your deposit, Pete."

"Nothing I can do about that, is there?"

Why did he always have to converse in questions. I looked at Stephanie who was eyeing the two of us warily.

"Oh, well. But Stephanie is coming, aren't you? With Ronan?"

Pete answered for her. "Apparently. But she knows I don't like it, don't you, Steph?"

"I know," she said calmly. "But I'll be with Mum, with my family."

I hated the look he gave her, wanted to defend her from it, but she didn't react. "You'd just better behave yourself, okay?"

"Meaning what exactly?" I asked him quietly.

"Mind your own business, In-Law." His charming name for me. "Steph knows what I mean. Exactly what I mean. We all know that *you* put it about a bit, In-Law. But Steph… She won't be packing any bikinis. She won't be out late clubbing. She won't be alone with a man during the whole fortnight. I'm looking to you to see to that, In-Law. Do you hear me?" He was smiling now, realising that I was offended by his allegation. He also knew from experience that I wouldn't rise to his bait, because angering him could put Stephanie in danger. There were still thumb marks on her neck from his last attack, thumb marks she dismissed to everyone but me as love bites. Love bites, indeed.

This was the first time he'd let her go away without him since they'd met. I was amazed. But I was delighted. And I was scared.

"I hear you. Shame about the bikinis, because she'll miss out on sun-tanning."

"No prob, Mum," she interrupted quickly. "I'll have a St Tropez before I go."

Pete nodded appreciatively. "That's my girl."

I hated what he had done to her. Where was my sunny daughter? Who was this wary young woman? And him, he'd changed too. He was proud of his power over Stephanie, whereas once he'd concealed it.

Oh, well, don't interfere, Linda. At least Georgina and Mark still seemed delighted with each other, if a bit wary about the holiday I had booked. Not about the villa on a golf complex near Fuengirola, but the inclusion of Douggie.

"I think he could cramp our style," was Mark's objection.

"Nonsense." Georgina, crisp, in control of everything except her ability to reproduce.

"Georgie, imagine us in the club house, right, and Douggie comes in, right, and you try and introduce him, right. It will be bloody embarrassing."

"Nonsense again. You worry too much about what other people think. We'll be in Spain. Who needs introductions? It's more laid back there, more accepting. Forget about Douggie. For us, it will be sangria, paella, flamenco, sunshine, golf, markets, and no commuting to London. Glorious."

"But all of that is only when you get out of bed." Mark knew my daughter well.

"True. Well, it will be up to you to get me out of bed, won't it, Fuzzy Bear."

Mark glanced at me, probably uncomfortable at Georgina's open use of her affectionate nickname for him as a result of his currently unshaven look. But I pretended not to hear her, nor to see him put his tongue in her ear. It was time for me to leave. "Good then, that's settled. I'll meet you at Stansted, near the check in."

Mark was easing me towards the door of their trendy Brighton apartment, obviously in a hurry to be alone with Georgina. "Right. And Stephanie?"

"She's driving me and Douggie to the airport."

"Right. Result. See you there."

"See you next week, Mums." I couldn't see her, but I could hear her, a bit muffled as if she was pulling her sweater over her head. Ten years and they couldn't get enough of each other. Any other couple would have had four or five kids by now. I sighed. No point going there.

Douggie, predictably, wasn't over keen on a holiday or on going abroad, because he preferred the familiar and the formulaic. But once he was reassured that he could take his clock, his laptop, his Game Boy and some of his books, he was ready to plan his schedule. We did a timetable together, dividing time between the beach, the markets, the swimming pool, a bit of sightseeing around Malaga and Mijas, a trip to the flamenco, shopping and eating. I think he would have preferred more time indoors with his screens, but he seemed quite fascinated by the thought of flying, of travelling at speed, up 'in space' and over more miles than he had experienced in his lifetime.

The flight was a doddle. I have to admit that I had been a bit worried about how Douggie would cope with so many new experiences being thrown at him at once, but he genuinely seemed to enjoy every moment. He was fascinated by the on-board television monitors, by the plastic food containers and especially by the changing flight information telling us the height, speed and temperature. This was far more interesting for him than the view from the window, which was what I liked to marvel over while thinking about Jeff.

Stephanie was sitting behind us, Ronan on her lap, alongside Georgina and Mark, the two girls giggling together like children and Mark nodding off behind his designer sunglasses to avoid thinking about flying. He did more flying than any of us in his job as a sales executive for an international software designer, but he hated it, and had been delighted that Pete hadn't joined us, for Pete would have laughed at the white knuckles and pained expression.

"Thirty thousand feet. Four hundred and seventy five miles per hour." It was almost a mantra.

"Does he have to read it out every thirty seconds?" Mark asked, leaning forward between the seats.

"Bit unnerving for you, is it?"

"No need to be cheeky. I'm thinking of all these passengers, right."

"Of course you are. But don't lose any sleep over it. I'm sure they have better things to think about. There are worse things – crying babies for instance." One in particular had been whining almost since we sat down. Why on earth did the parents not bring enough toys or whatever they needed for little Johnnie or Ruthie or whoever? I often loaned out toys to such families when travelling with the girls nearly thirty years ago, but so many still hadn't learned how to make life easier for themselves, and for everyone around them.

"Drink."

"Okay. Look, the stewardess is just coming."

"Drink now."

"I know. But look, see how she's giving out drinks to those other people? Soon be your turn."

"Don't want a turn."

I retrieved an emergency carton of orange from the depths of my ancient Gladstone bag. "Here. Have this. I'll replace it when she gets to us." Which was only some ten minutes later. There again, for Douggie, ten minutes was an issue.

"What can I get you, sir?"

"Twenty-seven thousand feet."

"Sorry?"

"He'll have an orange juice, please. Preferably without pieces of flesh and pith floating about in it…"

The hostess smiled knowingly. "Aah. A man who knows his orange juice."

Was she being condescending? Probably not.

Douggie ignored her completely. I doubt if he knew she was talking about him.

Hearing me order Cava, Stephanie and Georgina followed suit but with two mini bottles apiece compared to my *uno*. They were definitely in holiday mode, leaving Mark in sensible mode, which would do him no harm at all. He had arranged to drive the people carrier waiting for us at Malaga airport, not the easiest place to find your way out of. Ronan, my pride and joy, slept all the way.

There was unanimous delight with the villa. Four bedroom detached with views over the golf course and glimpses of the sea from upstairs. Even Douggie was pleased with his double room which, like the others, had its own en-suite.

"Douggie's toilet. Douggie's sink. Douggie's shower. Another toilet."

"No, it's not a toilet, bro'."

That was Stephanie, trying to avoid the passionate noises already apparent through the none-too-thick walls. I was less inclined to her level of tolerance and gave the wall a hearty bang. "Hey, you two, keep it down. There's plenty of time for that later." The rumpty-tumpty stopped immediately and I winked at Stephanie.

Douggie was running water into the bidet. "What is it? What is it?"

"It's called a bidet." Stephanie put a bare toe under the running water. "It's to wash your feet."

"Stephanie!"

"Linda say."

"There. He doesn't believe you."

126

She laughed and gave him a hug before moving over to his balcony. "Linda say."

"It's… yes, it's for washing your feet."

I saw Stephanie's shoulders shake and then Georgina's spiky red-gold hair appeared around the door. "Spoilsports. Just because you're not getting it. What are you up to? We're off to the pool."

"Underwater nookie?"

"Ho, ho, ho. Very funny, young Steph."

"What's nookie?"

Georgina laughed aloud. "Now you've done it. Come on, join us. All of you."

"I need to get Douggie sorted, but take Stephanie with you."

"I'd rather unpack first, Mum."

"Boring." Georgina briefly displayed her glorious, if pale, body, in its minuscule leopard print bikini. "Not bad for thirty four," she said, patting her flat tummy.

"Come on, sexpot. I've got to get out of here. I'm sweating big-time. Is there any air conditioning, Linda?" Mark had come in, looking very vulnerable in his swimsuit, although he was not as white as his wife, thanks to his naturally olive skin. They made a stunning couple and seemed to me to be even more in love – and in lust – than when they'd married. Perhaps the absence of children had preserved their original attraction?

"Look, you two – go, go. I'll sort the air conditioning."

He gave me a damp hug. "Thanks, Linda. You are a swell chick."

"Well, thanks for the 'swell chick'. Too many Hollywood movies, young man."

"And thanks for the 'young man'. Come on, Georgie."

"Drink." Douggie's priorities were unchanged.

Stephanie shooed Mark and Georgina away. "Go on, get out of here. We'll come and find you later." She didn't seem in a hurry to start her unpacking. There was a bottle of rioja in the hamper left for us on the kitchen table by the villa management team and I poured us out a drink so we could just crash out for a while with Douggie in the kitchen.

We could keep an eye on Ronan who was toddling around the room, investigating the contents of cupboards..

"Ronan is such a happy child. You are so lucky."

"It's Georgina who's lucky," she said, more to herself than to me, I think.

I could feel my eyes filling up but she wasn't looking at me. "Steph ..."

"No, I don't want to talk about it."

"Talk about what?" Douggie had finished his orange squash.

She ruffled his hair. "Unpacking."

"Where's Douggie's clock?"

"It's in your case." We'd checked the packing together countless times.

"Forgotten about *The Italian Job*."

"Well, that's where you're wrong. It's in your hand luggage with the laptop."

"He's brought his laptop? Isn't it too heavy for hand luggage?"

"I don't know. I didn't ask."

Douggie was pulling me, literally, into his bedroom, obviously to check up on the information I had given him.

Clock, laptop, discs and books were all found, sorted and housed as a priority before Stephanie and I did our unpacking. I noticed that Georgina and Mark had left their suitcase on their bed, its contents sprawled in colourful disarray. "Do you think they'd like me to see to it?"

"No, I don't, Mums. I wouldn't want anyone ferreting through my g-strings, that's for sure. No, not even you."

"What don't you want to talk about, Stephanie?"

"You know perfectly well, Mums."

"I suppose you mean Pete. Or, rather, you and Pete."

She started painting her toe-nails, perched on a kitchen chair, leaning forward so that her curls hid her face, reminding me exactly of my mother. Exactly. "This is quick dry, so we can soon explore."

"Stephanie." Three pairs of dark eyes looked at me, not used to the tone of my voice.

"Sky now." Douggie had discovered the television in the lounge.

"Okay, but only five minutes. Then we're going out."

"Six."

"I said five."

He settled for five and started channel hopping.

"Darling?" I kept my voice down this time.

"Don't, Mums."

"But what are you doing about it?"

She screwed the top of the nail polish back on, very slowly and carefully before speaking. "There's nothing I can do. That's Pete. I've told you before. He can't help it. And I don't care, anyway." She pouted, reminiscent of the wilful child so ingloriously tamed. "I'd do anything for him. I'll be anything he wants. I'll give him anything he wants. For better or worse remember?"

"Listen to yourself. It's so… demeaning. What happened to you?"

"I turned into Pete's wife. I turned into a hairdresser. I turned into Ronan's completely useless mum…"

"No." I had to interrupt. "Don't say that. You're not useless. Ronan's a spectacular success."

"But not because of me. I couldn't breast feed, remember?"

"I think you mean *wouldn't*."

"Whatever. I couldn't wait to get him into a nursery because I hated spending day after day with him. You know how difficult it's been for me. I'm just not a natural at this parenting thing. I've turned into everything you probably hate. And I don't want to talk about it, I told you. Because you'd never understand, not in a million years."

"Stephanie. You're probably right. I'll never understand. I'm not concerned about understanding, don't you see? I'm concerned about your safety – and Ronan's."

"Pete would never do any real damage."

"Bullshit." We were going over old ground, not getting anywhere.

"Mum, seriously. Things have improved since Ronan was born. One hundred per cent. I'm here, aren't I? He'd never have allowed that before Ronan came along."

"You mean he thinks you're trapped."

She glared at me. "Look, I'm here on holiday, to recharge my batteries. He'll miss me, he'll welcome me back with open arms and we'll be just fine. You'll see. That's it. End of conversation. Now, I'm going to see if my mobile works. He'll be expecting to hear from me."

"Okay." It was no use. "If it does work, can I borrow it to phone Jeff?"

"Of course." She winked. "When do I get to meet him? He sounds very fit, Mums."

"I don't think Pete would appreciate those sentiments, you little horror." My youngest, my wild child. A real man-eater till Pete came along. The world in her beautiful hands, her modelling potential spotted by an agency scout, making up her mind for her, and which could have led to great things – with a different husband.

Douggie interrupted my thought process. "Switched it off. News." Oh, well. "DVD player. Look."

"Oh, I didn't realise. What a pity. We could have brought some of your favourites."

Douggie was looking at a colourful leaflet sitting on top of the DVD player. "Shop. Get DVDs."

"Let me see. A hire shop. Great. That's what we'll do then."

"Now."

"We don't have to do it now. We can do it after lunch."

"Closed."

I looked at the leaflet again. He was right, of course. Closed 1-5. "Okay, then, we'll pick up a DVD before lunch, but we won't watch it until this evening. Okay?"

"What time?"

"Give it a rest, Douggie." Stephanie was offering me the mobile. "Yes, it works."

"Did you speak to… him?"

"Can't say his name, huh? No, I got his voice mail. He'll be at work for a while yet. I forgot about the time difference. I sent him your love, though."

"Darling." I could see I'd upset her.

"Oh, don't start again. Come on, Unc. Let's go to the Video Shop."

"DVD. Not video. DVD."

"Whatever. Let your sister make her phone call in peace."

"Who's on the telephone?" Douggie was still incurably nosey.

"Jeff."

Stephanie looked from me to Douggie. "So you know him, do you? Interesting. Come on, Douggie, you can tell me all about him." She picked up Ronan plus Ronan's security blanket, but I noticed the child was looking at Douggie, not at her.

"You'll be lucky," I called after them as they moved away slowly, Douggie reluctant to leave my side. Stephanie hadn't really spent much time at all with him over the years, even less than Georgina. Recently of course − thanks to the ubiquitous Pete − she hadn't spent time with anyone male other than her son, but even prior to that there had been a reluctance to be associated with the family misfit, the family odd-ball, words she had actually used as a teenager, although she didn't use them now. Probably since she'd passed that important thirty milestone a few years back, becoming more accepting, more tolerant of everyone except herself.

I had to leave a message, too. "Miss you already. Miss your mouth, your voice, your eyes, your… think of me later. It's too hot to wear anything in bed here." What a tease I was turning out to be. Grossly unfair. I hoped I'd reached the right voice mail.

So much for tolerance. "Mum. You take him to the bloody shop. He won't even go out of the gate."

Douggie was standing in the garden, looking at his feet, biting his knuckles in a way he had to relieve tension. "What's up, Douggie? What do you want?"

He gripped my hand tightly. "Sunglasses."

"But it's not even bloody sunny. I told him."

"If he wants sunglasses, then it's sunny enough for him. Just get them, Stephanie. They're in my backpack, beside my bed.

"It's okay, Douggie. Stephanie's getting the sunglasses. Silly old Linda. I forgot." The tension dissipated and disappeared completely when Stephanie and sunglasses arrived.

"You're very good with him, Mums."

"I've known him longer than you, that's all."

"No, it's more than that. I would no way have the patience. And as for visiting him in that home…" She shuddered. "There's something about it, something spooky."

"Funny you should say that. I've been wondering myself if it's the right place."

"Oh, I don't know about that. Is there a right place? I doubt it. Anyways, if you're taking him to the shop, I'll find our lovebirds and dip my toes in the water. What do you think, Ronan? Fancy a dip?"

"Oogle google," replied her son. Or something like that.

"Tell them it will soon be time for lunch. I'd like to stick to Douggie's schedule as far as possible."

"Oh, for Chrissake."

"What harm does it do? It means a lot to him and makes not a blind bit of difference to us."

Stephanie shrugged. "Okay. Okay. I'll tell them."

I was holding Douggie's hand as we approached the DVD hire shop, and we almost bumped into Georgina. "I suppose there must be a restaurant on the complex somewhere," I asked her idly.

"Of course there is. By the pool. Why don't you go and join Mark? I'm just going back to get a couple of towels. Be with you soon. The restaurant specialises in seafood, yummy."

Douggie decided to express his opinion on the subject: "Don't like seafood."

"Tough" was Georgie's indifferent response.

"There's no need to talk like that. He doesn't understand what you mean, it's not explicit enough."

"Don't lecture me, Mother."

This was a very different Georgina to the one giggling in the bedroom less than an hour ago. Something had happened. Already. "Come on, Georgie, you're a film buff, let's go in the shop and you can help Douggie and me choose a couple of DVDs."

"But I was… oh, okay."

She didn't speak again until we were in the comparative quiet and cool of the hire shop and Douggie was preoccupied by a row of Tom and Jerry DVDs: his favourite. "I'm sorry. I know I shouldn't have spoken to Douggie like that. I never know what to say."

"It's okay. Just try and think before you open that big mouth of yours."

"Easier said than done… and there's something else."

"Hmm?"

"At the pool. Lots of them."

I turned away from the ceiling-high stack of films and the Technicolor array of posters surrounding me. "Is this a riddle?" But no, it obviously wasn't a riddle. My bossy daughter was crying. "My God, Georgina, what is it?"

"Babies. I've never seen so many in one place. Plump and happy. As if being on holiday with Ronan isn't bad enough."

"Oh, Georgie." I put out a hand.

"No, don't. I'm being absolutely pathetic. Pathetic. I know it. But the look on Mark's face. Oh, Mum." She sobbed on my shoulder.

"Five Tom and Jerry DVDs. Four hundred and fifty eight minutes."

"The voice of sanity," she mumbled, and we both laughed.

"That's better."

"Thank God for Douggie."

"No God."

"What?"

"No God."

"Is that so, Uncle? You must tell me how you arrived at that conclusion. I mean, tell me how you know."

"Philip Pullman."

"You've read *Northern Lights?*"

I put her out of her (stunned) misery. "Well, not exactly. I gave him a condensed version."

"Priceless."

The tears had gone. The moment had passed. But… "I'm afraid we have to face the pool area again, Georgina. If that's where the restaurant is…"

"Of course. I'll just get those towels, but I'll be fine. I'm a big girl."

"Señorita no big."

The Spanish Hire Shop Manager beamed at all of us, not differentiating between intellects as happened so often at home.

"Enjoy, señor, señoritas. The cat, the mouse. Is funny. For all ages."

"Absolutely. Pay the man, Douggie. Count out the euros. That's it. Well done."

Douggie was pleased with himself, at his prowess with euros and at his success in finding Tom and Jerry fifteen hundred miles from home. And the seafood restaurant was more than happy to provide him with a plateful of chips and a 'fish burger', while we indulged ourselves with prawns, calamari and salad.

Ronan slept through it all, happily, blissfully unaware of his aunt's love-hate feelings for him. No, hate was a bit strong. But Georgina would never love him as much as she was capable of until she was a mother – even a foster mother – herself. She was just too in awe of him and, whether she faced up to it or not, a tad – or more – jealous of Stephanie. Just as Stephanie would never love him as much as she was capable of while the demanding Pete was around.

There we all were. The 21st century family on holiday.

Chapter Thirteen

May 2004

The happiness that Douggie exhibited on holiday was, to my mind, unprecedented. I had never seen him taking any sort of interest in the outside world, but in Spain he'd taken charge of Mark's state-of-the-art camcorder as soon as he'd seen it and he really enjoyed following us around as if we were in a reality television show. Mark was the one who had to capture the views and the atmosphere of the area, however, as this was outside Douggie's level of interest.

Certainly, he had seemed reluctant to let me go when I'd taken him back to Dunkirk House. I wasn't totally confident that he was as happy there as he might be. There was something, something I couldn't put my finger on. But I couldn't be there twenty-four hours a day to assess the situation, or to reassure myself that he was just fine.

I made a point of discussing the whole holiday experience with Moira Paul. She seemed surprised: at Douggie's ability to join in – "he doesn't do that here" – at his ability to take responsibility for the camcorder – "I think we'd be a little wary of that here" – at his willingness to try different food and different experiences, such as the flamenco evening – "oh, he likes his routine here". Okay, so she and everyone at Dunkirk House wanted a peaceful life and so did Douggie, but I didn't like the idea of limiting his experiences.

She was not at all happy when I expressed my concerns. "Isn't it a bit late for that?"

"Sorry?"

"He's been living in residential care for thirty years, Mrs North."

"And?"

"And, as a result, he has had limited life experience. Absolutely. But you have had every opportunity to take him on holiday before now, to expose him to the outside world."

"Is that some sort of criticism?"

She waved me into a chair and sat down beside me, so we weren't confrontational across her desk. "Of course it's not. Douggie is lucky to have you. You have been the abiding force in his life." She paused to let that sink in and I realised that she was paying me a compliment.

"I'm sorry. It's just…"

"Mrs North. You don't have to explain. We can't, and we shouldn't, live our lives for other people. I think the job you do now is remarkable… remarkable. And you'll have seen for yourself how few people receive the level of love and attention that you give your brother."

"I still don't think it's enough. I think that's what I'm trying to say."

"Has he ever said he is unhappy?"

"No. The concept is difficult for him. Even you and I would have trouble defining 'unhappy', don't you think? And if it existed, but if it was fleeting, would that make it any less undesirable?"

"What do you want me to do? We could insist he accompanies us more often when we go to the local PHAB club, if you like. Or the pub perhaps, although he isn't interested in beer of course."

"No. Socialising is not really something he needs, or wants, to do."

"What then?"

I sighed. She was trying to help but I'd seen her glance at her watch. "I thought he could move in with me for a while. On a trial run." I don't know where the idea had sprung from, but it had sprung.

"That's quite a dramatic gesture. Have you given it serious thought?"

"I must admit I haven't." But I knew it was more than a gesture.

"You'd need help. Even if it is for a trial run."

"Yes. I know."

"And if it doesn't work out, then it could be quite a negative experience for Douggie."

"But if it did work out?"

"That's different, of course. Mrs North…" She was trying to find the words. "You have a life."

"Absolutely. But I also have concerns."

"About Douggie, you mean?"

"Yes."

"Well, I don't know what to say. You are not telling me what your concerns are, so it's very difficult for me."

"I know. I'm sorry."

"If you want to take Douggie on, then I'm sure it could be arranged. There would be the usual reports, assessments, forms, meetings – of course, you know the score. But I beg you to think about it for a few days at least. Think about your life."

"I will. But I've always been more of a doer than a thinker."

"And think about the effect on Douggie."

"I'm sure it will be a positive experience."

She glanced at her watch again.

"I'm going to see Douggie now. I'll come again next Sunday. I'll come by car so I can take his things with me."

She laughed then. "Nothing is going to happen that quickly, I can assure you."

"No. But in the meantime we'll call it a holiday. He's coming to stay with me for a holiday."

"Whatever you say, Mrs North." She paused and licked her lips. "Of course, homes such as this are being phased out to encourage a culture of care in the community. So it might be a good idea to make plans in advance. Just in case." She was giving me a way out, a loop hole and I appreciated it. She wasn't a bad sort at all.

I felt suddenly elated. I felt like some kind of knight in shining armour, as if I was rescuing Douggie. From what I had no idea.

"Douggie. Listen. Next Sunday I'm taking you back to Barking with me. For a little holiday. So we can talk about the future."

"Year 3000."

"Well, not that far into the future."

"How many years?"

"Perhaps the next forty years or so."

"Douggie will be ninety years old."

"Yes."

"How many verys of old is that?"

"Oh, twenty verys."

"2044."

"Yes. Well. It's a bit difficult to know about the future. No one knows what will happen. To you. To me. To the world."

"Linda knows."

I ruffled his hair. "No, Douggie. I wish I did. No one knows."

"Douggie just had a holiday."

"Yes. But this is different. This will give us time to talk."

"Playstation better than talking."

"There will be time for Playstation, too."

"How many hours?"

"I'm not sure yet. We'll work it out. But we need to talk about the best place for you to live."

"Douggie lives at Dunkirk House, Fisherman's Avenue, Southend on Sea, Essex, England, the United Kingdom."

"Yes. But people are making changes. Important people. The Prime Minister. The Government."

"The Queen?"

"No. Not the Queen." Oh, dear, this wasn't going to be easy. "You could live with me perhaps."

"Live with Linda?" His face lit up. So much so, that I came close to breaking down there and then. But I knew I couldn't commit. It might not work out. I would need to source additional care. I'd got used to living alone, after all. Then there was Jeff. What was I going to do about Jeff? Was this a way of keeping him at a distance? I didn't know. I just knew it felt right.

"We could try it. But we could look at other ideas."

"No more Dunkirk House?"

"Do you want to stay here?"

"Douggie likes Dunkirk House."

I wondered if Moira Paul was right about this place being in danger of closing. I had tried to blot out the idea up to now, but certainly this was one area where that could happen. "Do you like it all the time?"

He didn't answer.

"Where would you like to live?"

"On the moon."

"Seriously."

"Yes. Neil Armstrong landed on the moon, July 1969. Not crowded. No shouting. No dogs. No library man."

There it was again. "Not the moon. It's not a safe place. No oxygen. No electricity for the television."

"Douggie needs electricity."

"Exactly."

I thought momentarily of a finca in rural Spain, Douggie spending his time fishing, gardening, walking. But it was no more than a thought. He would hate life without 'screens'.

"Eighty per cent."

"What do you mean?"

"Douggie likes Dunkirk House eighty per cent."

"Eighty per cent? Of the time? I see. Right." Not a bad score. Most people probably scored similarly on how much they liked their own lives or lifestyles. "So, we can do better."

"Ninety per cent is better."

"Yes."

"Ninety five per cent is better."

"Yes." This could go on for quite a while. "So, before I see you next week, you can think of something you would like ninety five per cent of the time."

"Living with Linda."

"That's one possibility."

"Daphne is going to live in Southchurch Boulevard."

"Sorry, who?"

"Daphne. Number Six."

"Oh. So what's in Southchurch Boulevard?"

"Don't know."

"Who will she be living with?"

"Don't know."

"Her family?"

"No."

Perhaps I would investigate the mysterious Daphne's plans.

"Care in the community," he said carefully.

"Is that what Daphne said?"

"No. Daphne doesn't talk. Just like Douggie."

"But you do talk."

"Talk to Linda."

That wasn't strictly true, but I didn't press the point. I would take up a little more of Moira Paul's time before I left and ask her about Daphne.

First, Douggie and I had a bracing walk on the pier. He liked walking when it was windy, as it was today. The downside was that he asked, "How many miles per hour is it now?" – the wind, that is – every few minutes. The wind was of far more interest to him than looking at the view over to Kent, the fishermen, the boats, the surf board enthusiasts, the sparkle of the sea when the sun came out. What excited him most of all was the fact that it seemed to get windier the further out you walked from the shoreline. I would rather have been spending time in the Pier Museum, but Douggie had never been that interested in the past. Perhaps someone would build a Museum of the Future one day.

We got back in time for tea and cakes in the communal lounge area. Only a few of the residents were around, and one of them, a blonde girl with very thick glasses, came over to me. "You don't live here." The tone was aggressive.

"No. I'm visiting Douggie. I'm his sister."

"Douggie," she yelled across to him. "You didn't tell me you had a sister." She smiled at me, sweetly now, and pumped my hand. "I'm Vanessa. I'm twenty nine. My mum is coming to see me next… month."

"Pleased to meet you, Vanessa. And I'm pleased to hear about your mum."

"Who told you about my mum?" Aggressive again.

Before I could answer, she pumped my hand again. "My name's Vanessa. I'll be thirty soon."

I wondered if Daphne was even less able to communicate than Vanessa. Care in the community indeed. I left Douggie with a plateful of Swiss Roll slices. "More than one? Please. More than two?" Hopefully someone – though probably not Vanessa – would stop him from eating more than three.

Moira Paul was hunched uncomfortably over a computer, muttering, and she didn't look pleased to see me again. My enquiries were dealt with very quickly and I got the impression she didn't take too kindly to my taking an interest in anyone other than Douggie. Fair enough.

It appeared that Southchurch Boulevard was a warden controlled complex. Seemingly, the mysterious Daphne, who was approaching retirement age, was going to be looking after herself with the help of a part time carer paid for by direct payments. This was a fairly new idea that some of my clients were involved with. I hadn't thought about it for Douggie, hadn't thought beyond Dunkirk House until today really. But certainly it was another possibility. The independence, perhaps, without the potential for neglect.

When I got back to say goodbye, it looked as if Douggie was eating a fourth slice of Swiss Roll. He had carefully unrolled it first and I remembered how we would do that as children, because it seemed to make it last longer.

It would be nice to share more of these moments. It would be nice to share his life, and not just be a Sunday visitor. I started to convince myself that it was a good idea, something to look forward to. I just hoped he would feel the same.

Stephanie and Georgina were not impressed. 'Absolutely insane', 'bloody idiot', 'damn fool', were just some of the milder epithets they volunteered.

"Surely he's settled?" asked Georgina, in genuine bewilderment.

"Yes. But I've felt a bit, oh I don't know, unsure about the suitability of the place, for a while. And I'd rather make a change now, before it's sprung on me, on us, a year or two from now."

"Haven't you got enough on your plate?" This from Stephanie, who felt my job was already a drain on my emotional resources.

Their reactions were pretty much as I'd anticipated. But at least they were thinking of me. And Douggie.

Jeff, on the other hand, seemed more concerned about Jeff. "What about me?"

"What about you?"

"It's going to be difficult for me to see you with Douggie around."

"I don't see why. It's not as if he's going to be in the way while we writhe around in bed."

"Unfortunately not. I'm still working on that. But I meant the dinners for two, the cuddles on the couch, my massages…"

"Honestly. Listen to yourself. I thought you liked Douggie. I thought you understood."

"I do like him. I do understand. I can see what you are trying to do. But I want our relationship to develop. Without constraints."

"So Julia's not a constraint then?"

We were lazing around, full of chicken curry, watching a quiz show. He stood up and turned off the television "Julia is not a constraint. Has it escaped your notice that it's Saturday night?"

"No."

"Did you notice that I didn't have to rush off after Thursday's class?"

"Yes. And I was delighted. Just as delighted as I am to see you on a Saturday night."

"Don't you want to know why?"

"I did wonder. I was thinking you were getting careless, but I didn't want to mention it in case it reminded you where your duty lies, and you might be more careful in future."

"Julia is not coming home tonight. His name's Adam. She's told me all about him, all the gory details down to the colour of his pubic hair.

She's told me what they do, when, how, how often. She's told me that I'm a boring old fart who can't get it up."

"But just because she's sleeping with someone else, doesn't mean…"

"She's getting ready to leave me, Linda. Oh, it won't last. He is a personal trainer apparently. She's told him she's twenty five and he believes her, so he is obviously besotted. But when he's had his fill, I'm not going to be there waiting. She knows that. It was always going to be part of the deal."

"But I thought…"

"Don't think. You don't think like Julia. You know what she said? She told me that she didn't care if it didn't last, because ten minutes with him was better than ten years with me."

"Jeff, please."

"No, let me finish. It's okay. It wouldn't be okay if you said it, but… it's okay. And something else that you might find interesting. She said that she'd happily divorce me, because the stigma of divorce was less than the stigma of being single. In fact, she seems to be looking forward to it, as if it was glamorous instead of what it really is – tragic, messy, upsetting." There was the slightest wobble in his voice.

"Jeff. I'm so sorry."

"Don't be ridiculous, woman. This is what we've been waiting for. Or at least what I've been waiting for."

"Did you say she's not coming home tonight?"

"I did. But not because I expected you to invite me to stay."

"Thanks. I need time to sort myself out. Everything seems to be happening at once." I wanted to sleep with him, and he knew it, but I held back. It was bloody difficult, because he was just standing there, looking at me, waiting for me. He had been so patient.

"How much time do you need?" His voice was suddenly hoarse.

I stood up and went over to him, kissing the frown away from between his eyes. "Does thirty seconds seem reasonable?"

He lifted me into the air with a whoop. "Linda! You mean it?"

"Of course. Although I'll understand if you can't get it up, you poor old fart."

"It's already up."

"I love it when you talk dirty."

"You ain't heard nothing yet."

The night was too memorable for me to need to record it in my journal. I'd never known anyone make love to me as Jeff made love to me. It was my first physical relationship since Rick had left me. And I was oh, so ready. Okay, so my body has a few problems – cellulite, love handles, the usual stigmata – but Jeff seemed oblivious, and I loved him for it. To say I felt eighteen again is absolute Gospel.

I'd set the alarm for the next morning as I had to be off early to collect Douggie. And there was a momentary shock to see Jeff's beautiful blond head, his sharply chiselled features, so close to mine when I woke up.

"We've used four condoms, you dirty girl," he muttered to me as I leaned towards him.

"There's six in a packet."

Jeff insisted on accompanying me to Southend later. I did the driving so that Douggie would at least have the familiarity of the Metro. Jeff, next to me, used his right hand to great effect every time I paused in traffic. Admittedly, my remonstrations were a bit feeble, and he obviously didn't believe me when I asked him to stop.

"Look, I think you'd better drive. I can't concentrate."

"Only if you can keep your hands off me."

"I'll try. Hasta luego."

I did manage to keep my hands off him, but it wasn't easy. All I could think about was how good the sex had been, when I should have been thinking about Douggie.

As we pulled up outside Dunkirk House, he took my hands and kissed each finger tip slowly. "I love you."

"I know."

"You told me you loved me for the first time last night, do you know?"

I flushed with embarrassment. "Of course I know."

"So it wasn't just in the heat of the moment then?"

"No."

"Listen. Before we go in. There's something…"

"I have to do this. Nothing's changed. Just because we…"

"Linda, you're jumping to conclusions. Everything's changed. But I'm not talking about that. I wanted to ask you something quite different. About your mother."

"What the hell has my mother got to do with us?"

"I'm not talking about us. I'm talking about Douggie. Why don't you find her? If you want Douggie to be part of a family again, then perhaps his mother… "

"Don't be ridiculous. Firstly, she may be dead for all I know. Secondly, she may have another family, other grandchildren, that I don't know about. Thirdly, if she left him as a child, she certainly isn't going to want to know him as a fully grown adult. Fourthly, she's in her mid-seventies by now, and won't want her boat rocked."

"What about Douggie's boat?"

"No, she's of no interest to him. Believe me. Not because she's made him angry or upset, because that's not it. He's written her off. Years ago."

"And her?"

"Meaning?"

"She's in her mid seventies, you said. Don't you think she may want to tidy up her life?"

"No, I don't think so. And I bloody well don't care either way."

"Don't be angry, baby." He kissed me and kept on kissing me until the tension had disappeared from my body. "Although you're even more beautiful when you run your fingers through your hair. It gives you a tousled bedroom look."

"Stop it. Someone's looking out of the window." I pushed him away and jumped out of the car.

It was Douggie who was looking out of the window. I waved at him and he disappeared. He was obviously looking out for me. But whether he was looking forward to today, or whether it was just because I was five minutes later than the time I'd given him…

Someone had helped him pack. "Well done, darling. Jeff will carry the case for you. Do you remember Jeff?"

"Linda's friend."

"Yes."

"Is Rick Linda's friend?"

"Rick was Linda's husband. Now he's her friend. But I'm her best friend." Jeff had stepped in to help me out.

"You know, I'm the one who works with people with learning difficulties, and yet you always know the right thing to say."

"Jeff didn't go to Spain with Linda."

"No, you're absolutely right. I wanted to. But I was working. And your holiday was a family holiday."

"Friend. Not family. Rick is family."

"Not any more, sunshine."

"Families don't change."

I could sense him struggling with this lack of order in his well ordered world. This was something else for him to learn: "Sometimes they do."

"How many verys of a shame is it?"

"A million. At least."

"Linda is family."

"Yes, darling, I'm family. And that's not going to change. Now, have you got everything?"

"Holiday. In the town. Not the seaside. Is it mixed up?"

Jeff laughed and picked up Douggie's case. "Very, very, very, mixed up."

With Douggie moving into my home and Jeff into my bed, life was becoming very complex indeed. I had realised that I needed Jeff, but also that Douggie needed me – the difference being that Douggie didn't know it.

Chapter Fourteen

July 2004

Douggie's 'holiday' in Barking was a success. In fact, he didn't go back to Dunkirk House. I decided that was too unsettling, so I went to Southend on my own to collect his things while Jeff took him to the cinema to see *Shrek 2*, which to my surprise, Jeff rated as on a par with *Shrek*. Not something that happens every day.

When Douggie came back to the flat and saw all his things, he thought it was 'magic' but made no objections, asked no questions. "No more Dunkirk House." And that was that. For someone who didn't like change, or the idea of change, he was so very accepting when it happened.

I'd had to take a few weeks off and sort out a care package. It would have been impossible without the contacts I had built up, but I did it. Douggie approved of everyone I picked to help in his care when I was working or socialising. It was important that I continued to have a life and the situation with Jeff was such that we had more time together now, and we spent it differently, frequently in his bed or mine, glued together magnetically by the novelty and urgency of lust.

Jeff embraced Douggie far more than did Stephanie or Georgina, or their families. Certainly, at the moment he was desperate to impress me, to keep the sex going. But there was more to it than that. In fact, I felt that Douggie was helping minimise the stress Julia was causing in Jeff's life. She had found out about us, naturally, and was not a happy bunny. 'Cake and eat' springs to mind.

"You know, I used to feel sorry for Douggie. Big time," he told me one evening when we were tangled up in my sheets, Douggie gently snoring at the other end of the flat in my – no longer – spare room.

"And now?"

"I think he's lucky. To have you, of course. But to live a simplistic life. His needs taken care of. No ambitions. No unrequited love."

"What do you know about unrequited love?"

"I had a past before Julia, you know. And while it is not something I would care to resurrect, it is something that I remember."

"I know what you mean. There was a boy at school…"

"Exactly." He glanced at my middle aged body, hidden thankfully by the bedding. "I bet you were edible at school."

"You can eat me now, if you like." Was that me?

"Steady, tiger." He laughed and rolled over so his eyes were looking down into mine. "I'm lucky, too. I've got you. And I've acquired the brother I always wanted, but one with a bonus. One who doesn't ask the 'why' question. What a blessing in life."

"Why?" I was laughing at him, and he put his hands under my rear and pulled me onto him. I was the lucky one.

On nights such as these when Jeff stayed, he often left in the mornings before Douggie woke up. Yet when Douggie asked, inevitably, "What time did Jeff go home?" I always said "eleven o'clock" or "half past eleven." For some reason I couldn't say, "six o'clock this morning." It was odd. Douggie was unaware of the physicality of our relationship, which would in any case have been irrelevant. He was not judgmental. Obviously there was only an element of guilt attached as far as I was concerned.

As I prepared Douggie's breakfast – two Weetabix, two spoonfuls of sugar, warm milk, always in the same bowl – I thought about what Jeff had said about Douggie. Guilt was probably an attribute – or a failing? – that I could happily do without, that pricking of conscience ingrained in my pores that Douggie didn't seem to have. Was he lucky?

I looked across at Douggie but he was too engrossed to make eye contact. "Sharon will be here at half past eight, Douggie."

"Sharon's turn."

"Yes, darling. Do you like Sharon?"

"Sharon sings too much."

I grinned. "Okay. I'll tell her off."

"No, don't tell her off."

"You don't want me to tell her off?"

"No." He thought for a moment. "Is Jeff coming here for dinner again?"

That 'again' caught my attention. "No. He's working late. But he said he'd call round later. Is that okay?"

"Linda's friend."

"Yes. And Douggie's friend."

He didn't respond to that. But at least he didn't say, "Not Douggie's friend."

"I'll be home early tonight, pet."

"What time?"

"By five o'clock."

"Is Linda going to watch *Richard and Judy*?"

"I don't think so, darling. Why?"

"Douggie can watch *Home Alone* DVD."

"Okay. But only once."

"Ten times."

"Twice."

We carried on bargaining until Sharon arrived, reaching a compromise of three. Because he jumped from frame to frame, lingering on his favourite bits, he didn't actually watch the whole thing over and over again. So it wasn't such an ordeal, and at least it was one of the DVDs that I rather liked, too.

Sharon. Tim. Kelly. Ashwan. Cameron. A whole army of people now came in and out of the flat, taking Douggie to the shops, the library, the supermarket, the park, ten pin bowling, even bingo, although most of the time he apparently forgot to mark off his card. When I'd suggested that the exercise might therefore be pointless, the long haired, sweet natured Tim had convinced me otherwise.

"But, Mrs North, he loves being surrounded by numbers. He likes handling the cards, hearing the calls, looking at the screen, counting the money, everything about it."

"Okay. Okay. As long as he's not bored."

"If he was bored, he'd be saying 'how many minutes?'."

Absolutely. So it seemed that my motley crew were broadening the range of his experiences and Douggie was getting used to going out more instead of being stuck in front of his screens. I didn't mind him spending a few hours in front of his treasured DVD at the end of the day if I thought he'd been reasonably active. It even seemed to me that he'd lost a bit of weight around the middle. So, so far so good.

My mobile rang the moment I reached my office chair. "Darling, I forgot to tell you. I've got us tickets for *Cinderella on Ice* tomorrow."

"What about...?"

He could finish my sentences for me by now. "Douggie? I've got three tickets. I'll bring them over later. Love you. Think about me every single moment you are alone. You hear?"

"I will. I do."

"Think of me kissing you, licking you... whoops, my office line is ringing."

"What a shame."

"Love you."

Hearing the dialling tone, I thought briefly about all those months I had put him off, all those months that we could have been... Oh, well. Never mind. We were making up for lost time now. He didn't seem to mind all of those outward signs of ageing. If anything, it just made his love making more urgent, as if aware of our mortality, of the amount of time we had left. A pity I couldn't give him children; I would have loved to have his children.

My mobile again. I used it strictly for personal phone calls only. The caller's name came up on the screen. Stephanie.

"Mum. Could you look after Ronan for me for a couple of hours tonight? Pete wants to take me out to dinner."

"Oh, and what are you celebrating?"

"Nothing. Can't my husband take me out to dinner occasionally without it being a celebration?" My question had made her ratty. But I knew Pete. Perhaps he was also on a guilt trip. Not that I'd ever seen any signs of it, but Stephanie assured me that it happened each and every time he raised his hand to her.

"Of course he can, darling. I didn't mean to pry." I was being mean. Things did seem to have improved since Ronan came along.

"I'll cut your hair for you, if you like," she offered.

"That would be nice. Thanks, darling."

"See you about six then. Will Jeff be round?"

"You might just miss him."

"Pity. Gorgeous hunk." She giggled. "See you later."

I switched off the mobile. There was a mound of post and eight answer-phone messages to deal with. Plus I had to prepare for a meeting with Social Services at eleven to persuade them of the necessity for increased respite for a stressed mother who had a brain-damaged daughter as well as three other under tens to look after. Just because the family were able to afford to go on regular holidays seemed to make them think that mum – and the siblings come to that – did not need respite. Far from it. That level of care didn't go away just because you moved it to Butlin's or Euro Disney.

I checked my e-mails, and wished I hadn't because now I had something else to think about:

> *Traced your mum. Lives alone in Bournemouth. I won't forward telephone number and address on to you until you confirm you actually want them. Some people would rather not know! Invoice in post. Regards. Neil Green.*

Oh, hell. I found myself wishing that she had died, or, at least, gone overseas, or just proved untraceable. Bournemouth. Oh, hell.

Let's face it, by hiring the Bournemouth equivalent of Neil Green, Mum could have found Douggie, or me for that matter, if she'd wanted to. But it was that guilt again. That feeling that, perhaps, I should make some sort of attempt at contact. Douggie wasn't capable; she was ageing; but me, I had no excuse.

I e-mailed him back quickly, saying that I would like the address. After all, I didn't have to do anything with it. And I tried to put her out of my mind, which was pretty crowded at the moment.

I managed to pull off another two days a month respite for my family-in-need. It wasn't much, but it was double what they had now and was one of my more successful outcomes. Mum, Lucy, was over the moon. Her kids were her life, and her husband wasn't as much help as she would have liked, having his own fight with depression. But she never put an ounce of blame on to him; she was the one 'not coping'. She now had two more days a month, not for herself, but for her other kids. There were amazing people out there, unaware of their strengths and capabilities.

Jeff was the only one I could talk to about my work. Without naming names of course. Stephanie felt if she could cope with Pete, then anyone should be able to cope with anything. A sad but true illustration of how her mind worked. And Georgina just felt that anyone I was helping who had children was already 'blessed' in a way that she wasn't, and should 'be grateful' for what they'd got.

"You mean they should be grateful even if they have got a child with cerebral palsy?"

"Of course. They wanted a child. They got one. They took the chance that something could go wrong..."

"Do you know how few mothers even think about things going wrong? How often does it go wrong in novels, at the cinema, in soaps? Do you know, it's not even touched on at ante-natal classes?"

"I didn't know. Not that it makes any difference. More fool them to take on such a responsibility blindly. Look at the statistics." She couldn't be shifted, however often we had the same debate.

I knew that Georgina would rather have a houseful of disabled children than have no children at all. But she was rare.

Jeff didn't get on as well with Georgina as he did with Stephanie. Georgina couldn't understand his choice to be childless, Julia or no Julia. He had once tried to talk to her about it, but she wouldn't listen.

I had to admit that Georgina was blinkered in the way that some people are about religion, or about vegetarianism, or modern art.

Even Stephanie and Georgina were growing apart since Ronan's birth. I felt so sorry for my eldest daughter, so sad for her. She was destroying her relationship with Mark, especially since he'd been confirmed as having a low sperm count. Inevitably, this gave her a place to lay the blame, something she needed to do.

"Low sperm count doesn't mean no sperm count."

"In our case, it might just as well."

These were the kind of exchanges they had openly in front of me, Jeff, Stephanie, Pete, and Old Uncle Tom Cobbly. Everyone had to know about her pain and it was becoming something of a ball breaker for Mark.

Was Jeff perhaps right? Was the happiest member of my normally dysfunctional family Douggie? Surely no one could be happier than I was at the moment. Being loved and lusted after by someone you cared about was more important than I had wanted to admit.

I still didn't tell him I loved him except in bed, and I knew that was beginning to annoy him. But with Rick I thought everything would last forever and so I was happy to commit, whereas with Jeff I knew that relationships formed cracks and broke down and I was less optimistic about our future. Not because I didn't care about him, but because I'd grown up. Apart from that, he was a lot younger than me, although he never reminded me about it, and I didn't want to repeat the experience of being dumped for a younger model. I believed him when he told me he loved me, but whether that love would last was a different issue for me.

Later, Stephanie cut my hair into a more youthful, feathered style which I must confess I rather liked. Douggie wasn't so keen, of course. "Linda should have the same hair."

"It's nice to have a change, Douggie."

He shook his head. "Same hair. No change. Same hair forever."

"It's only my hair that's changing, pet. Nothing else. Just a little bit shorter and a little bit curlier."

"Douggie has curly hair."

"Yes."

"Stephanie's curly hair all gone."

"Yes." She grinned at him. "I don't need to hide behind my hair any more."

I looked over from where I was shaking hairs from a plastic wrap into my kitchen bin. That remark was obviously more for me than for Douggie.

"So where is Pete taking you?"

"The Belle Piazza. New. Italian."

"Douggie had spaghetti bolognese."

"Yes. So I see. It looked good."

"Douggie likes spaghetti bolognese."

"I might have exactly the same a little bit later."

"Douggie likes curly hair."

We were going around in familiar circles. "Good. So don't keep telling me off for changing mine, then. Because now my hair is curlier than Stephanie's, you should be happy."

To change the subject, I put Ronan onto Douggie's lap. Ronan immediately grabbed Douggie's curls as if he had been, bizarrely, following the conversation, but there was no adverse reaction from my little brother. I had often wondered if Douggie had a high pain threshold because I'd noticed when he put his hands under very hot water, or bashed his knee, it seemed to have no effect on him, other than red skin or a bruise the next day.

"Douggie." It was one of Ronan's clearest words.

Douggie smiled at him. Actually smiled *at* him. Stephanie glanced at me in surprise. She had noticed it too.

"Unker Douggie."

Great Uncle, actually, but close. "And you'll soon see Unker Jeff," I told him encouragingly.

Roman showed off a few new teeth in a happy smile. "Unker Jeff."

Stephanie glanced at her watch and quickly gathered her hairdressing things together. "Blimey. Nearly seven. I must be going. Thanks Mum."

"Will you be very late?"

"Shouldn't think so. Just settle Ronan in his buggy and he'll be fine. I'll try not to, er, disturb you." She winked, and I, to my embarrassment and her delight, blushed.

"Oh, go on. Have fun. Enjoy your meal."

"I'm looking forward to it. Apparently the restaurant is candle lit, with live opera." It was good to see her so animated.

"Sounds fantastic. Well done that son-in-law."

"You see. He's not so bad." She wanted me to agree with her.

"No. Now shoo. Shoo. Say goodbye to your mummy, Ronan."

"Goo bye, Mummy."

Douggie lifted him up and held him out to me. Enough was enough as far as he was concerned. *Home Alone* could wait no longer.

I hadn't even finished clearing away before Jeff arrived. Just a few months ago, I had been coming home to an empty flat day after day, grabbing crumbs of comfort from Jeff's ability to fit me in, looking forward to seeing my daughters once a week or so, visiting Douggie. But now there was always someone here. I was never alone. I thought I would hate it, but I loved it. I felt a part of the real world.

Of course, when Jeff heard about the e-mail, he thought I should contact my mother straight away.

"I'll think about it," I said as we enjoyed our favourite Rioja after Douggie had taken himself off to bed at his regular half past ten watershed. This was an inheritance from the homes he'd lived in and, although I told him he could stay up later, he was used to the idea of ten thirty. I let him have a small portable television in his room so it looked more like his previous rooms had looked, but he didn't use it at night, although sometimes he'd watch *You've Been Framed* or *Mr Bean* while I was cooking dinner so that I could watch the news, his 'unfavourite' programme.

I listened now to see if it was on. But no. So we kept our voices down. Douggie had excellent hearing, some kind of compensation, perhaps.

"Why not go to visit her? Lay a few ghosts. I'd be happy to go with you."

"What about Douggie?"

"Take him with you. You don't have to tell him who she is, if you don't feel it's a good idea."

"When she visited him that time in Margate, she was 'Audrey', not 'Mummy'."

"That was over twenty years ago, wasn't it?"

"Are you thinking he won't remember? Because Douggie will. He remembers everyone who has passed in and out of his life. Believe me."

"So why didn't he remember his mother?"

"Because he was only five when she left. But he'll remember Audrey all right. I have to admit that I feel a bit guilty keeping her from him, but in my terms, not his, as he never mentions her – or Dad. They are his past. They don't encroach into his present or his future."

"Are you sure you haven't signed up for Guilt Classes as well as Spanish?"

I didn't answer him and he came and sat by my feet so I could massage his shoulders.

"That feels fantastic. But don't forget your drink. I need you to be well lubricated for my plans later this evening."

I didn't want to spoil his plans, but: "Don't forget Stephanie will be back to collect Ronan."

"Oh, Gawd. I'd forgotten."

"How could you forget when you were the one who bathed Ronan and put him in his pyjamas?"

"I know. But she leaves Ronan with us so often that sometimes it feels like he's ours."

I didn't answer.

"That was a compliment. It feels like we're a family. I love him. I love Douggie. I want us to be a family. Say something."

"Julia."

His head jerked back. "She wants a divorce. Fast. Before Adam loses interest. She can get her hands on a bit of money if we can sell the house, and bribe him into staying with her."

"You're being very unkind."

"No. Realistic."

"Are you proposing?"

"Of course I am."

"And you've thought about the fact that you are of an age when you can have lots of little Ronans, but I am shot."

He turned round, still kneeling, and took the glass out of my hand. His own smooth brown hand insinuated its way under my skirt, up over my knees, and in between my legs. I started to part them but he shook his head. "No, let me. And while I'm doing this, I want you to think about what you just said."

"About lots of little Ronans?"

"About being shot."

Chapter Fifteen

August 2004

I sent Mum a letter in the end. Quite brief, updating her about Douggie and me. I didn't mention Dad's death, on Ivy's assumption that she knew, even if she didn't attend the funeral. I also didn't put my ex-directory telephone number, because I didn't want to deal with a surprise telephone call. What the hell would I say?

> *So, if you think any useful purpose would be served – for any of us – by meeting up, then drop me a line. I've said nothing to Douggie, so we could make a trip to Bournemouth to visit Audrey as far as he is concerned. I hear the town's worth a visit. I've never been. I enclose snaps of Stephanie, Georgina and Ronan. Yours etc.*

A bit on the distant side, but what could she expect? The quicker I put it in the post, the less chance there would be for me to tinker with the content, or even change my mind about sending it. I had been persuaded by Jeff, who had this rosy image of a reunion in his mind's eye, but I was still not convinced. So, if she didn't reply, that would be fine. And if she did, I would still have time to think about it. I had made no commitment.

Nor had I made a commitment to Jeff. "Linda. I want to make a public declaration of how I feel."

"So go find a rooftop to shout it from."

"That's not good enough. You deserve everything. The ceremony. The honeymoon. Our lives won't change, not even our address. But I want you to be Mrs Brooks, not Mrs North."

"Jeff. Please. It's too soon. I can change my name if it's a problem."

"You're over simplifying."

"No. You are. You think marriage will mean happy ever after. If only life was like that. Look at Stephanie. Look at Georgina. Look at my marriage, and yours. Look at my parents."

"My parents have been happily married for over forty years, did I tell you?"

"Happily?"

"Well, they've had their ups and downs. Everyone does. But, yes, happily."

"And is she nearly twenty years older than him?" I exaggerated – a little.

"There you go again." This would be the point when he would generally pull a face and move on. Thank goodness.

Douggie always got a birthday card from Auntie Ivy, as did I. But this year she'd enclosed a cheque for fifty pounds instead of her usual fiver.

> *I've been a bit remiss about the cost of living. Forgive me. At least with the enclosed you will be able to buy a computer game or some such, instead of little more than a coffee and doughnut.*

Back came the guilt. Ivy had been the only person, apart from me, who had visited Douggie over the years, but since I'd immersed myself in Douggie's life, and removed him from his institutional setting, I had been unable to 'fit her in'. It was remiss of me, given that Bethnal Green was really not far at all.

Remembering that I'd only enclosed a nostalgic bookmark with the card I'd sent to her, I felt mean and ungenerous. So I phoned her immediately. "That was very generous of you."

"Do you know, dear, I was in Woolworth's the other day, and I stopped to look at some of the games that I know Douggie likes. And I was just horrified to see how much they cost."

"Ivy. Really, you don't have to send him money. We manage really well. I work full time now, and Jeff is very generous."

"Ah. Jeff."

"Would you like to meet him?" I asked rashly.

"Has he moved in with you and Douggie, then?"

"No. But I think he will be. Soon."

"I see. So, why not bring him to tea on Sunday? And Douggie."

"I think we agreed to baby sit for Stephanie."

"Oh, well. Another time."

Even more rashly, I found myself suggesting: "On second thoughts, we could bring Ronan, Stephanie's son, with us, if you like. You haven't seen him either, have you?"

"No, dear. Well, that sounds very exciting. Will I have to get, er, Ronan, something special to eat? Is he on solids?"

"Oh, Ivy, of course he is. He'll eat pretty much anything, so don't worry. He's two now. Just keep anything breakable out of his reach, that's all."

"Oh. Right. Yes. Is three o'clock all right for you? You remember how to find me?" From anyone else, that would have implied a criticism. But not from Ivy.

"Yes. Is the lift working?"

"It is. At the moment."

"Would you like us to bring you anything? Is there anything you need?"

"That's kind of you dear. But no, I have good neighbours, good friends, who look after me."

It was a hot Sunday. And the lift was smelly and claustrophobic. Although the faded sign read 'Maximum 8 Persons', it was cramped with the four of us, and I was glad I didn't have to use it on a regular basis.

"Wonder why she stays in this high rise," I said to Jeff as we emerged into the marginally fresher air of the communal landing.

"At eighty plus? It's easier than moving," he muttered.

Ivy was outside her front door, hair newly rollered, slighter and greyer than I remembered, the henna long gone. She smiled widely to reveal less teeth than the last time I'd seen her. But, while she was obviously more frail, marred by give-away liver spots, she seemed to be successfully looking after herself, having presumably managed to avoid the nastier of the ailments that old age usually delivered. She was a good advertisement for the single life.

"Well. Well. Well. This is lovely." She kissed us all as we filed in through her front door, seeming genuinely pleased to see us. I handed her a large slab of Douggie's birthday cake, surreptitiously, so that Douggie wouldn't see me. He didn't like me giving 'his' things away – to anyone, regardless.

"Thank you, dear. He looks very nice."

"What? Oh, you mean Jeff? Yes. He is. Very nice."

"Toilet. Which room?" The flat had been extensively re-vamped over the years, with new doors and décor, so Douggie was obviously initially confused and needed to re-establish the territory.

While I gave him a tour, which didn't take long, given the size of the flat, I could hear Jeff introducing himself to Ivy, admiring the fresh flowers in her fireplace, the locket around her neck, the tapestry cushions. He was doing a good job of ingratiating himself. "You did these cushions yourself? Really? They look as if they've come from an antique shop in the South of France."

"Schmoozer."

"Don't knock it, dear. It's a dying art."

Jeff's reprimand made us laugh, except Douggie who didn't get the joke. "Stop laughing."

"Okay, grumps." While I settled him into a seat where he could see the clock, the door – for a quick exit? – and me, Ivy made a fuss over Ronan. There were a few dust free circles on the top of her mahogany sideboard so she had obviously taken my advice about moving breakables.

I was surprised to see birthday cards on the tiled fifties mantelpiece.

"Ivy, wasn't it your birthday weeks ago?" Surely I hadn't got the date wrong all these years. After all, by now she was over eighty.

She looked up. "Yes, dear. The 20th of June. Gemini. The same star sign as Audrey, but we couldn't have been more different. I hope you like fish paste sandwiches. Suitable for both milk teeth and dentures..." She smiled, seemingly unaware that she'd mentioned Audrey so casually. "Oh, you mean the cards." She'd realised where I was coming from.

Douggie had noticed them, too, and he now began to pick them up one by one, reading the messages.

"How many verys of nosey is it?" He was smiling at the idea of being seen to be misbehaving.

"Don't worry, dear. I have no secrets. As for the cards, I like them. I leave them there till Christmas and I leave the Christmas cards till my birthday. So there's always a nice display. I expect you think I'm eccentric." Now she was addressing me – almost apologetically.

"Not at all. And even if I did, I'm a big fan of eccentricity. For me, it means original, the opposite of boring."

"Hear, hear," Jeff chimed in. "I'm quite looking forward to retiring so that I can grow my hair and wear tartan slippers in the street. I might even learn to spit."

Ivy laughed, more approving of Jeff than ever. I wrinkled my nose at him, appreciatively.

"Don't laugh." Douggie said again. *"From Audrey, with love."* For some reason, he chose to read that message out loud. But he then just put the card down and picked up the next without comment.

My eyes met Ivy's. "Yes," she said quietly. "She sends a card. She always sends a card."

"But you said..."

"I have no contact? And that's true. I don't. She doesn't include a letter, not even an address, and that's what you asked me."

"Well, there would at least have been a postmark."

"Would that have helped? I hadn't realised..."

"No. It doesn't matter."

"Did you get anywhere?"

I admitted I had, "…but only recently."

"And?"

"And nothing. I've written to her. Do you want her address?"

She shook her head. "I don't think so, dear."

"Biccett." That was Ronan.

"Biscuit?" He shook his curly mane, but I think he meant to nod.

"Drink." That was Douggie.

"Oh, dear." That was Ivy.

Jeff sprang to the rescue. "Shall we cut the cake?"

"Fish paste sandwiches first," I suggested.

I found myself glancing at Audrey's card as we sat and chatted about bunions, the merits of salmon fish paste versus tuna, East London, markets, and Human Rights. So she sent her sister a card. She knew Ivy's address. But did she know that we kept in touch with Ivy? Perhaps not.

"Would you like me to show Jeff the photo album, dear?" Ivy knew where my thoughts were.

"Douggie likes photos."

"Fo's." So did Ronan it seemed.

"Sounds unanimous." I smiled to show her that I wasn't apportioning any blame and she retrieved the bulky faux leather tome from an overflowing bookcase on top of which was perched what looked remarkably like a Bakelite radio.

The three boys leafed through the album. Jeff made all the right noises. Ronan made a mess, thanks to the fish paste. But Douggie… I should have realised. "It's Audrey." Oh, no.

I glanced at Jeff, grimacing, annoyed with myself that I hadn't foreseen the consequences, especially as I'd only just been thinking abut her. Douggie was very good at putting two and two together.

Ivy came to our rescue. "Yes. Audrey is my sister," she told him.

"Sister. Douggie's got a sister."

"Yes. And here's a photo of Linda when she was the same age as Ronan is now."

Douggie was happily side tracked by black and white, and brown and white photos of us as children and Ivy managed to direct him away from those snaps which included Audrey. She found one I didn't recognise with me, Dad and Douggie digging sandcastles on Ramsgate beach.

"Dad. Linda. Douggie." Pause for thought. "Who's holding camera?"

"Ah. Good question. I suppose it must have been me." It certainly wasn't Ivy, but she got away with it.

I looked down at a world half a century away and I wanted to sob my heart out, for what we'd lost. But I couldn't. Ivy closed the album.

"I guess we've had enough."

"And this young man's mummy will be looking for him soon." I picked up my smiling grandson from the floor. "Shall we take a photo before we go? Something for Ronan to look back on. To those lost days."

Jeff's mobile was also a digital camera, and the technology fascinated Ivy and Douggie both. He was able to manage a couple of great pictures. "I'll send you copies for your album."

"Oh, thank you, young man. And remind my niece to come again. She'll listen to you."

"I will. Thank you so much for your hospitality." Jeff kissed the loosened skin of her cheek without reluctance as if she was a member of his own family. I was so proud of him. He wasn't just trying to impress me. He was a genuine gentleman with a giant heart – as well as a love machine.

Because we'd been stuffing ourselves with sandwiches and Douggie's left over birthday cake, dinner was not planned for Sunday evening. But Douggie sat down at the table at six as usual, so we toyed with some crisps, cheese and olives, and we opened the bottle of Sangria that Antonia had given everyone at the end of the Spanish course just a few weeks ago.

"You know what would be nice this evening?"

"I bet I can guess."

"You think I have a one track mind." Jeff reproved me, and we were smiling at each other like idiots, thanks in part to the Sangria, and in part to the double entendres that we knew went over Douggie's head. It added just that little frisson to the conversation, even while it was sad that Douggie lacked any sexual awareness. Or was it sad? According to Jeff, that just made him even luckier.

"I meant it would be nice to go to that open air jazz concert in Valentine's Park."

"Douggie doesn't like live music, you know that. And especially not open air concerts." For Douggie, music belonged inside. Everything in its proper place.

"I do know. I meant just us."

"You should have said earlier. I could have contacted one of the carers."

Jeff sighed and stretched. "It's a shame we can never do anything spontaneous."

"There you go. That's life in this house."

"When my divorce comes through and we've sold the house…"

"Well?"

"We could buy a bigger house. Perhaps something with an annexe."

"Put Douggie in an annexe?"

"What's an annexe?" Douggie always showed an interest when his name was mentioned, naturally.

"It's a kind of joined-on flat," Jeff explained.

"Douggie doesn't like annexes."

"Quite right. You tell him. Annexe indeed." I wrinkled my nose at Jeff.

"How can he say he doesn't like something he knows nothing about?"

"Because it's not the same as what he's got now. And he likes what he's got now. Q.E.D., he won't like the option he hasn't got."

"Would you mind if I went alone then, just for an hour?" I hadn't seen that coming.

"To the jazz? Of course not. It's a lovely evening. Ideal."

"You really don't mind?"

I probably did. Just a little bit. The thought of him enjoying himself, while I stayed at home with Douggie and the television. "Don't be silly. How long will you be?"

"A couple of hours tops. A shame for us both to miss it."

"I agree." Well, I nearly agreed.

"Keep it warm."

"As toast."

"And wet."

"As a warm flannel."

He nuzzled my neck and kissed my ear. I was never going to need H.R.T. at this rate. Hormones were never a problem when Jeff was around.

When Douggie was in bed, I couldn't concentrate on the new Lesley Pearse novel, a very unusual situation for me to be in. I put Russell Watson on the C.D. player, quietly, and thought about Jeff's annexe.

I wondered if it had just occurred to him this evening, out of the blue, or if he'd been thinking about it. I had known from the outset that spontaneity could be a problem with Douggie around, but did it matter? Wasn't it a small price to pay to see Douggie settled and happy? And to rid myself of at least some of the guilt that I had been carrying around for too many years?

Buying a house together, annexe or no annexe, was in any case a commitment that I wasn't ready for. A joint mortgage was as much of a tie, in its way, as a marriage contract. There was a joint dependency there that I didn't much care for.

I was dealing with a case at the moment whereby the parents had bought their learning disabled son a house and he was using his own housing benefit to pay them rent. It seemed a win win situation. I had accepted Douggie into my home without looking into the financial implications, and certainly without looking to benefit financially. Would an annexe be a good idea financially, perhaps?

However, Douggie would not then be living in a family unit. Which was what I had been trying to provide for him. Okay, not the usual family unit, but family nevertheless.

An annexe would be right next door. There could probably even be direct access. So was it so different? Did it offer a compromise beneficial to us both?

No, Douggie would not benefit. That was one thing I could say with a reasonable amount of certainty.

But, perhaps I should also be considering myself. And even Jeff. And Douggie had to be prepared for the possibility that I could die before him, in which case my home would no longer be his, as I had children of my own to consider. But an annexe, if self-contained, could perhaps prepare Douggie for a more independent life at some point.

More change. Did I really want to even consider more change where Douggie was concerned? Wasn't there a limit as to how many changes he would go along with amicably? And how would I explain the decision, assuming I ever made such a decision?

My head was whirling. I had the last glass of Sangria, which didn't help at all. There were grey areas here for me to look into. As an advocate, there were always more answers to find out, usually for other people, but in this case for me. And the answers would stand me in good stead, I was sure of that. One thing I would have to do, which I always advised my clients to do and hadn't done myself, was to set up a trust for Douggie rather than just leaving him money which he couldn't handle – assuming he outlived me that was. But I had to do it, just in case. There was only five years between us, but accidents – and worse – happened, and happened all the time. Dad had been shrewd enough and able enough to sort out Douggie's future to pre-empt a crisis, and I needed to do the same.

Jeff got back just ten minutes later. A box of chocolates appeared around the door before he did.

"What the…?"

"Peace offering." He didn't look like a man who had been out having fun.

"You didn't need to do that."

"No. But I wanted to."

I kissed him, and he stood back and looked at me, holding my shoulders.

"Linda. I love you. I'm sorry if I want too much. I'm sorry."

I kissed him again and this time he kissed me back.

"I can taste the Sangria," he said.

"Yes. I feel distinctly woozy."

"It would be a shame to take advantage of you."

"But that's when I love you best."

He stood back again. "You said 'love'."

"Yes. Love."

"I'll have to go out and leave you alone more often. Or is it the booze talking?"

"No. I haven't wanted to admit it, you know that. But I do love you. Lots." The expression on his face was indescribable. I hadn't realised I had the power to instil that level of happiness. "Now don't get excited. I don't hook love and marriage together the way you do."

"Wow. Linda North loves me." His voice definitely choked. "I've made progress."

"I think it's me that's made progress." And I jumped on his bones for a change.

I was watching Jeff getting dressed early the next morning. It had got to the stage where he kept an office outfit in my wardrobe. I watched him tucking in his shirt, zipping up his fly, every movement full of eroticism in my eyes. Some people could make any movement sexy and he was one of those people.

"You should advertise ice cream on television," I said lazily, hugging the mug of tea that he'd brought me in bed.

"What?" He paused, mid tie-tying.

"Nothing."

He turned suddenly, as if making a decision. "Linda. I've been wondering whether to tell you or not."

"Tell me what? And keep your voice down. Douggie's still asleep."

"Sorry. I forgot." He dropped his voice obligingly. "I suppose I should have told you last night. I saw Pete at the jazz festival."

"Did he speak?"

"No. Too far away. But he saw me. He was with a blonde, but I could see that it definitely wasn't Stephanie. Too young."

"And?"

"And nothing. He saw me, raised a hand in a blokey kind of way, and they moved off."

The conclusion was pretty obvious. "I'm glad you told me. I think. But I certainly wouldn't want Stephanie to know."

"So he hasn't got a sister then?"

"It's nice of you to clutch at straws, and although as it happens he has, she's brunette, much older than him, lives in Wales somewhere, I think."

He sat on the edge of the bed. "I thought things had improved there."

"They have, according to Stephanie. It may have meant nothing. Did they seem like an item?"

"I couldn't really say. I didn't see them again. He made sure I saw him put his hand on her bum, but as I say he was doing his blokey thing. He always does that when I see him. As if we were two of a kind."

"The mind boggles."

"I've got to go, darling." He removed my mug of tea and pushed me back down on the bed, pulling down the straps of the flimsy nightie I always wore in his honour. "Unfortunately."

"So go. And no sexy text messages. I've got meetings all day, and one this evening, so I need to stay focused. And your messages just put me off."

"Okay." He winked. "But I am delighted to hear it."

"Go. Go. And don't forget to get those photos done for Ivy."

"I won't. And I'll do copies for you and Stephanie."

I thought about Pete when he'd gone. The girl was unlikely to have meant anything, because the one thing I did know was that he was besotted with Stephanie. Okay, so maybe his way was a possessive and disparaging way that I disapproved of, but I had never had any doubts about that aspect of their relationship. And they had a sex life only rivalled by my own at the moment it seemed. Not that Stephanie gave me any gory details: daughters didn't do that. But the Sunday afternoon they had spent together while we babysat Roman was definitely spent in bed; and she often showed me the underwear that Pete bought her, which revealed as much about their relationship as it revealed of Stephanie's flesh.

In fact, if anything, it was Georgina and Mark who worried me more at the moment. Her obsession, like Pete's, was damaging their marriage. She was still absolutely dismissive of I.V.F., or adoption, even surrogacy. And Mark was now only performing to order, as she called it. So that was making her even unhappier.

"Wash and clean teeth."

"Yes, Douggie. Good morning. You use the bathroom first."

I knew I wouldn't get a 'good morning'. The niceties of social exchange were not part of Douggie's make-up.

He peeled off his pyjamas as he moved along the hallway, leaving them where they lay. It didn't seem to matter how many times he was told, he still needed to be nagged every single morning to pick them up. I watched his naked unembarrassed rear disappear from view. Carers always had to be warned about his lack of sexual awareness. For him, sex was merely the distinction between the male and female of the species and nothing more. Certainly not an act between two people. Although he knew, biologically, how babies were made, thanks to some graphic books on the subject, he didn't equate this with 'sex'. Nor did he equate baby-making with 'love', whatever he understood by the word. But that wasn't unusual in this – or perhaps any – day and age, and in itself was hardly an unusual viewpoint.

That made me think about Pete again. Perhaps he'd just met the girl at the festival. Perhaps he was just being blokey as Jeff pointed out. Interesting that Jeff hadn't told me straight away, though. He must have felt, instinctively, that there was something more to it.

The combination of too much thinking and last night's Sangria were beginning to have an effect, and I needed to be really alert today to fight other people's battles.

I heard Douggie making his way back to his bedroom to get dressed, leaving me just enough time for a shower before we had breakfast together. He didn't like it much when I worked on into the evening, because it meant that we didn't eat dinner together. He behaved very differently when he had dinner with one of the carers, or even with Jeff, who had taken on the role from time to time. With me, he had to have a spoon, he refused to use a knife, he always asked which part of the food was the hottest so he could leave that until the last, he refused the addition of tomato ketchup or any other condiment, and he had to sit on my left. None of those things applied if I wasn't around. It was as if he knew I, but only I, would accept his need for rituals. I had long given up trying to change them. I didn't see them as particularly damaging, especially as he modified his behaviour in the presence of others.

Douggie, of all of us, led a life not dictated by other people. He didn't feel an obligation to please anyone, or to be cheerful or polite if he didn't want to. He was oblivious as to what other people thought of him. I had never been able to explain duty or obligation to him, it was like explaining a foreign language. In fact, it was worse, as he had managed to grasp a few words of Spanish when I had been doing homework not so long ago.

So was Jeff right? Was he lucky?

"Are you lucky, Douggie?"

"What's lucky?"

"Do things go right for you? Do you get what you want?"

"Douggie lucky."

"So you think so, too. Perhaps you're right. Don't forget your orange juice."

"From Spain."

"Sorry?"

"Oranges."

"Oh. Yes. Do you remember seeing the orange trees when we went to Spain?"

"Douggie's been to Spain. Douggie lucky."

"Yes. Perhaps we'll go again."

"Don't want to."

"I thought you liked it."

"Been to Spain."

"So that's it. You've been there once. And once is enough?"

He drained his glass. "What time Linda coming home?"

We established the timetable of his day together. Tim was due this morning and should have arrived by now. *Please don't let him be late.* Unpunctuality didn't just make Douggie twitchy, it had a similar effect on me when I had a busy day stretching in front of me.

"Tim's here." Douggie spoke before the doorbell had even rung. Spooky. But he was right. Tim and the postman had arrived together.

"Sorry, Mrs North. Traffic."

Now there was a word you didn't hear too often: *Sorry.*

I left Tim to talk to Douggie, smiling at their instant debate as to who was going to do the washing up.

There was one letter. Postmarked Bournemouth. I propped it behind the alarm clock on my bedside table and glanced at it a few times while I tonged my hair away from my face, pencilled in my eyebrows and darkened my eyelashes. Vaseline would suffice for my lips. The letter would have to wait.

It was nearly ten o'clock when I got home. I'd put Jeff off for tonight so that I could catch up on the sleep I had been losing thanks to his overnight presence of late. It also gave me the chance to spend a little time alone with Douggie before he went to bed. And to read the letter, which, as it turned out, wasn't very long.

> *Dear Linda,*
> *How very pleasant to hear from you after so long.*

I had to smile.

> *I don't get out much these days because of my arthuritical (sic)*
> *hip. So it seems very unlikely that I would ever be able to get to see*
> *you in Barking. If you wished to come here, of course, that could*
> *be arranged, although I only have a small one bedroom luxury*
> *apartment near to the seafront.*

'Could be'... not exactly encouraging. 'Small apartment'... for which read: 'so there's no room for you'.

> *Thank you for the photos. What a lovely family you have. They*
> *really don't seem like my family at all.*

Which was hardly surprising.

> *I have no regrets, you know. I have had a wonderful life. I have*
> *travelled, I have spent a lot of money, and there have been many*
> *men. None of them quite like Frank, of course. He was the love of*
> *my life, although I would understand if you don't believe me.*

You saddo.

> *Although I own this apartment, I have no other money, so I've*
> *never bothered to make a will. Perhaps I should.*

That's not why I contacted you, you silly woman.

> *I often think of you, and especially of my damaged Douglas.*
> *But if I had stayed, you know, I think I would have hated him*
> *because he reminded me of my failure and hated you because you*
> *were always going to be lovelier, brighter, and more caring than I*
> *could ever be.*

Not just silly then but feeble, selfish, and twisted.

> *Yours truly, Audrey*

Yours bloody truly.

I read it again. And again. The love of her life. Dad would have liked that. It wouldn't have made any difference to how he felt about her, but yes, it would have pleased him. Being loved is always pleasing regardless of where it comes from.

No guilt as far as she was concerned. No 'sorry'. All my life I'd felt guilty and she had been able to discard us without a look back. I didn't believe she 'often' thought of us. And I was amazed that she made no pretence to have loved us, her children, but saw us as extensions of herself that she obviously didn't much care for. I'd always believed that there was another man. But now it seemed that it was down to Douggie and me. Yours bloody truly indeed.

I showed the letter to Jeff the next evening.

"Have you shown this to anyone else?"

"Like who? No, I haven't."

"I suppose you're angry." He was getting to know me very well.

"Yes. And disappointed. And annoyed that I bothered to contact her, because it has obviously been a complete waste of time."

Douggie came into the kitchen where we were sitting, the letter on the table between us. I snatched it up before he saw it.

"Drink."

"Okay, pet. How about some milk for a change."

"Blackcurrant."

"Okay. Here, take it with you."

"What time Linda watching television?"

"In about half an hour."

"Half past eight?"

"What's on?"

"Place in the Sun." He seemed to know the whole schedule off by heart.

"Good. Yes, I like that."

He left us alone, waving his mug of blackcurrant around oblivious to how full it was. Thank goodness for wooden floors.

Jeff took the letter from me and opened it out. "I don't see it in quite the same way as you do."

"Jeff, you're an accountant not a psychologist. And this is my selfish mother we're talking about."

"I know. I know. You've no need to attack me. It's interesting that she mentions a will."

"Not to me, it's not."

"I wonder if she had other children."

"I don't know. And I don't bloody care."

"I think it's important. Because if she didn't, then she probably has thought of you often, a lot more often than if she'd started again with a new family perhaps. Especially as she's got older. People think much more about the past as they get older."

"Perhaps." Although he was right, of course.

"No, they do. Remember, my parents are still alive. If I think about the conversations we have these days, it's all getting very nostalgic. I suppose they don't want to think too much about the future, because of what's waiting for them – and I don't suppose your mum is so much different."

"Didn't you notice the word 'hate'?"

"Didn't you notice the word 'if'? She didn't stay, did she? So there was no chance of hate developing. She's talking hypothetically."

"She wouldn't even know what that meant." I knew I was sounding bitter.

"But you do. She's alone now, it seems."

"And that's how she wants to stay."

"I think you're right." He handed me back the letter. "But that doesn't mean it wouldn't make her happy to see you."

"You think I care if she's happy?"

"Now who's being selfish?"

My eyes blurred over, and I bit my lip in an effort to contain my emotions. This was not something that he could understand. No one could. Not Douggie, for obvious reasons. And not my daughters, who had never met their grandmother. And not him, with his cosy, privileged background as an only child.

"Don't cry."

"I'm not bloody crying."

Douggie came back at that moment to rinse out his empty mug. "Linda said bloody."

"Yes. Sorry."

"Linda said it."

"Yes. And I'm sorry."

He smiled. "Bloody."

"It's not funny. So there's no need for you to say it."

His smile widened.

"Don't you dare."

"How many minutes before *Place in the Sun?*" Jeff changed the subject adroitly.

"Twenty minutes." And off he went.

"Right. Time for a cup of tea." He put the kettle on while I answered the phone. It was Stephanie.

"Pete said he saw Jeff at the Jazz Festival. Alone. Is anything wrong?"

"No, darling. It was a last minute decision, so we didn't make plans for carers, that's all. Is everything alright?"

I had a feeling she wouldn't have phoned if Pete hadn't mentioned Jeff. She started off very much on the defensive.

"I was there, too, you know."

"Really?"

"With Ronan, asleep in a buggy."

"That's interesting."

"I don't suppose Jeff saw me."

"No, as a matter of fact he didn't."

"But, from the tone of your voice, I suspect he saw the girl Pete picked up."

"He mentioned a girl, yes," I said carefully.

She couldn't keep it up any longer. "Oh, Mum," she wailed. "He said he needed a wee, and we waited for him in the beer tent."

"And?" I felt the anger rising and I could see silent concern in Jeff's face.

"He seemed to be gone a long time, and I was just beginning to wonder... when he came back with her. She couldn't have been more than sixteen under all that heavy make up." She took a deep breath. "He didn't say anything. Just stood there in front of me, grinning, while she clung on to him, fingering his biceps. Then he told her to piss off, poor cow. And I slapped his face. From both of us."

"Which I suppose you paid for."

"When we got home. He would never hit me in public."

"Oh, Stephanie. Listen to yourself. You're making it sound like a good quality. Are you badly hurt?"

"Of course not."

"And did he justify showing off his... pulling power?"

"Do you know what he said?" Her voice wobbled. "He said that it proved how much he loved me, because he didn't give her one. So my reaction was completely out of order. Does he have a point?"

"Darling. I don't know what to say. The man is disgusting. Are you all right?"

"Just a bit sore."

"Where is he now?"

She managed a laugh. "Where else? The pub."

"Did you phone earlier?"

"Yes. But I didn't want to leave a message on your Voicemail... oh, Mum..." She broke down completely. "I thought we were doing all right. I really did. It's the drink. He needs help."

"So do you."

I listened to her sobbing, feeling helpless. My expression must have said it all, because Jeff grabbed my left hand to attract my attention. "Do you want me to take you over there?" he mouthed.

"Stephanie. Do you want me to come over?"

"No! If he comes back and you're here..." The sobs abated as she fought for control.

"Did Ronan see him hit you?"

Silence.

"Oh, no, Stephanie. You have to do something. You have to. If it's the drink, there are solutions out there. Do you think he'd talk to Rick?"

"You're joking. Dad thinks it's sorted. If he thought anything else, he'd be round here with his hands round Pete's throat. Do you think Jeff would talk to him?"

"Jeff? I'm sure he would, though I suppose talking may not be enough…"

"Mum. It's a start. And he thinks the world of Jeff."

"Okay. What do you want him to do, just call round?" I pulled an apologetic face in Jeff's direction.

"Yeah. Nothing formal. I've got a girlfriend coming over tomorrow night for a haircut. If he could just sort of drop by…"

"He's here. I'll ask him."

Jeff agreed at once, but when I had finally hung up on a calmer Stephanie, he voiced his obvious surprise at her request: "But he hardly knows me."

"He is a good judge of character, it seems. A quality I wouldn't have thought he possessed. In fact, I can't think of one redeeming quality."

"You're biased."

"Yes."

Once I'd told him about Pete's irrational behaviour in the beer tent – not to mention the fact that he was still unable to keep his hands off Stephanie whenever she upset him, he came up with an idea.

"I'll try and get him to agree to meet Ian."

"Ian?"

"My ex-business partner. Used to be an alcoholic. Then moved on to hard drugs. Now he's on tonic water and Vitamin C tablets. He re-trained as a social worker. Great bloke. Fantastic wife, looks like Cameron Diaz, also an ex-druggie. They met at some clinic or other."

"Wow. You have some interesting friends."

To compensate for my lack of family. By the way…" He reached into his briefcase and brought out some estate agents' details. "Have a look at these. Properties with annexes."

You know, he'd timed it just right. How could I deny this man who was helping me sort out my own life. He was already sharing my family as well as my bed. Nothing phased him. My age, my brother, my daughters, my sons-in-law, my ex-husband, my mother, my job, my lack of domesticity. He even shared my fondness for Spanish guitar music and Russell Watson. What more could a middle aged crone ask for?

"Place in the Sun."

"Right, Douggie. What are you going to watch?"

"Want to go on the internet now. Find all the Fletchers living in New York."

"New York? Okay, whatever. You can have it on for an hour. Is that okay?"

"Ninety minutes."

"Seventy five."

"Okay." He was happy.

As for me, I wasn't exactly happy, but Jeff was definitely a great person to have around in a crisis. And it seemed we were lurching from one crisis to another at the moment.

And Jeff? I hadn't asked him about Julia lately, or whether she still figured in his present as well as his past. He was happier than I'd ever known him. It was almost as if he relished every new problem that cropped up in my life, given the absence of them currently in his own. While it wasn't my gratitude he was after, both of us knew that it wouldn't do our relationship any harm.

Chapter Sixteen

October 2004

I humoured Jeff by going to see some of the properties he thought would suit us. But they were very expensive, and I wasn't any more ready for the financial than I was for the moral commitment. And it was just too much change in one year for Douggie.

I knew that once I'd committed to Jeff, then we would need to do something about the domestic set up. There was obviously a lack of freedom while Douggie was around; freedom not just to go out when we wanted to, or to go on holiday without making elaborate plans. There were lots of smaller things: freedom to invite friends over because Douggie generally didn't approve and made it plain, which made it, in turn, uncomfortable for the friends, however forewarned they were. Freedom to indulge our lust before Douggie's watershed – Jeff likened the situation to having a baby but worse, because babies at least slept more than Douggie. Freedom to watch a television programme or read a newspaper without being interrupted with requests for a drink, requests for clarification of a word he'd seen or heard, and with questions that needed answering that could not wait, as in "People from India have straight hair and people in Africa have curly hair. How mixed up is that?"

Then there was Douggie's need to appear and disappear again on occasion, seemingly checking up on what we were doing or merely to check that we were there. Why wouldn't we be? There again, Audrey had disappeared. Then Dad. Then the people in first one home and then another.

What I needed was for someone to give me the sort of advice I handed out on a daily basis. Making my own decisions meant that it was difficult to be objective, and impossible to apportion blame in any other direction than at my own head.

I was still writing in my journal, although on a very occasional basis, and I made a list of the decisions that needed making on a Jeff-free evening when Douggie was hogging Sky, leaving me with only the soaps for – dispiriting – company.

Marry Jeff?

Move?

Change Douggie's domestic arrangements?

Meet my mother?

The answer to all these was: 'Not at the moment'.

Then there were decisions over which I had no control, but which affected me and my family. Thankfully, Pete had met Ian a few times, and Stephanie was encouraged by this. But she seemed unable to relax, not afraid exactly, just tense. Was the fact that Ronan was growing more fractious connected, or just a normal developmental phase. It was so long since my own girls had been babies, it had all become a blur, and in any case surely boys and girls behaved differently, even during the terrible twos period...

And Georgina had become equally fractious with Mark. Was their marriage in danger because they hadn't had children? Why couldn't she see what it was doing to him, that she wasn't the only one suffering?

I couldn't make decisions for my daughters. It seemed to me that Stephanie was trying the hardest to save her marriage, while Georgina had the marriage that better merited saving.

Did dysfunctional families produce dysfunctional families? Or was this just marriage in the 21st century? I thought of the families I was trying to help at Mencap, divided by arguments over care, over responsibility, over money, over lack of control, lack of the power to make decisions. I had the power, but I was still torn.

The journal had no answers.

"Linda make it better."

"What's the matter?"

Douggie had sat himself down next to me and was peeling off a grubby white sock. I made a mental note to ensure they went into the laundry bag.

Although, when I saw what he had uncovered, the mental note was erased by a loud alarm bell. "Douggie! That looks really painful."

The big toe was swollen and inflamed, and the source of the problem was obviously the long, chalky toenail that had grown up and around its tip, cutting into the skin, causing a suppurating, open wound.

"Special stuff."

The 'special stuff' – a tea tree stick that I usually used for cuts and bruises - was not going to make any inroads on the mess I was looking at. More bloody guilt. Why hadn't I noticed before? Why hadn't I checked his toenails the last time I cut his finger nails? I was always around when Douggie had a bath or shower, and I usually made sure the clothes he chose to wear were free of stains from toothpaste or bolognese sauce, and I should have noticed.

As he followed me into the kitchen where I went on a hunt for TCP and bandaging, I noticed that he was limping. I hadn't even noticed his limp. How the hell did I get to be so unobservant? What had happened to me?

"Douggie, this is only a temporary bandage. We'll go to see the doctor in the morning."

"Go now."

"I'm sorry, darling, but the surgery's closed. And if we go to the hospital, we'll just be waiting around for hours. This is hardly what they'd call an emergency. Are you in pain? Do you want some paracetamol?"

"Para...?"

"Aspirin. Pain killers. Medicine." I scrabbled around for the right words.

"Only special stuff."

I dabbed on the tea tree lotion to keep him happy, but the nail was too embedded for me to want to try and cut it myself. With a bit of luck, our G.P. would do it there and then. I set to with the clippers on the other nine, however, all of which needed attention. Perhaps I should arrange for him to have a general overhaul, because if he did have any medical problems, he wasn't going to tell me, and certainly not anyone else, until they caused him a real problem in his day-to-day living. It wasn't just pain, which he tolerated well above the average. Although that sounded a good thing, pain was there for a reason, a warning, and if you didn't heed the warning, then…

I telephoned the Mencap office and left a message on the answer phone explaining that I had to take Douggie to the doctor, and I also spoke to Sharon who was due to come over in the morning. She offered to take Douggie to see Dr Patel but it was the very, the absolutely, least I could do.

"Had you noticed a limp at all?"

"I don't think so, Mrs Fletcher. Nothing. Poor Douggie."

Poor Douggie. Obviously no one had noticed. I started thinking about septicaemia, about gangrene, about stuff I knew nothing about. Had he had tetanus injections? Did he need them? Jeez.

I thought Dr Patel might be unhappy about our arriving without an appointment, but he was very understanding, once he'd laid eyes on Douggie's foot.

"Ouch. Oh my goodness. Yes, we can do something about that. Can you come back at the end of morning surgery? I can do it here, although he'll need a local anaesthetic."

Douggie clung to me. "What's happening?"

"You need an injection. Like, like… the dentist. Only this time the injection will be in your foot."

"Douggie doesn't like injections."

"No, I know. But it's the only way to make the toe better. See you about eleven o'clock, then, doctor? Thank you so much."

"Going home now."

"Yes. But we're coming back. At eleven o'clock."

"No injections."

"We'll talk about it."

Dr Patel smiled. "He'll be fine."

"Tell him, not me," I reprimanded.

"Sorry. Douggie, you'll be fine."

I felt a bit mean. He had been very kind. "Of course he will. See you later."

I let Douggie watch a DVD – *Home Alone II* – which would just about take him up to the time we had to leave again. In the meantime, I managed to get our transition advocate to see one of the families that were booked in to see me that morning – it wasn't really a transition case as their son, who had Down's Syndrome, was already at residential school, but I knew Ronnie could try and relieve the family's concerns which mainly revolved around a lack of stimulation. It would be a shame to take Billy-Bob out of the college now that the funding was in place, if the situation could be resolved. Billy-Bob! It just kind of added insult to injury, somehow. He had been bullied at school as much for his name as for his appearance and mental capacity. But that, at least, did not seem to be an issue at college.

So many families with so many problems. Should I be doing this? Shouldn't this kind of work be reserved for those with boring, empty lives who had the time, energy and optimism that I never seemed to have. There again, those people didn't have the experience or people skills that people like me had. It was a dilemma.

My telephone rang but I let my answer phone click in. It was Jeff. "Your mobile is switched off and you're not at work. Is anything wrong? I'll keep trying…" I picked up.

"There's no need. I'm here."

He sounded really concerned, bless him, but was soon laughing at the in-growing toenail explanation.

"There's nothing funny about an in-growing toenail."

"I know. I know. I'm laughing with relief. That it's nothing more serious."

"It could have been."

"Been what?"

"Something more serious. It's got me thinking."

"Darling, my internal phone is ringing. I've got to go. I love you. Don't worry. I'll come over after work and I'll bring presents for you both."

"You don't have…"

"I want to. What else is money for?" I could hear someone laugh in the background. Jeff wasn't saying the usual stereotyped platitudes of an accountant.

I even had time to phone Stephanie and Georgina, although Georgina was at the nursery and couldn't speak for long. Not to tell them about Douggie, which was not their problem, and wasn't such a big problem anyway, but just so they knew I was thinking about them.

Jeff brought us both books. He'd been to W.H.Smith in his lunch hour. Sweet. Mine was Carol Ann Duffy's *The World's Wife*, Jeff's impressive idea of an introduction to poetry for Essex Girls. And Douggie's was the *Big Book of Yuk*, which had everything disgusting you could think of, including, would you believe it, an in-growing toenail in a far worse state than his own.

Dr Patel had done a good job, and although Douggie's limp had worsened, it was obviously Douggie's idea of what he should be doing rather than a necessity. I don't know how I knew that, but I knew it.

"Say thank you for the book, Douggie."

"Yeah."

Jeff shrugged, used to Douggie's ingratitude. "I can see he likes it, so that's the main thing." That was true. He was already engrossed. If he hadn't been interested, it would have been tossed straight on the floor. You knew exactly where you stood with Douggie when it came to presents.

While Douggie was preoccupied, Jeff gave me a full-on kiss, waiting for me to respond to the little flicks of his tongue. "I missed you," he said thickly.

"Jeff. It was one night."

"Meaning you didn't miss me?"

"Of course I did."

He held me by my shoulders for a moment and looked at me until I ran my finger very slowly over his lips. "That's better. You can show me later how much you missed me."

That was all it took. Just one kiss and a look. I tried not to wonder about how long it would last, this mutual power for arousal, given my earlier thoughts about the transience of loving relationships.

"Something smells good."

"Rive Gauche."

"Not just that, although thank you as I presume it is in my honour. I meant in the kitchen."

"Gammon and pineapple."

"Douggie doesn't like pineapple." He looked up.

"No, the pineapple is not for you."

"Have we got time for a drink first?"

"Douggie's busy so yes, of course. Come in the kitchen."

He threw his tie on the floor, reminding me of Douggie, and followed me, fondling my breasts from behind as I poured two martinis with tonic water, a newly acquired taste for both of us.

"I've been thinking."

"About us?" He came even closer.

I turned around holding the full glasses so that he had to release me. His attention was welcome but it would soon be time to dish up.

"Not just us. Everything. I've been wondering if I'm trying to do too much, to be too many people."

He perched himself on one of the two bar-type stools. "Of course you are."

"But there again, it's important for me to be busy. I like doing something rewarding. What's wrong with that?"

"Nothing. Do you know what I want you to be?"

"I can guess."

"I didn't mean my wife. I was thinking more of my woman." He put down his glass and beat his chest. "Just my woman. Nothing else."

"Sounds spectacularly selfish."

"Yes. I don't want you to think about anyone else but me. I don't want you to spend any time with anyone else but me. I don't want you to do anything that isn't concerned with me. I want you to think of me when you choose your perfume, your clothes."

"You know who you sound like? Pete."

"Ah, but the difference is that Pete actually expects as well as wants. And he gets annoyed if he doesn't get what he expects. I'm realistic. I'll settle for whatever I can get."

Douggie came in, also looking for a drink, of the soft kind. "How many minutes before dinner."

"Ten minutes."

"Christmas is coming."

"Do you like Christmas?"

"Douggie likes Christmas." He left us alone and Jeff raised an eyebrow.

"There are Christmas ads on the television already," I explained.

"Oh, yes, of course. Where were we?"

"You lay the table and I'll dish up."

"No, I mean we seem to have been sidetracked. You were telling me that you do too much, and I was agreeing. So what are you going to do about it?"

"Probably nothing."

"You know, Confucius he say that he who does less, does it better."

That made me laugh. But he was right of course. "Perhaps if I worked just one or two days a week, with less cases."

"Or why not do something less demanding? In a supermarket, perhaps? Not because it will stretch your mind, but I bet the money is comparable, and the pressure is virtually non-existent. After all, isn't your job nowadays just a form of respite? A way of escaping from Douggie's twenty-four-seven presence?"

I had to think about that. "I suppose so, in part. But I don't like to think about it like that."

"Either way, you would still have your respite, but you'd be able to concentrate on him, on me – hopefully – on your daughters, and the rest of your personal baggage. Perhaps do that O.U. course you mention periodically."

"I see what you mean. But then I'd feel guilty about leaving my clients behind."

"Let's face it, whatever you do, you feel guilty. It should be your middle name. But remember when you applied? There were plenty of other applicants."

"So?"

"So, they'll replace you. Painful fact but a fact. Like all of us, you are not indispensable. Except in one department."

"What is that?"

"Except to me."

I hadn't seen that coming and it made my cheeks hotter than they were already as a result of my proximity to the oven.

Douggie came in to join us, kicking off the one slipper he was wearing. Obviously to these two very different men I looked like just the type of person who was happy to spend my leisure hours wandering around the house picking up male apparel. Whereas I felt I looked like a person who could save the world and his wife. I'd have to read that poetry volume.

"Which one is the hottest?" The predictable question.

"The gammon."

"Which one is the coldest?"

"The sweetcorn."

He made inroads into the meal without further ado. I was relieved to see that he was behaving quite normally even as regards his appetite. One less thing to worry about.

"Ian's taking Pete out tonight." Jeff was bringing me up to speed.

"Good. Presumably somewhere with no alcohol?"

"You could say that. He's taking him to a shelter for battered women."

I nearly choked on my pineapple. Douggie thumped me on the back, far too vigorously, but it worked.

"And he agreed?"

Jeff shrugged. "Why not? I think Pete knows he has a problem, and this is Ian's idea for making him face it. He won't want Stephanie to end up somewhere similar."

"Over my dead body."

Douggie looked at me. "Who is dead?"

"No one, darling. We're talking about… the future." Douggie was well aware of mortality, even if he didn't understand it.

"Don't want Linda to be dead."

"Okay. I'll try." I patted his arm, reassuringly.

"I asked Ian to ring me here later, because I know you'll want to hear what happened."

"Good. Thanks, Jeff. You are…"

He poised, the forkful of roast potato halfway to his mouth.

"…a pal."

"Is that all?" I think he said, but his mouth was full.

Chapter Seventeen

November 2004

The month of lists – cards and presents. And of shopping. And of planning. But this year, I made some more important decisions. I didn't want to start 2005 with a completely undefined future. Adventure was fine if you were footloose and fancy free but I was not either, and probably never would be. Disability in the family was a constraint, of course, but it was more optimistic to look on it as a focus for planning and structure. Such a focus was not a bad thing. It brought order out of chaos.

The first decision was for me to contact my mother and invite her over pre-Christmas. Although Jeff suggested Christmas, I thought that was too major an invitation for me – and probably her – to handle, and would be too disruptive for Douggie and the sort of Christmas he was used to, *sans mère*. Jeff offered to collect her and was even happy to go all that way alone. The details could be sorted if she accepted. I had a feeling that she probably would. And yet I kind of hoped she wouldn't. "Mixed up" as Douggie would put it.

My letter was as brief as hers, with no trace of the criticism or angst I felt. My restraint was only brought about by my all-pervading guilt. Perhaps I had been the reason she left. Not Dad. Not Douggie. But perhaps me. Perhaps I was responsible for Douggie losing his mother, for Frank losing his beloved wife. It was unthinkable. No, it wasn't, because I thought it. Not often, because there was nothing I could do about it, and I would never know the truth, but whenever I thought about her leaving, I wondered.

Sometimes I re-read my 1957 journal which I had kept all those years. There was no trace of guilt there. Just anger and bafflement. Hold on to that. It was infinitely preferable to the alternative that had grown in my adult psyche.

The second decision was to accept Jeff's proposal. We had gone to a firework display locally, and Douggie was completely absorbed in the spectacle, while we were absorbed in each other.

"I've made a decision."

"About a take away curry?"

"No. About marrying you."

The smile disappeared from his face. He licked his lips, and I watched red and gold stripes reflected on his skin momentarily from the overhead whorls and sprays. He didn't look at me but lifted his face to the sky. "And?"

"You are good for me. You are part of my family. But …"

He closed his eyes, face still turned upwards. "But?"

"I'd like to be more than your woman. I'd like to be your wife. Not now. When your divorce dust settles. When we've found a suitable house."

He opened his eyes but still didn't look at me. "Next year. No later." His voice was very calm.

"Okay. It's a deal. Is that it, then? No great crushing hugs or Whoopees?"

He didn't answer me, but the next flash lit up the tears on his face and I kissed him gently, tasting the salt. He seemed unable to move. "I want to savour the moment. Every November 5th, I will remember this time, this place. I will remember the happiness and relief that I'm feeling now." He kissed me then.

I was so lucky to be so loved for a second time. Some people never even had this experience once in their life.

Douggie became aware of our extended embrace. "Too much kissing."

Jeff laughed and pulled away. "Spoilsport."

I kissed Douggie so that he wouldn't feel left out but he rubbed the receiving cheek like a child who's been kissed by a hairy-chinned aunt. "Too much kissing."

Jeff nodded at the back of Douggie's head. "Do you want to tell him, or shall I?"

"There's no need. When we've made, er, marriage plans, then we can tell him together. Because you know he's part of the deal." I spoke quietly, my words further dimmed by the sound of fireworks, but Jeff was watching me intently.

"Of course I do. He's infinitely preferable to a hair-shedding slobbery large dog or twin teenage sons with a drug problem or…"

"Okay. I get the idea. And you'll settle for stepfather instead of father."

"I'll settle for anything that includes you. Although I still like the idea of an annexe."

"I know. And it probably is a good idea. As an advocate, I know it would be the route I would be promoting."

Douggie had turned back to us. "Ten o'clock. Go home now."

"The fireworks haven't finished, Douggie."

"Ten o'clock. Had enough."

"Okay. I must admit, I can't wait to get your sister home."

It was too dark for Douggie to be able to see the embarrassed expression on my face, but he didn't comment, the remark going over his head.

The first love only had me to take on, with a future populated with children, not with issues relating to care. Rick and I had thought, if we'd thought at all, that Frank would look after Douggie until such time as Douggie went into a home, and that would be that. We hadn't thought about homes closing, carers in short supply, and we especially hadn't thought about the possibility of guilt or responsibility featuring in our lives as we grew older, faced with our own mortality.

And here we both were, with younger models. Except in my case my new man was prepared to take on an appendage. Douggie. From living a life with only a hedonistic wife to worry about, he now had me, my brother, and my guilt to live with.

The 5th of November prompted one of my occasional journal entries. Just six words: *'Accepted Jeff's proposal at firework display'*. But I knew I only had to look at those words to remember the tears on his face, and the heightened tenderness of the lovemaking that followed.

"You know what I'm looking forward to?" he whispered at one point. "I'm looking forward to 2007 when I can make mad passionate love to a pensioner."

"You'll make an old woman very happy," I murmured.

Journal, 12th November: *'Got the job at Sainsbury's.'*

I had been over qualified – in terms of my experience – for a couple of the jobs I'd applied for, so this time I under-played my background and my office skills, the first time I'd had to do something like that. It was a shame. But still. I got the sort of job I'd decided was right for me at the moment. Two days a week, in the stock rooms.

The money was not great, but Jeff was behind me. "I'll be supporting you soon financially, so why not now?"

"Because I've got used to supporting myself, that's why."

"So, here's your chance to be on the receiving end for a change. And don't worry, I can think of lots of ways for you to thank me."

"Sex maniac."

"And whose fault is that?"

I often wondered if marriage would kill off our active sex life in the way that it gradually had with me and Rick. But when I broached the subject, Jeff was dismissive.

"You worry too much. And in any case, I would still want you, even if you turned celibate on me."

"I don't believe you."

He shrugged and gulped down coffee on his way out of the door, late as usual, trying to adjust his tie and smooth his hair simultaneously. "When have I ever lied to you?"

"I won't be able to spend so much money on underwear, perfume, the things you like."

"So I'll do the spending. I'll enjoy it. Trust me. Bye."

"Bye, Douggie," he called out, hearing that he was awake. Douggie had come across Jeff in my bed for the first time the morning after the firework display, because we had all overslept. But he had said not a word, and had not registered even the mildest surprise, so Jeff didn't pretend for Douggie's benefit any more. I wasn't sure if I felt less, or more, guilty about the revised situation.

"Jeff is Linda's friend," he remarked now, coming into the kitchen. "Good morning."

"Jeff is friend or family? Choose."

I was glad he'd brought up the subject. "Friend now. Family next year."

Douggie made one of his rare attempts at prolonged eye contact, always a sign that he was concentrating especially hard.

"Rick's not coming back."

"No, darling. Rick has a new family."

"Douggie doesn't want a new family."

"There will just be one extra. That's all."

"Jeff is extra."

"Exactly."

He smiled and looked away. "Family getting bigger. Ronan. Jeff."

"Yes, pet. How many Weetabix?"

"Two."

Silly question. He wandered off to the bathroom. We were getting there. I braced myself to give in notice at Mencap, citing the additional time I felt I needed for Douggie and for Jeff. But in the event they were all so excited about my plans to re-marry, that they expressed little regret at my impending departure.

Of course, they were a bit disappointed that I didn't have a ring to show them, but Jeff and I were going to choose one the next day. I had agreed to the conventionality of an engagement ring as long as we didn't have to have a party and, although I sensed his disappointment – "I'd so wanted to show you off" – he had agreed.

"You can show me off at the wedding."

Engagement parties at my age just seemed naff, and I was a tad concerned that if I saw all Jeff's thirty-something and forty-something friends that I would be forcibly reminded of my age. Although that was just as likely to happen at our wedding, it would be too late for me to cry wolf then. Naturally, I hadn't told Jeff my true reasons, because I knew he would pooh-pooh them.

He'd insisted on a family party the following evening at *The Mews*, and he had invited Stephanie and Georgina without telling them what we were celebrating. Auntie Ivy was going to babysit Ronan and Ashwan was going to take Douggie ten pin bowling. I thought this was more for Ashwan than Douggie but they went regularly and Douggie was getting quite good, apparently.

Saturday afternoon saw us, with Douggie, in Hatton Garden. Douggie was fascinated by the number of jewellery shops, as was I, even though some of them were closed. I had tried to persuade Jeff that a local shop was perfectly okay, but he'd insisted on something a bit special. I'd always liked emeralds rather than diamonds, which seemed a bit predictable, even boring, and we eventually settled for an emerald surrounded by diamond chips.

"Douggie likes green."

"That settles it then," said Jeff, to the amusement of the booted and suited assistant who served us.

"Jeff. It's just beautiful. Shouldn't we be saving for a honeymoon, or a new bed, or something."

"Don't worry. I will never do anything rash where money is concerned. You forget what I do for a living."

Douggie wanted me to wear it there and then, but I said I wanted to show Stephanie and Georgina first, which kept him happy. He did insist, however, on holding the box, and peeping at the ring occasionally, which was quite an unnerving experience on the District Line. But we made it home without incident.

A few hours later and Stephanie and Pete were already at *The Mews*, waiting for us. "Hello, In-law. You've fallen on your feet there." Pete nodded at Jeff. "A good bloke." Praise indeed. I noticed they only had a jug of water on the table.

"You're looking fantastic," I told Stephanie, truthfully. The black ballerina top looked like suede, and the trousers looked like leather. Her bleached days had slowly been replaced by softer highlights and, although her thick curls were controlled by straighteners, they were unable to remove the bounce. Particularly important was that there wasn't any bruising to be seen on her face or arms.

"I feel it," she said proudly, touching Pete's arm briefly. He looked round at her admiringly, as if butter wouldn't melt. They made a striking couple. I hadn't met Ian – not yet – but he seemed to be doing a good job.

"You look alright yourself, In-law," Pete told me gruffly, in his inimitable fashion.

Jeff laughed as he pulled out a chair for me. "Alright is one hell of an understatement. They could pass for sisters."

My hair had a few red streaks for the occasion and I was wearing a sage green satin slip dress. "Are you sure I don't look like mutton?" I had asked Jeff before we came out.

"Mutton is my favourite meat, didn't you know?" So he was a great help. But I felt good and that was the main thing.

Georgina and Mark arrived soon after, and she had chosen a damson embossed velvet suit. Mark's business was obviously doing well because it looked like a very expensive outfit, though not particularly flattering – it made her look a bit heavy. And they seemed much happier together than they had of late, although I could have been imagining things in the euphoria of the evening.

In the flattering candlelight, I felt that Jeff could be right about us passing for sisters. And the girls were far more excited by our news, and by the ring, than I had dared to hope.

Georgina cried openly, and had to be comforted by Mark. "I'm sorry, Mum. It's just that when Janine and Dad… when they… I know how devastated… I thought… I'm so glad."

A beaming Stephanie proposed a toast, but I noticed that Pete held up his water glass while the rest of us had poured wine. No one commented, even when he asked for ice and lemon as if to disguise what he was drinking. We all knew. We all wondered. But no one wanted to spoil the moment.

"So when are you getting married, Mum?" Stephanie was glowing. I was flattered that they were both so pleased. Obviously Jeff had proved a hit.

"I don't know, darling. We haven't decided."

Jeff picked up my hand and kissed the palm before responding with "The sooner the better." I caught an exchange of looks between my daughters. Could they be just a tad jealous?

"That's just Jeff. But I want to get the domestic stuff sorted first."

"What will happen to Douggie?" Mark, ever practical, raised the concern.

"Nothing. We may move to something with an annexe. But Douggie will still, to all intents and purposes, live with us; will still hopefully have the same carers allowing for the usual turnover, in the same area, near places he's becoming used to, and near enough to visit all of you." I grinned at Georgina. "You're the furthest away, but Brighton is not a problem, if you ever invite us."

"Mum. You don't need an invite. Jeez."

"And I'm changing to a less demanding, part time job, so I can spend more time with my family."

"Which includes me," interrupted my new fiancé, now kissing my newly adorned finger without the least sign of embarrassment.

"Oh, don't start getting soppy," protested Stephanie.

Georgina laughed. "Now, I'd like to propose a toast. I'm afraid I'm going to steal some of your thunder here, Mummy."

I looked at my oldest daughter in surprise.

"Here's to the future Mrs Linda Brooks and her new granddaughter."

She stood there, glass raised, smiling at me, while it sank in. I glanced at Mark and he nodded reassuringly, his eyes suspiciously damp. Stephanie had her mouth wide open.

"You mean…?"

"Yes. I mean. Mummy, I'm three months pregnant. And I couldn't wait any longer to tell you. I'm so sorry. Have I completely spoiled your evening?"

"Idiot. You have made it perfect. Just perfect."

Jeff called for champagne. "But not for you, mum to be. For the rest of us. We're in shock. Do you want water or pineapple juice?"

"Pineapple juice sounds good."

"And for me. I won't feel such a nonce if there are two of us drinking the stuff." The fact that Pete could make jokes about his struggle was a good sign.

I felt everything was coming together. Everything. Georgina's news had just blown me away.

"And it's a girl? You know that?"

"Yes. The scan."

"So we're looking at, what, May?"

"Yes."

"We'll avoid a May wedding then." Jeff was grinning.

"Oh, don't fit your plans round me," she said, suddenly concerned.

Jeff was still grinning, as was I. "It will be a pleasure. So, to Georgina and Mark."

"And to my granddaughter." Georgina's earlier tears had been brought on by a combination of emotion and hormones. The drink and the occasion were having a similar effect on me. "Ruby."

"What?" Georgina and Mark spoke together.

"I've always liked the name Ruby."

"Ruby!" They looked horrified.

"Or Daisy?"

"Mum, leave them to decide the name. They don't have to decide now. There's plenty of time."

Stephanie was right, but, "I don't want to think of her as 'it'," I protested, startling near-by diners.

My girls looked at each other, sharing the 'oh God' moment.

"Tell you what, Mum. Her middle name will be Linda. So think of her as Linda."

My cup runneth over.

As did Douggie's. He was still awake when we got home, probably sensing that something special had happened. I went in to him to show off the ring as soon as Ashwan had left. And I told him Georgina's news.

"Uncle Douggie."

"Yes. Well, great-uncle. But uncle will do. For the second time. This time it will be a little girl."

"Niece."

"Great-niece." A new word for him. I didn't have to explain any further. He worked it out straightaway. Even I didn't always give him the appropriate credit, whether stone cold sober or not.

"How many verys of a big family will Douggie have?"

I hugged him. "Fifty seven."

"Is it a lot of verys?"

"No, darling. It's just the right amount."

Chapter Eighteen

December 2004

Sunday the 19th. Ten a.m. She was due at midday for lunch. I had invited Ivy, too. But my daughters would come over later, giving us time to talk. Jeff had decided to take his parents out for a traditional roast as a pre-Christmas treat, but he planned to join us afterwards.

I was even more nervous than I thought I'd be. But it did seem better for the family to join us later. It could have been overwhelming for Audrey. Not that I felt the need to be particularly considerate, but I wanted to face her accompanied only by the people she knew. If she had anything emotive to say, she wouldn't be inhibited by the presence of strangers, and I wanted to know if she did have anything to say of any significance.

In the event, she and Ivy arrived within a few moments of each other. They had obviously both been to the hairdresser recently, the two grey heads stiffly styled. Although no longer slim, Audrey was wearing a flattering trouser suit and I could see that she had looked after her skin – not a surprise, given her earlier preoccupation with the mirror.

To my surprise, she had driven. I wasn't expecting that. And we had to fluff around for a while sorting out parking, because I had only one parking space, and the street had double yellow lines, necessitating my moving out into the street and using the disability badge that Douggie's presence provided. Douggie was fascinated by her SMART car, and also by its registration which included a D, an F and a 52. "Douggie Fletcher. Age 52. How much of a coincidence is that?"

Then she wanted a tour of the flat and showed an interest in every detail – the coving, the light fittings, the bedding, the taps. So far, conversation after an initial "Linda! Well, well, I would have known you anywhere," had been restricted to, "Oh, this is lovely," and, "Very nice," and, "Very smart."

She hadn't yet spoken to Douggie, who had been following her around. "When are they going?"

Ivy spoke before I did: "Oh, we'll be gone by five, won't we Audrey?"

"Yes." Audrey looked at me. "So, he didn't acquire any manners, then." It was a statement, not a question. Although I could have read it as an accusation, I tried not to. I had promised myself I wouldn't let her get to me. I just smiled.

In response, she moved towards Douggie and tried to hug him, but he backed away. "Have you told him who I am?" she asked me.

"You're Audrey. Friend of the family."

"I see. Probably a good idea. You haven't said hello to me, Douggie, and now you want me to go. It's not very friendly."

"Don't take it personally."

"No. I won't." She was treating the three of us like strangers, which, let's face it, I should have expected. For, to all intents and purposes, that's what we were.

Ivy took Douggie into the kitchen to "help" pour out some drinks, diplomatically leaving us alone in the lounge.

"You look well, Linda. I'm pleased."

"Are you?"

"You have a lovely little place here. And you're obviously doing a good job with Douggie. Though I can't imagine why you've taken on that kind of responsibility."

"No, I don't suppose you can." I wanted to ask so many questions. But it didn't feel right. I didn't feel comfortable.

"Frank did a good job. Better than I would have done. I knew he would."

"Yes. I miss him."

"Best not to rake up the past, don't you think? Too much heartache."
So why are you here? What is this about? "That looks like a very new,
shiny ring you are wearing on your left hand."

"Yes. It is." I tried to keep my voice as cool as her own. "His name's
Jeff. You'll meet him later."

"Good. And there's a great-grandson – Ronan? Is that right?"

Ivy came in with a tray. "He's a sweetie."

"Oh. You've met." She seemed surprised. "Douggie, come, sit with
me." She patted the seat next to her on the sofa but Douggie sat next
to me, watching her. She shrugged as Ivy joined her instead.

"They have turned out very well, haven't they?" Ivy asked her
brightly, but Audrey just smiled.

"Nice for you. To have them so near. You must feel like a surrogate
mother."

"Not at all. We don't see that much of each other. They lead busy
lives. But sometimes I baby sit for Stephanie."

"At your age? Still, I expect you find it pleasurable, dear." She
seemed to lose interest and changed the subject abruptly.

"Lunch smells good."

"Lasagne. We don't have a traditional roast any more. Too much
like hard work."

"Really? I thought you probably thrived on hard work."

Was it just me? I glanced at Ivy but she was sipping her martini,
seemingly oblivious. "Perhaps once. Not any more. I'm approaching
retirement, you know."

"Don't remind me. The thought of having a pensioner for a
daughter…" She laughed out loud then, the old infectious laugh I
remembered.

Douggie's head jerked up. "How long has Mummy been away?"

She stopped immediately. Douggie had recognised the laugh, too. I
should have guessed that he would realise eventually, or that something
would be said. Should I have told him? Shite. I tried not to react.
"Forty-seven years, darling."

"Is Mummy going to live with Douggie?"

"No, darling. She's just visiting."

"Douggie has a new family. Ronan and Jeff," he said conversationally. I caught Ivy's eye. She grimaced, no doubt wondering if, like me, the crisis was over.

"Why don't you tell me about Ronan?" Audrey asked him quietly, also, thankfully, not reacting.

"Why is not a good word for him. Tell Audrey, er, Mummy, about Ronan."

"Ronan is Douggie's great-nephew." Audrey and Ivy exchanged glances. "He is two years old. He can walk. He likes Goofy, and… chips. He has a pudding basin haircut. He has been in an aeroplane to Spain."

"And have you been in an aeroplane to Spain?"

"Yes."

"Did you enjoy it?"

"Aeroplane flies at over 500 miles per hour."

"And what about Spain?" Audrey's question was polite, just making conversation.

"Too much outside. Douggie likes inside."

I laughed, relieved at the normality – in our terms – of the conversation. Douggie was amazing. He could take the most devastating revelation in his stride, as if it was an everyday eventuality.

I went to dish up the lasagne, and signalled for Ivy to follow me. "You're happy to leave them alone?" she murmured as we sorted crockery and cutlery and salad.

"I am now. Now that he knows. And I'm so relieved, Ivy, that it's out in the open. I don't have to pretend any more."

She nodded. "You remember when she visited him, in Margate?"

"Of course."

"I wonder he didn't suspect then."

"He doesn't have a suspicious mind. Perhaps now he knows, perhaps now he wonders about Margate. But he doesn't talk about the past. Never has. It's not such a bad way to approach life."

"I agree. That's the problem with age. Too much dwelling on the past. I think of us when we were young, sharing a bed, going to Sunday school together in darned white socks, singing a song about Clark Gable and Betty Grable. Far more vivid than where I went last weekend. In fact, where *did* I go last weekend?"

I laughed and kissed her cheek. "You must ask Audrey if she remembers the song."

She put a hand on my arm. "Is it difficult for you to call her Mum?"

"Not difficult. Impossible."

"Yes. I see."

Lunch was more successful than I'd dared hope. Not just the food, but the atmosphere. We talked about the past, about the East London of Saturday morning pictures and hopscotch in the street. We talked about the future and Georgina's coming baby. Audrey referred briefly to a life of thwarted hopes. She'd tried her hand at acting, at writing, at singing. There had obviously been quite a few men, and I was not that surprised to hear that she'd married and divorced another three times. But there had been no more children. "Birth control came along, dear girl, thank God. Put an end to all that fidelity nonsense."

"Is that something to do with hi-fi?" Ivy was getting giggly, obviously not used to afternoon martinis.

By the time the rest of the family arrived, we were all – Douggie excepted – a tad on the giggly side. Douggie had become enamoured with a *Lilo and Stitch* DVD, a Disney cartoon about an alien, an orphan and a social worker. A psychologist would no doubt have had a field day.

After the introductions, Audrey and Ivy gave us a rendition of *Sisters*, a 1950s hit for the Beverley Sisters, and then Audrey went out to her Smart car to retrieve a bagful of Christmas presents.

Her brief absence gave me the opportunity to reassure everyone, especially Jeff, that the 'reunion' had been a great success, at least superficially. Okay, so there were still lots of questions, but they could wait. And even if there were never any answers, life was like that. Life was a series of questions, unless you were deeply religious, which I wasn't.

Jeff offered to drive Ivy home, as it was getting a bit too dark for public transport, and a taxi would have been prohibitive. Their departure seemed to signal the end of the afternoon for everyone, leaving a smiling Audrey alone with me and Douggie.

"I enjoyed that, Linda. Thank you so much for asking me."

"Yes. I suppose I should have done it sooner," I said grudgingly, not sure if I believed what I was saying.

"It's not your fault. It's mine. I've been a complete arse."

I laughed at the unexpected choice of language. "Coffee, I think."

"Yes. And a favour."

"What's that?"

"I'd like to spend a bit of time alone with Douggie. Try to explain. I know it won't be easy. But I'd like to. Would you mind if I took him out for a drive. We won't be long."

"You mean now? But you've had too much to drink. Tell you what, I'll sit in the kitchen or something while you say what you want to say. But remember to keep it simple."

"I know how to talk to him, Linda. He is my son. Sorry. Silly thing to say. But if you go into the kitchen, it seems to me that he'll just follow you rather than be alone with me."

"Okay. Tell you what, I'll put the kettle on for your coffee, and then I'll go down to the garage on the corner to get some milk, because we're about to run out after all those cups of tea we had this afternoon. I'll only be about ten, fifteen minutes."

"Okay, girl."

I left her trying to persuade Douggie to turn off, or at least put on hold, the DVD. Twelve minutes later, to the minute, I was back. And she was gone. In her car. With Douggie.

I didn't even have my key to get in. I'd expected her to open the door for me. I didn't have the keys to my car. I didn't have my mobile. I just stood there, leaning against the front door, my brain whirling, sweat breaking out along my upper lip and hairline.

What the hell was going on? Where had she taken him?

Action returned to my limbs. I ran down the few stairs at the entrance to my small block of flats, and into the road. No sign of her, but she couldn't be far. I ran back and put the milk on the doorstep. Then out into the road again. Where was the nearest phone box? I'd never had to use one, but where the hell was it? Yes. I could see one, a hundred yards away – but no. Vandalised. Bloody typical. And then I ran in the opposite direction, back to the garage, hoping they would have a pay phone. They didn't.

"Everyone has mobiles now. We don't need it."

"Well, I bloody need it."

"There's no need to swear," objected the elder of the two Asian staff.

"There is. That's just it. I have to phone the police."

"Well, why didn't you say so."

One of the customers and the garage shop staff all offered mobiles. I grabbed the nearest, but its owner had to help me because the technology required was different to the basic level that my own mobile offered.

"Police? My brother's been kidnapped. Yes, kidnapped… Yes, I know who, and I can describe the car she took him in… part of the registration number, yes, there's a D, an F and the number 52… Yes, I said *she*… His mother… Yes, I said his mother… Please, it's a long story. You've got to find them… Okay. But I'm locked out. I don't know when my boyfriend will be back with a key… but surely… Oh, for Chrissake, okay, but hurry. Please hurry."

I gave my address and rang off. "Any chance I can make another call? Sorry," I said nervously, but the guy with the dreadlocks, the owner of the mobile, grinned amicably. "No sweat. Free calls all weekend."

I tried dialling Jeff, but his mobile was switched off. Shite.

"Thank you." Everyone in the garage shop was looking at me. A little bit of drama in their lives. "I've got to go."

I ran again, wondering if perhaps she'd just gone for a drive as she'd suggested, and the two of them would be back at home waiting for me. Of course. I had probably made a complete fool of myself.

I was out of breath now, but also less panic-stricken. I was also not prepared for a long wait outside on a cold December evening, and had to hug myself close to increase the warmth of the leather jacket I was wearing. But the world was carrying on in front of me, cars, passers-by, Christmas lights going on in neighbouring flats and houses, a lone cat, a boy whistling on a bicycle. Everything was as it had been half an hour ago. She'd be back soon. Probably before Jeff, so I wouldn't have to tell him what an idiot I'd been. She probably thought I had a key on me. Although, there again, would someone really go for a drive with that much alcohol inside them?

I took a deep breath. And another. It was going to be all right. Forty minutes. The police obviously hadn't taken me too seriously. No sirens, no flashing blue lights. Fifty minutes. The panic was returning. A few more minutes and I saw Jeff's Nissan turning into the road, passing the bright lights of the garage I'd thrown into disarray. He saw me and pulled up sharply. I ran over to speak to him through the window.

"She's gone. With Douggie."

"What? Audrey? What do you mean *she's gone?* No, hang on. Go in and let me park up, and then tell me what's happened."

"I can't get in. I'm locked out. I've been locked out for nearly an hour." The panic had been replaced by numbness. And I knew that soon, very soon, the guilt would be back with a vengeance.

He parked quickly and messily so that he could jump out and let us both in. I looked around for a note. She might have left a note.

"There's no note."

"Why should there be a note? What the hell happened? Where have you been?"

"Trying to get help. She wanted to be alone with him. Just for a few minutes. It had been such a good day, a worthwhile day. I didn't think... I didn't dream... She said she'd like to take him for a drive but she'd had too much to drink, so I went to the garage to get some milk. Just for a few minutes. Twelve bloody minutes. Oh, Jeff."

"So, she's taken him for a drive anyway. Damn fool. But I'm sure she'll be back soon. She'll bring him back. Of course she will."

"I phoned the police, Jeff. But they haven't turned up."

He shrugged. "Not a lot they can do. What did you tell them?"

"I can't remember. Something about kidnap."

He smiled wryly. "She doesn't want him, you know that, so she's not going to take him, is she? Be sensible. She'll be back. I just hope she can handle her drink behind the wheel. Especially at her age."

I looked at the untouched cup of black coffee. "She didn't even stay for her coffee." I could feel the control slipping away again. "She's got Douggie. What have I done?"

He held me close as we stood in the kitchen, hoping for the best, fearing the worst, confused, baffled. I began to whimper, blaming myself.

"Stop it. Stop it now. You're not to blame. Everything is going to be all right. I'll check the answer phone. You check Douggie's room, see if he's taken anything."

Just having something to do helped. But there was no message, and Douggie's room was undisturbed. He had removed his DVD and put it back in its casing, but no one would have been able to prevent him doing that, however much of a hurry they might have been in.

"I'm going to phone the girls. And then I'll phone the police again."

"They're probably busy. Or perhaps short handed. It's Sunday evening. Or maybe grown up sons disappearing with their mothers doesn't take priority."

I knew he was right, but I phoned anyway even though neither Georgina nor Stephanie sounded concerned. I tried to sound more reasonable than I had the first time I'd called. "It is only a little more than an hour, Mrs North. Hardly a missing person. Or persons. Where does your mother live?"

"Bournemouth."

"So perhaps they've gone there."

"You don't understand."

"Mrs North. You are on our list. If we can spare someone, we will. In the meantime, if there are any further developments, let us know."

There was a 'further development' all right. One much worse than even I had imagined in those darkest moments.

At nine o'clock, we were still sitting in the kitchen, drinking endless coffee, trying not to talk about what could have happened, trying – not particularly successfully in my case – to think of rational explanations. The doorbell rang, and I could see the unmistakable flashing of a police car through the glass panel.

"Thank God. They're here."

The two uniformed young men on the doorstep did not smile when I opened the door. "Mrs Linda North?"

"Yes."

"May we come in?"

"Thank God you're here. Come in. Please."

They glanced at each other before following me inside. "You've been expecting us?"

"You're here about my brother, aren't you?"

One looked at a notebook. "Is your brother Douglas Fletcher?"

"Yes."

"And you know Audrey Norton?"

"Audrey Norton? You mean Audrey Fletcher? Oh, I suppose she could be the same… My mother. What's going on?" I felt Jeff behind me, gripping my shoulders.

He took charge. "Can you tell us why you're here and forget about why we think you're here?"

The – marginally – older P.C. looked confused for a moment by Jeff's brisk question, and then looked back at me. "Mrs North. We have some very bad news."

I knew what they were going to say. Before they said it, I knew. I sat down, and Jeff sat down with me, still holding on to me, shifting his grip.

"There's been an accident. On the dual carriageway. Two fatalities, the female driver and a male passenger."

He asked me if I could confirm the make of car and the registration number. I could, by nodding mutely. But I was on auto pilot, hearing only the words *two fatalities, two fatalities*, over and over again.

"The driver's handbag has ID in the name of Audrey Norton. The male passenger has a donor card in the name of Douglas Fletcher."

I couldn't say anything. Not a word. I tried. But nothing happened. Nothing was functioning. My body seemed to be closing down. I was thinking about Douggie and his donor card, the one he had carried since 9/11 for a reason he could not explain. Jeff squeezed me hard. "Fatalities? Both? And you're sure about the identities?"

"Well. We'll need verification. When Mrs North feels able."

"Could I do it?" he asked, trying to be helpful.

"And you are…?"

I could hear the conversation. About identities. Fatalities. This couldn't be happening. I found myself thinking that it was nearly Christmas. I was thinking about Audrey's presents.

Then I heard them talking about organ donation. I felt sick.

"Are you next of kin, Mrs North?" I must have nodded. "We'd be happier with your permission."

"I can't. I can't do this." I'd found some words. "He – they – can't be… they can't be."

Jeff let go of me. "Strong tea. Stay there. You don't have to do anything or say anything."

I was beginning to shake, and one of the policemen removed his helmet and knelt down in front of me. "I'm so sorry."

Was that me wailing? It was. It was me.

What followed is, thank goodness, a blur. A lot of kind faces. A lot of tea. Questions. About the car. About the drink. Forms. Inquests. Funerals.

As for Jeff and the endless conversations that followed before and after the formalities… He seemed to think that what had happened was actually good for us! Oh, he didn't actually say that, but one word he did say, that sticks in my head, was the word 'relief'. That, more than anything, made me think, about him, about everything. Did anyone – could anyone – understand? And if he didn't understand, then what hope was there for us, us as a couple. Did love exist without understanding?

Douggie, what have I done? Guilt upon guilt upon guilt. Relentless. Guilt that has, let's face it, been lurking there for as long as I can remember. Will it ever go away?

Chapter Nineteen

April 2005

Javea, Costa Blanca

Dear Georgina,

Just a line to let you know that everything is fine. The sun and the solitude are just what I needed. Of course it's not really solitude. There are plenty of people here, and perhaps too many Brits. But the villa is not overlooked. So I can pretend. And there are views of the mountains in one direction and the coast in another. Well, let's just say that Ilford it's not.

I'll be back to see you before the baby's due, don't worry. I wouldn't miss it for the world.

Jeff phoned to tell me that he's found a buyer for my flat, so he's done well and been a great help. I think I'll probably start looking for a more permanent address here. It's as good a place as any. And you can all come and see me for long holidays. I'd like that. Give him my regards if you see him.

I'm catching up on my reading. "Cloud Atlas" by David Mitchell. Clever, but a bit too demanding. "Girl with a Pearl Earring" by Tracy Chevalier. A little gem.

Isn't it good news about Stephanie? I'm writing to her next – I need Pete to send me some more books! Another grandchild by Christmas. I'm beginning to feel like a real grandmother. Another baby will be good for Stephanie and Pete, I'm sure. I'm really pleased for her. For both of you.

Give my love to Mark. And little Ruby (only joking).
Love, Mum.

What I didn't mention was that I had a letter in my hand, in Jeff's writing, that had arrived that morning. Why had he written and not phoned? We'd had several friendly conversations on the phone recently.

It seemed there were always difficult decisions to make. To open or not to open the letter? I made a simpler decision: to go for a swim before lunch. I needed the exercise and the pool was of an Olympic standard.

Two words from the coroner's report repeated themselves over and over in my head, keeping pace with my strokes: 'Advanced carcinoma'. I had kept those words to myself. Locked them away.

But I had spent a lot of time thinking about D-Day. Death day. Douggie day. Devastation day. And thinking about my mother's 'advanced carcinoma'.

So was it a deliberate act? I'd never know. No one would ever know. I could live with the guilt. I had no choice. But I wouldn't be taking any prisoners with me. Not anyone.

No doubt the girls were disappointed that there was going to be no wedding but Jeff and I…? There could not be any Jeff and I, not after I'd stormed out on him and left him to pick up the pieces. I'd had to get away. I knew Jeff couldn't and wouldn't understand. That had become our problem. What had started out, for me, as a heart-warming experience that had left me feeling desirable and loved, had ended with a breakdown in communication. I had found it impossible to explain the importance of Douggie in my life.

Leaving Jeff had hurt. It had hurt both of us. I had spent most of my life feeling guilty about my brother's life and now I had the additional burden of guilt at abandoning Jeff. I could live with the guilt. I had no choice.

I was fast approaching another milestone and that word I was dreading - 'pensioner'. It would seem that this was what was left of my little life. It would just have to do.

I would read Jeff's letter later.

ALSO BY DEE GORDON:

Fiction:
Meat Market, 2004, Vanguard Press

Non-Fiction:
People Who Mattered in Southend and Beyond, 2006, Ian Henry Publications

Southend Memories, 2006, Sutton Publishing

Foul Deeds in and around Southend on Sea, 2007, Wharncliffe Books

Infamous Essex Women, 2009, The History Press

Essex's Own, 2009, History Press

Little Book of Essex, 2009, History Press

Voices of Stepney, 2010, History Press

Southend at War, 2010, History Press

Little Book of the East End, 2010, History Press

Haunted Southend, 2012, History Press

Little Book of the 1960s, 2012, History Press

Not a Guide to Southend-on-Sea, 2013, History Press

Secret History of Southend-on-Sea, 2014, History Press

Essex Land Girls, 2015, History Press

Poetry:
Bad Girls, July 2008, Troubador (self-published)